"Ellie, why don't you like me?"

Ryder's question was so sudden, so sincere, Ellie almost dropped the teapot she was holding.

"I—I don't know you well enough to *dis*like you, Ryder. I mean, you've been wonderful with Zak—this afternoon, and then tonight—"

"But I make you nervous."

"Yes. I mean, no. I mean, I guess what makes me jittery is that I don't—don't know what you want. Why you're here."

"Do I have to want anything?"

"Mr. Sloan, I'm sure you're a very nice man, but . . ."

"You trust me about as much as you would a shark in a feeding frenzy, right?"

Dear Reader,

Welcome to Silhouette **Special Edition** ... welcome to romance. Each month, Silhouette **Special Edition** publishes six novels with you in mind—stories of love and life, tales that you can identify with—romance with that little ''something special'' added in.

This month, Silhouette **Special Edition** is full of special treats for you. We're hosting Nora Roberts's third book in her exciting THE CALHOUN WOMEN series—*For the Love of Lilah*. Each line at Silhouette Books has published one book of the series. Next month look for *Suzanna's Surrender* in the Silhouette Intimate Moments line!

Silhouette **Special Edition** readers are also looking forward to the second book in the compelling SONNY'S GIRLS series, *Don't Look Back* by Celeste Hamilton. These poignant tales are sure to be keepers! Don't miss the third installment next month, *Longer Than...* by Erica Spindler.

Rounding out August are warm, wonderful stories by veteran authors Sondra Stanford, Karen Keast and Victoria Pade, as well as Kim Cates's wonderful debut book, *The Wishing Tree*.

In each Silhouette **Special Edition**, we're dedicated to bringing you the romances that you dream about—the type of stories that delight as well as bring a tear to the eye. And that's what Silhouette **Special Edition** is all about—special books by special authors for special readers!

I hope you enjoy this book and all of the stories to come.

Sincerely,

Tara Gavin
Senior Editor

KIM CATES
The Wishing Tree

Silhouette Special Edition

Published by Silhouette Books New York

America's Publisher of Contemporary Romance

To Linda Wallerich and Kate Bush,
two die-hard fans.
And to the Chicago Cubs—
if it takes forever.
Also, with special thanks to Kate Bush
for drawing Zakary's map.

SILHOUETTE BOOKS
300 East 42nd St., New York, N.Y. 10017

THE WISHING TREE

ISBN: 0-373-09687-9

First Silhouette Books printing August 1991

KIM CATES

is an incurable fanatic, addicted to classic tear-jerker movies, Chicago Cubs baseball and reading and writing romances—both contemporary and historical. Married to her high school sweetheart, she divides her time between her writing career and enjoying her nine-year-old daughter, Kate, from whom, Kim insists, she learned everything she knows about the temperament of royalty.

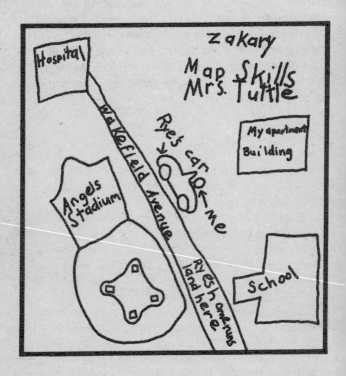

Chapter One

He was late.

Ellie MacCrea raked slender fingers through her hair, her face aching with the effort it took to keep her mouth schooled in a reassuring smile. But it was impossible to keep from swearing inside as her gaze flicked from the apartment window to the small figure of her son on the faded chintz couch.

Dozens of baseball cards depicting a game Zak might never play again were grasped in fingers that could once throw a pitch more accurately than any other kid in the neighborhood. Skin that used to glow beneath its spattering of freckles was now drawn too tightly over wan features.

An Atlanta Angels cap was pulled low over the seven-year-old's eyes, eyes Ellie knew were now shadowed with uncertainty. Pain. Not just the shadow that had clung to them ever since Zak had been stricken with nephritis.

But a new pain. One that whispered of the long-ago days he had perched on the fire escape, watching, waiting, for his father to come for visitation.

Ellie ground her teeth, hurt and anger welling white-hot inside her.

The nuns at Immaculata Elementary School had tried to drive patience into Ellie during the years she had spent beneath their yardsticks. But at times like these, she knew they'd failed miserably. Patience? she thought grimly as she looked at her son—she wanted to kill someone.

And that someone was Ryder Sloan, star third base-man of the Atlanta Angels. The most narcissistic, hedonistic, brainless lump of pure male ego ever to be dropped in the middle of a baseball field—*if* she were to believe the headlines screaming from the sleazy tabloids at the grocery checkout lines. Not that she ever really read the blasted things. . . .

"He will come, Mom? Ryder Sloan, I mean." There was a tremor in Zak's voice that was all too familiar. "Jed said that those Wishing Tree people promised. . . ."

Promises . . . who was it who had said they were made to be broken? Ellie turned away, struggling to find the right words. "Sweetheart, Jed wanted to do something real special for you when he wrote to the Wishing Tree Foundation," Ellie said, remembering how delighted her lanky eighteen-year-old student had been when he had dazzled Zak with the news that the organization for granting wishes to seriously ill children had decided to realize the boy's most cherished dream. "Jed knew that Sloan was your favorite player, and—"

"The greatest third baseman in the history of the game, with a .314 batting average and forty RBIs this year, and it's only the middle of June—"

"Yeah, Sloan's great all right." Ellie tried to keep the cynicism out of her voice as she remembered what Jed had privately cited as Sloan's most impressive average of all—that of big-busted groupies drooling over his gorgeous bod. She mentally jammed a catcher's mask onto the image of Sloan's cocky grin.

"Zak, I just want you to understand that sometimes people like Mr. Sloan get real busy. Things come up."

"Like with Daddy." Zak said it in a small, dull voice that made Ellie wince. It was a statement, not a question. And it made her stomach churn.

It had been almost two years since her ex-husband Daniel had disappeared from Zak's life, a respite Ellie had been grateful for. Divorced the year before that, she had sat helplessly, watching as Daniel had broken promise after promise to the boy, saddling him with countless disappointments, until at last Daniel had vanished altogether, without a word. And certainly without child support.

Zak had been heartbroken for a while, but he had healed. Until now, when it seemed he was to suffer more of the same, compliments of Ryder Sloan. This day, which should have been so wonderful for a child who knew too much about hospitals and needles and dialysis machines, would rank right up there with the birthday outing that had "slipped" Daniel MacCrea's mind.

Ellie cursed herself. She never should have agreed to let the Wishing Tree arrange this meeting—to set Zak up for such a crushing fall. But Kate Maxwell, the organization's dynamic founder, had been so convincing, so sympathetic, so warm, Ellie had almost believed...

She crossed the worn carpet, curling up close to the child. She slipped one arm around him, and was glad when Zak snuggled close. Ellie looked down into that small solemn face and wished she could sweep away Zak's hurt with a few easy platitudes. Wished she had believed that was possible. Daniel certainly had. God knew, he had tried it often enough. But even before that first day the doctors had come into the room to give Ellie the diagnosis she had so dreaded, she had been honest with her son.

And in the endless year in which she had watched Zak's kidneys slowly fail, watched him become steadily weaker, she had continued to meet the boy with a truthfulness that she hoped had calmed at least some of the fears they both lived with every day.

"You know what?" she said, her voice thick with unshed tears. "I love you, munchkin."

Zak made the required grimace for a tough third grader whose Mom insisted on calling him by a baby nickname, but he nuzzled closer.

"Tell you what, kiddo. How about if I grab a bottle of Astro-Ice Cooler and a bag of pretzels and we pig out watching . . . what was that monster movie we taped last weekend? *Godzilla Meets the Swamp Squasher?*"

Zak groaned, but his lips tilted in a wobbly smile. "The swamp stomper, Mom."

Ellie shrugged. "Squasher, stomper, what does it matter? Godzilla always wins." She got up, straightening her full, old-fashioned skirt as she started toward the sunshine-yellow kitchen. But at that instant, she heard a commotion outside the apartment building. Catching her lower lip between her teeth, she hurried to the window, praying, threatening, pleading with the fates to let it by Ryder Sloan.

She should have been grateful when her gaze fixed on that thick mane of dark hair, that notorious million-watt grin and those drop-dead gorgeous features three stories down. She *would* have been grateful. Except that when her gray eyes locked on the debacle being played out below, she felt as though someone had hit a fastball into her stomach.

Photographers' flashes popped in bursts of light, journalists scrawled notes and screamed questions, while two rival television stations thrust microphones toward Sloan, their video cameras rolling. The crowd of about a hundred fans jostling amongst the paparazzi might as well have been waving palm leaves and shouting "hosanna," they appeared so worshipful. And Ryder Sloan—he seemed to be sucking up the adulation like a soda through a straw.

"What in heaven . . . ?" she said to herself. "It's a damned circus!" *What did you expect,* a voice jeered inside her. *An egomaniac like Sloan would hardly come without his adoring throng.* And, of course, the publicity from his magnanimous gesture wouldn't hurt when they negotiated the next contract on his sports car commercials.

The thought of Zakary, and his wish, being turned into some crass commercial publicity stunt sickened Ellie, infuriated her. She had expected Sloan to be an arrogant jerk, had expected him to preen under Zak's adoration. But she had thought the man would stride up the front walk alone, had hoped in some tiny part of her that he would care—really care—about seeing the little boy she loved so much.

"It doesn't matter," she tried to convince herself, "as long as he's here. And he is. *Finally.*" She had almost decided to let him live. Almost. Then he made a fatal mistake.

Those devilish eyes that had twinkled from countless magazine covers flicked to the expensive gold watch strapped to Sloan's wrist. Ellie saw his lips tighten in irritation as if he were already late for his next appointment. Then his eyes flashed up to the window above the fire escape, his gaze locking with hers. It was patently obvious he thought she was one of his slavering fans, as his mouth widened into a sensual grin, but it was the suggestive wink he shot her that made Ellie wheel, thirsting afresh for his blood.

"Mom, is that Ryder?" Zak cried, skittering off the couch and rushing toward her.

"Zakary MacCrea, sit down!" Ellie hated herself for the edge in her voice and forced herself to soften it. "Yes, munchkin. It's Sloan, but—"

An army of mothers couldn't have kept Zak from the window. "Awesome, Mom! He came! He really came! I knew he would! He's the greatest third baseman in the history of the game!"

Ellie cringed at the light in the boy's eyes. That innocence, that happiness, could be shattered by one careless word from the hero the child so worshipped.

Oh, no, Mr. Sloan, Ellie resolved with a surge of militance. *You're not going to turn this into some blasted publicity play. Not if you want to live to grandstand it through another baseball season.*

She glanced down in time to see Sloan pause to pose for a photograph with two giggling sixteen-year-olds in leather miniskirts. Ellie thrust out her chin with resolve. "Zak, if you don't calm down you'll never get to meet Mr. Sloan. Now, I need to go down and…and show him the way to the apartment."

"I'll go! Let me—"

"Zakary, sit down!"

"All right," Zak moaned, sinking back onto the couch in surrender. But Ellie was already out the door and down the stairs. She flung open the building's main door, intending to charge out at the same instant someone else seemed set on charging in.

She slammed into a rock-hard chest, heard a rumbling laugh as strong hands steadied her. "Whoa! No need to kill yourself. There's plenty of time to sign an autograph."

Approving laughter rippled through the crowd and a shrill voice called out from somewhere, "Bet she wants lots more than your signature, Rye!"

"The only *autograph* you're supposed to be signing here is the one to *my son,* Mr. Sloan," Ellie said, eyes blazing as she pulled from the baseball player's grasp. "Or have you forgotten?"

"Ooh! Hey, lady..." Murmurings of outrage rose from the crowd, but Ellie scarcely heard them. Blindingly blue eyes pierced her, and she knew how a tree must feel when it's been felled by lightning.

Sloan's grin faded. "Your son?"

"Zakary MacCrea. Tell me, Mr. Sloan, do big-league jocks know how to tell time, or do you have some lackey to do it for you? It's four o'clock now. You were supposed to be here when the little hand was on the three and the big hand was on the twelve."

His deeply tanned cheekbones washed red as Sloan's gaze darted away. "There was a hang-up at the airport." The jauntiness faded from his warm-bourbon voice, and a line of puzzlement creased between his straight dark brows.

She hated the look of surprise, of innocence, in eyes that should have been jaded.

"Don't bother making excuses, Mr. Sloan," she snapped. "I'm not with the media. I know what you really are, but you see, my son thinks you're a hero. And you're damn well going to be one for the next hour, even if it kills us both."

He regarded her levelly. "Mrs. MacCrea, I didn't rush back from Chicago to disappoint your boy." Quiet, words were so quiet. The sting of guilt made her crazy.

"I'm glad we both agree on that, at least. Now, Zak has probably worn a path in the carpet running back and forth trying to catch a glimpse of you, so you get up there, and be charming. It seems to be one thing you're good at."

Sloan's lips quirked in a disarming hint of a grin. "I'm good at lots of things, Mrs. MacCrea. Infielding. Hitting home runs." His eyes traveled to her mouth for a moment. "Stealing bases."

Her cheeks burned. "You better hope you're damn good at gauging the time," Ellie said, eyes blazing, hating the tingly sensation washing through her beneath Sloan's lazy gaze. "'Cause this much I promise you. You look at that watch of yours once—just once in the next hour—and it'll take every team of surgeons in Atlanta General to pry the pieces of it out of your wrist."

She saw two photographers jockeying to get through the doorway, heard them start babbling questions. "Just a few shots with the kid, Ryder—some bleeding heart stuff."

Ellie's cry of fury was cut off by Sloan's voice, its tones surprisingly hard, unyielding. "Forget it, Fred. You might as well go develop your roll, 'cause you're not using any more film on me tonight."

"But, the mother, if we could interview—"

"Believe me," Sloan drawled, with an edge of amusement, "you don't want to hear what she has to say to you."

What slight softening Ellie had felt toward Ryder Sloan moments before vanished. She turned in a swirl of deep rose skirt and indignation, and swept up the stairs. She heard Sloan mutter a curse, then follow her up, but even her anger had to melt a little when she heard Zak's elated cry as they entered the apartment.

The boy bounded off the couch, then plopped back down, as if suddenly in the presence of some mythical god. Zak flushed, his eyes uncertain. "M-Mr. Sloan?"

There was enough white in Ryder Sloan's grin to cover the slopes in Aspen. He paced over to where Zak sat and hunkered down so he was at eye level with the child. "Zakary MacCrea?" he said softly. "I've been waiting a long time to meet you."

Ellie felt her stomach flip-flop as Sloan extended his hand to take the small one of her child. Zak's fingers looked so frail in the man's grasp, and his face was alight with awe and joy. But it was the expression on Ryder

Sloan's features that startled Ellie: a quiet empathy, an innate understanding of what it was like to be seven years old...and desperately sick. She hadn't expected that from a man like Sloan, but then Ellie had long ago stopped expecting anything from anyone.

As Sloan sat down next to Zak, she hovered nearby, ready to leap in at any moment should the man show signs of saying anything that might hurt the child. But after a while, she withdrew into the kitchen, the sound of their voices rising and falling in a companionable murmur following behind her.

It was a grudging sense of trust she had extended Ryder Sloan. An unwilling one. She wanted to give Zak the space to revel in the most exciting day of his life without his mother hovering over his every move. But she couldn't stop herself from stealing glances through the little space above the breakfast bar.

Sloan had looped his arm around Zak's narrow shoulders, and his dark head was bent over Zak's red one as they pored over the baseball cards scattered across the boy's lap. Baseball jargon flew between the two as they shared statistics with the relish only two diehard fans could have brought to it.

"I got your rookie card when you were most valuable player," Zak offered eagerly, holding out his most prized possession. "Had to trade Mr. Allison, our super, three Alex Craigs for it."

Ryder chuckled at the mention of his teammate. It had been Jed who had informed Ellie that Alex Craig was a backup catcher, a journeyman player who had been in the big league eight years. Craig's batting average had never exceeded his shoe size.

Ellie's mouth softened into a smile as she remembered the day Zak had brought the card home—triumphant, swelled up with pride at his canniness in trading. Even now, the boy had no idea that kind old Everett Allison had given him a collector's piece already worth more than Zak's allowance for the next three years.

Let 'im keep it, the elderly man had said when she had objected. *I 'member how I felt when I got my first Ted Williams.*

Ryder Sloan had taken the picture from Zak's hand, eyes holding an odd expression as he looked down at the image of himself, grinning at the camera twelve years earlier.

How many times had Zak told Ellie that that had been Ryder Sloan's banner year—the year the man had shot to instant stardom. Strange, Ellie thought now, regarding the man's face. He didn't look as though he were indulging in memories that brought him satisfaction. There was a wistfulness about him, a solemnity she sensed was rare.

She turned away as she heard Sloan begin to banter again with Zak, yet she couldn't shake the feeling that she had somehow intruded on something very personal, very private—if it were possible for a man as famous as Ryder Sloan to have anything private left.

Ellie nibbled at her bottom lip as she crossed to the refrigerator to pour two tall glasses of milk for the pair in the other room. The appliance's glossy finish reflected her image back to her. Her hair was tumbled. Her gray eyes still had that mother-grizzly expression. Her full mouth was a trifle sulky. But her cheeks were as pink as the plastic pitcher she held in her hand.

Way to go, Ell, her conscience niggled at her. *The guy flies halfway across the country to see Zak, and you treat him like he's an ax murderer or something.*

Well, how was I supposed to know he'd be a cross between Mel Gibson and Mr. Rogers? She grimaced. *And besides, he was late.*

And you've never been late in your whole life? You know how insane airline schedules can get. Their computers are possessed by gremlins who take pure delight in scrambling things up and watching the passengers trip all over one another trying to get where they're going.

Ellie sloshed milk into the glasses, then thudded the pitcher back into its place on the wire shelf. *Well, what about his entourage?* She made one last-ditch effort to defend her behavior. *Half of Atlanta is out in the front yard.*

Where would you be if you saw a guy who looked that good? Hiding in the trunk of your car?

Where had that come from? Ellie quashed the thought, irritated as heat flooded her at the memory of the way Sloan's eyes had lingered on her lips in the corridor, and at his words— "I'm good at lots of things, Mrs. MacCrea...."

I'll just bet. She forcibly stilled the tremor in her hand. *No doubt it's from all that batting practice.*

The ringing of the phone on the kitchen wall nearly made her jump out of her skin. She dove for the receiver, her eyes quickly flashing to Sloan. Guilt gnawed at her again, making her angry with herself, and with him for daring to be so all-fired . . . well, *tolerable.*

Jamming the receiver between her shoulder and chin, Ellie was relieved to discover that it was the ever-present, ever-phoning, ever-hilarious Jed.

"Ay, Mrs. MacCrea, did he come? Sloan? Is Zak going nuts? Does he look like he does in the TV commercials?"

"Zak's never been in any commercials that I know of," Ellie said wryly.

"Mrs. MacCrea!" Jed gave a long-suffering groan. "Don't start slapping that antecedent stuff on me in regular, normal-talking junk! You know what I mean."

Ellie thought about lecturing the boy on practicing in everyday life the English concepts he was having such trouble mastering, but it would have been an exercise in futility. He had already begun rhapsodizing upon the "wonderfulness" of Atlanta's third baseman. After fifteen minutes, Ellie couldn't bear it another second.

"Jed, I have to go now. I'll see you at your tutoring session tomorrow."

"Yeah. If I pass this Comp test in summer school, I'll be able to stay on the team this fall."

The team, the team, Jed's whole life was confined in one battered bit of pigskin. Sometimes she wanted to shake the boy and force him to see how much in life he was missing, devoting himself to a child's game.

"Terrific." She tried to infuse some enthusiasm into her voice.

"Oh, and Mrs. MacCrea... You haven't... haven't heard anything on that transplant thing for Zak, have you? I mean, last time I was there, you were hoping..."

"They lost the donor-kidney enroute to the hospital," Ellie said softly. "I guess it was damaged even before..." Her words trailed off as she felt again that awful, crushing sensation of defeat she had experienced after the call from the hospital.

"Bummer," Jed commiserated. "Oh, well, there'll be other chances."

If only Ellie believed he was right. But Zak's tissue type was so rare even her own kidney failed to match it. The chances of finding another one were almost nonexistent. And with each day, the time Zak could remain on dialysis dwindled.

She hung up the phone and stood there a moment, trying to gather her wits. The emotional roller coaster of Zakary's illness never seemed to end. She would just level off, and the bottom would drop out from beneath her. Each time she'd plunge deeper, farther, faster. Each time her terror grew that this would be the time she would hit the bottom. And life without Zak would be no life at all.

The sound of the child's eager laughter drifted to her, and she clung to it, dragging frayed threads of hope around her.

Gritting her teeth, Ellie picked up the milk she had poured earlier and carried the glasses out to set them on the refinished carriage seat that served as a coffee table. "Thought you two might be thirsty," she said as breezily as she could manage. "The way you've been talking, your mouths are bound to be dry."

"Mom...but Ryder drinks Astro-Ice Cooler, not milk!" Zak crinkled his nose, obviously mortified.

"Milk is one of my favorites," Sloan interrupted, ruffling the boy's hair. "How do you think I hit all those grand slams? But don't tell anyone my secret."

Zak beamed. "That's what my Mom says. That it's good for you and stuff."

"Your Mom is a real smart lady." Sloan downed the drink, his tongue stealing out to lick a clinging drop of milk from his upper lip. He gave her an appreciative grin. "Thank you," he said to Ellie. "I was so late running through the airport, I didn't stop to..."

His words trailed off. She looked away, and sensed he was looking anywhere but at her. He put the empty glass down.

"Umm, well, the least I can do is send you away from here without being thirsty. I... If you need to go... you've been here almost an hour."

"You mean I can look at my watch without fearing for my life?"

She wanted to keep it light, easy. Didn't want him to see the tremor in her hands, the worse trembling in her heart. "Your wrist is safe with me." Ellie met his gaze, saw the puzzlement in his eyes, as he regarded her. She looked away.

"Before I go, Zak, I want you to have this. Thought you might use it to break a few windows when you're feeling better." Sloan stood, digging deep into the pocket of his light team jacket. He withdrew a baseball, its white leather surface bearing a signature scrawled in what Ellie was certain was Ryder Sloan's handwriting.

"Wow Mom, look!" Zak bubbled with enthusiasm, his eyes brighter than they had been for months.

"It's terrific, sweetheart." She swallowed hard.

Ryder straightened his lean six-foot-three frame. "Zak, I have to roll now." There was reluctance in Sloan's voice. "But it's been great."

"Yeah."

"I...really am sorry I was late."

Zak shrugged. "It's okay. My dad...he was late all the time when he used to come to visit. But he's not anymore."

Ellie felt a sick tugging in her stomach and compressed her lips as Ryder's eyes caught hers in confusion.

"Not late?" he asked

"Not coming to visit," Zak said.

Ellie turned and fled through the doorway, stunned at the pain her son's matter-of-fact words had stirred up in her. She felt exposed, vulnerable, *humiliated,* as she leaned against the cool wall out in the corridor. She closed her eyes as she listened to the murmur of Ryder Sloan telling her son goodbye, and wished that she could slip between the cracks in the hardwood floor. But there was to be no such convenient escape as Ryder strode from the apartment.

She heard his footsteps pause, and opened her eyes.

"Are you all right?" he asked quietly.

Ellie forced a smile. "Aside from feeling like the biggest shrew ever to walk the earth? Yeah. I'm just dandy." She sucked in a steadying breath. "Mr. Sloan..."

"Ryder."

"Ryder, then. About...when you got here. The way I acted...I'm sorry. Usually I at least wait until I get people inside the door before I bite their heads off. It's just that...Zak... He's been disappointed so many times before. When you were late—"

"You thought he was going to be disappointed again." Ryder searched her face, and there was a strength in his eyes, and an empathy that seemed far too warm and real to exist in a face that had no doubt been splashed across every glossy sports magazine known to man. "If I had a kid like Zak, I think I'd kill anyone who hurt him."

"It occurred to me." The warmth in Sloan's voice was infectious, but Ellie was surprised at his words. She forced herself to straighten. "Especially when I saw every reporter in three counties trailing after you. I almost expected to see you leaning against that red sports car in your commercials, saying 'I love fast balls, fast women and fast cars.' It would have been great publicity."

"Publicity?" Sloan fingered a snap on his jacket and chewed at the corner of his lip as though considering something uncomfortable for the first time. "But I—"

Ellie shook her head. "It doesn't matter now. No matter why you came, I *am* glad you did, Mr. Sloan. It was the dream of a lifetime for Zak."

"I've never been anyone's wish before," Ryder said. "If only it were this easy to make other wishes come true."

He caught her eyes, held them for long seconds. Ellie's voice was shaky. "I quit believing in fairy godmothers a long time ago. And I'd give up every magic wand that ever was just to see Zak healthy again. Goodbye, Mr—Ryder—and thank you."

Hands strong and tanned from hours in the sun reached out, catching her fingers in a firm grip. "Sometimes you have to believe...." he said softly. "Even when you're afraid to.'' Then he turned and strode down the stairs. Ellie watched him go, wondering if a man like Ryder Sloan had any idea just how dearly believing had once cost her.

Chapter Two

Ryder leaned back against the limo's leather seats, trying to blot out the chatter of his agent conducting the postmortem of the visit to Zakary MacCrea. But Byron Crowell enthused on relentlessly. As relentlessly as the image of Ellie MacCrea's sad, pale face haunted Ryder's mind.

"A huge success." Byron beamed, shoving orange-rimmed glasses up the bridge of his bulbous nose. "Brilliant, playing up to the kid. I thought you were bonko to run through three airports and halfway around the city of Atlanta to spend an hour with him the night before a big game. But in the end—well, I should'a known you would play the crowd for all it was worth. Always did have the damnedest knack for it. Gave the boy the thrill of his life, and the publicity—"

"I didn't do it for the publicity," Ryder snarled.

"I know, I know. But where's the harm in gettin' a little mileage out of it? Gave the kid his wish, and it sure as hell won't hurt your popularity when they smear your face over every paper in three states. Even without pictures of the boy, people'll eat it up. And if they use the fact that you banned the photographers from the MacCrea apartment—God, what a touch of sincerity that'd give it. Tug right at the old heartstrings.''

''I did it for the kid.'' Ryder gritted his teeth, trying to withstand the urge to shut Crowell's mouth.

''Sure ya did, Rye. Damned nice of you, too,'' Byron agreed in a gratingly hearty voice.

Ryder wanted to snap a sharp reply, but in spite of his mounting irritation at the agent's brash attitude, there was enough truth in what he'd said to leave a bad taste in Ryder's mouth.

Especially with Ellie MacCrea's words still raking at his conscience. He closed his eyes, surprised at how clearly he could see her, still. Her autumn-red hair tumbled around features that had looked almost too fragile to be real. Wide gray eyes reflected the shaky courage of a child facing a thunderstorm.

Belligerent? Ryder had seen umpires with less grit than she had shown. Strong? How else could she have survived her son's illness? Yet at the same time she had appeared so vulnerable beneath that prickly facade. As if she were just waiting…bracing herself for the next blow to come.

And he, Ryder Sloan, had definitely been that blow. He squirmed inwardly, feeling like a kid who had accidently tripped a teacher on the playground.

She had thought his visit to her sick child had been nothing but a publicity stunt—something to further his bankability as an endorser for flashy cars, athletic shoes and men's cologne. She had believed he was using Zak, subtly, but using him nonetheless.

And she had come at Ryder, furious, in the entryway of her building—like a lioness defending her cub. He had deserved it. Every scathing word. Every scornful expression. Damn, the woman should have slammed the door right in his face.

That would have been one for Byron's papers, Ryder thought, rubbing at his gritty eyes with his fingertips. Ryder Sloan's Million-Dollar Teeth Driven Down his Throat by Irate Mother.

"Rye? Rye, did ya hear me?" Byron's voice intruded, the agent's beefy hand clapped him on the shoulder. "You must be tired. Been talking to you the last five minutes, an' you've been sitting there all glaze-eyed. Like you were at that all-night party when you and Marla—"

"I don't want to talk about Marla." Ryder jammed his fists against the rich upholstery, levering himself straighter in the seat. His mind filled with images of a face so sultry, so tempting, it would have been perfect in a picture of Eve with the serpent in the garden. And he had been a most willing Adam....

Every muscle in his body went rigid. And they already ached from the hours cramped up in narrow plane seats and hard plastic chairs in airline waiting rooms.

Byron harrumphed deep in his throat and fiddled with his signature tacky necktie. "'Course not. I didn't mean..." he stammered, then recovered enough to take on an accusatory glare. "I told you this'd wear you out. And you know, you've got the home game against Los Angeles tomorrow—"

"I know the damned schedule," Ryder snapped, glaring at the man.

"Yeah, and you also know that the Angels have the first glimmerings of hope for an Eastern Division title since the year you were born. And unless you're in top form, they can kiss it goodbye."

Relief shot through Ryder as the limo slowed, then came to a stop alongside the curb. Ryder looked up at the exclusive Atlanta high rise that was crowned by his

penthouse. Home. If anyone could call yards of concrete and walls of glass by so warm a name.

Ryder opened the limo's door without waiting for the
driver and slid his lean body out into the damp heat of
the late afternoon. He leaned against the vehicle's shiny
side.

"Despite what the sportswriters intimate, there are
eight other guys on the field besides me. And they've all
played damned good ball this season."

"But you've played *great* ball." Byron stretched like
a cat who had just raided a fish market. "Another season like last one and you'll be set for life, kid. Everything you've ever wanted."

"Not everything." He wished the words back as soon
as he'd said them, but he merely slammed the door and
turned to stride up to the building. The doorman greeted
him, ushering him in, but Ryder only gave him a quick
nod, his mind harking back to the bitterness, the hurt,
that had shadowed his first season with the Angels. His
rookie year. The year he had realized his most cherished
ambition. The year he had lost his most secret dreams.
Marla...

He shook his head, grimacing at the memory of the
green kid he had been. Naive. Idealistic. At least no one
would accuse him of those traits any longer. Now he
knew that people wanted something when they approached him. Women—the thrill of going to bed with
a professional athlete. Men—his money. Investment
schemes, tax shelters, a hundred and one ways to make
Ryder rich—and make themselves large dividends in the
process.

I feel sorry for you, Sloan, he griped at himself inwardly. *Real sorry. You want to look for real problems,
just remember where you were an hour ago.*

Ellie MacCrea's living room. Ryder felt a strange tug
in his chest. All warm rusts and cool blues, the room had

been, with plump patchwork cushions and half a dozen of Zak's toys scattered across scarred-up end tables.

The elevator whisked Ryder skyward, but he was still remembering the sunshiny kitchen and the way the light spilling through eyelet-curtained windows had snagged in the red of Ellie MacCrea's hair. Had she really thought he hadn't noticed her sneaking peeks at him while he talked to her son? Ryder had to smile. Her militant gaze had fairly burned into him, as if daring him . . . to what? To hurt Zak? To hurt *her?*

It had been a long time since anyone had regarded Ryder Sloan as persona non grata. A unique experience. One that should have been irritating, or at least amusing. But one that left him feeling as if a thin film of silt had drifted over his skin, leaving him tarnished in some way he'd never been aware of before.

The elevator slid smoothly to a stop, a discreet, pleasingly pitched bell announcing the top floor. Ryder stepped out into the entryway, let himself in to what he had once hoped would be his sanctuary.

Somehow he'd never realized that sanctuary was just another way of being alone. That celebrity meant being isolated, even in the middle of a crowd. And, God knew, he'd had enough loneliness and isolation to last him a lifetime.

He flicked on the light switch, and chrome-and-green-glass lamps set the cream-colored carpet and black furnishings aglow. Crossing to where the sliding glass doors opened onto the terrace, he peered out over the city.

Every one of his childhood homes had looked like this—sterile, elegant. Cripes, his mother had kept his bats and gloves in a walnut case, made specially for that purpose, his name engraved on a brass plaque on its side. Never could Ryder remember dashing in like Zakary MacCrea would have, tossing his glove onto the couch while running in to fling his arms around his mother, regaling her with the news of the grand slam he'd hit in the vacant lot nearby.

No, neither Arthur nor Andrea Sloan would have appreciated a rumpled, grimy little-boy hug, even if they had been around long enough to receive one. Even now, they much preferred watching Ryder play his games on TV—as far away as possible from the sweat and the noise and the crowd.

Ryder shucked off his jacket, hanging it in the closet concealed by mirrored panels. Had Zak MacCrea played ball before he'd grown too sick? Ryder found himself wondering. He could just see Ellie hauling lawn chairs to the ballpark, sitting with the other moms and dads drinking lemonade from blue thermoses. He bet she could give an umpire pure holy hell.

Ryder turned and paced into his bedroom. Kicking off his shoes, he sank down on the ocean-wide bed and closed his eyes. Byron had been right about one thing. Ryder did need to be at peak alertness, peak strength, when he took the field the next day. The division title was a dream everyone on the Angels shared. But since Ryder's rookie year it had held even more importance for him. Proof that he had been right—when he'd made that costly decision that had changed his life.

He had been dozing long enough for dusk to come when the phone rang. He reached over, mumbling hello into the receiver.

"Rye, darling, is that you?" The sexy feminine voice would have made most men ache in a very particular place. Ryder groaned inwardly.

"No, Tara, it's not me. No one's here but the plants."

"As if you could keep plants alive as much as you're gone, love."

Ryder could almost see Tara Lane's full lips curved into a pout.

"I've missed you," she purred. "I didn't realize how much until I saw that newsclip of you going to that little boy's place. It was so sweet of you to see him—"

"He's a terrific kid." If Ryder heard one more time what a "nice" guy he was for seeing Zak, he'd drive a bat through a plate-glass window.

"It's been a long season, Rye," Tara whispered cajolingly.

"And hopefully it'll be a longer one," Ryder mumbled to himself.

"I thought I might come over for a while. That we could steal, um, a few bases together."

"I don't think that would be a good idea." Ryder made a face as he shoved himself to a sitting position in the midst of the rumpled bedspread.

The thought of losing himself in Tara's luscious body for a few hours had lost whatever appeal it had once had. He was sure Tara felt the same way about the sex. However, the appeal of his seven-figure contract, it seemed, hadn't dimmed. "Tara, I've got an important game tomorrow, and—"

"It's always the 'and' that I worry about." Sulkiness had reached Tara's voice. "After this series, you have a few days off, don't you?"

"Listen, Tara, we've been over this before. I don't think—"

"Oh, goodness, look at the time!" Tara cut him off with a soft laugh. "No wonder you're so cranky. Poor baby! I should have checked before I called."

"No. I mean, yeah, I—"

"Must go now. Let you sleep like a good boy. Wouldn't do to let the manager find out I've kept you awake all night."

"Tara—"

"See you soon—maybe at the game Saturday. Bye."

"Tara, I wouldn't—" The phone clicked in Ryder's ear. He shook his head as he dumped the receiver back into the cradle, but in spite of himself, a wry smile twisted his lips. Of course Tara would be at the game Saturday. It was going to be carried on national television.

Glancing at the glow of the digital clock on the bed-side table, he uttered a soft curse. "Nine o'clock on a Thursday night," he grumbled. "I got to stay up later than this when I was in third grade!"

Third grade. The year Ryder's parents had spent four months on safari in Kenya. The year a serendipitous "calamity" had saved Ryder from months beneath the thumb of the stone-faced Sloan housekeeper, Miss Meerschaum, and had given him a summer of Cammy Rath instead.

A hollow laugh rose in Ryder's chest as he remembered how his parents had fumed over the fall that had left Miss Meerschaum with a fractured hip the night before they were to leave. They had acted as if the poor woman had sustained the injury on purpose—just to put a crimp in their vacation plans. And when they were not blaming Miss Meerschaum, Ryder had been certain they were blaming him.

Even then he'd suspected his parents wished they could just throw a sheet over him to keep the dust off, the way they did with the furniture. But since that was impossible, they had done the next best thing. His mother had put in a call to the man who tended the Sloan's gardens evenings and weekends, and had de-manded that he send his twenty-year-old daughter to take care of Ryder for the duration.

The first week Ryder had been more belligerent than ever—still stinging from his parents' tantrums. But in the end, he'd almost wished all air-and-water transporta-tion between the continents could have closed down through the next school term, stranding his parents even longer.

The eight younger brothers and sisters who jammed Cammy's parents' tiny tract house had ridden five miles on their rattletrap bikes to visit their big sister. But they had stayed to slide down the Sloan banister, teach Ryder how to throw spitballs, and climb the huge water tower in the vacant lot next door. That had been the year Ryder discovered Nazzereno's Pizza, cherry phosphates and the huge dill pickles at Orwitz's Deli.

Magical. Brimming with laughter. Ryder had prayed that summer would never end. But it had come to a crashing halt when his parents had returned. Andrea had immediately contracted migraines from the noisy Rath tribe, and Arthur had been enraged to see his son's name scrawled in model paint on the water tower's side.

Ryder still winced at the memory of Cammy's tearful goodbye. She had hugged him and told him that she wished she could take him with her—cram him into the triple set of bunkbeds in her brothers' tiny room.

Ryder had wished that, too. Badly.

Wished for a family, and love, and laughter. Wished that someone would want him around—even when he was tired, or cranky, or down.

Scads of people wanted Ryder Sloan now—ace third baseman, star athlete, crack hitter with a million-dollar smile. But sometimes he thought he'd still trade it all away for a set of cluttered rooms where he could get his heart warm.

He got up from the bed, pacing over to where ash-colored blinds obscured the window. He parted the thin slats, looking up to where the moon was floating in a faint red ring, but he didn't see the beautiful Atlanta skyline. Didn't see the gray clouds scudding across the tops of the buildings.

He saw a cozy living room, tasted foamy milk, saw Ellie MacCrea's slender fingers tousling her son's hair. Hunger gnawed inside Ryder, and for an instant he wondered what it would feel like to have those fingers smoothing over his hair, those wide, gray eyes glowing up at him.

Without the sadness. Without the dread that had lurked around Ellie MacCrea's mouth even when she had smiled. Though God knew, Ryder didn't blame her for being afraid. . . .

Zak's cheeks had been so pale, his frail hands holding the autographed baseball as if it were some treasure from the Taj Mahal. What would it be like to have a son like Zak, and be facing the possibility of losing him? And for Zak . . . how would it feel to be that young and not be able to run? Play?

Even now, at thirty-three, Ryder shuddered at the prospect of giving up baseball. And with each year that slipped away, he had only a limited number more that he could play the game that had been his whole life since he was Zak's age. But at least he had twenty-odd years of memories—of double plays and grand slams and the hot summer sun beating down on his jersey. Zak didn't even have that.

Cripes, Ryder thought in disgust, he hadn't even asked what was wrong with the kid. Whether or not Zak would ever be able to tug on a baseball glove again.

And suddenly Ryder needed to know.

He stared out at the night a moment more. Then he hustled into the living room to grab his jacket.

This is crazy, a voice inside him whispered. *Sloan, you've finally gone over the edge. Ellie MacCrea nearly had your head for coming when she expected you. You'll be lucky if she doesn't cream you with a vase for showing up now.*

No. There was always a way around a woman's temper. And Ryder was a master at circumventing such disasters. He should be. God knew he'd had enough practice with Tara. The grin the cameras loved quirked Ryder's mouth as he let himself out of his penthouse.

A peace offering...that was what was needed, he mused. Even the Apaches in John Wayne movies let the pale faces keep their scalps if the Duke came bearing gifts.

Chapter Three

The television's glow cast eerie fingers of light across the darkened living room, and the creepy background music made Ellie's scalp prickle.

She thought with a grimace that *Webster's Ninth New Collegiate Dictionary*'s definition of monster movies should read: Inventions of seriously disturbed minds whose sole intention is to drive parents of young children insane.

She glanced over to where Zak sat, grinning with delight as the creature from the Black Lagoon slid menacingly into the water. He could've been watching reruns of *Lassie,* for all the suspense that showed on his face. Nothing amused him more than the outdated costuming and makeup techniques used in the 1950s classics.

And nothing irritated Ellie more than her own less-than-sensible reaction to the very same films. Ever since Zak had discovered the *Thursday Night Creature Feature* on a local channel, she had endured chills skittering up her spine, her palms sweating at creaks in the night—a ridiculous affliction for a grown woman who could see the zippers on the backs of the monster suits.

Usually she was a good soldier—did her time with the same long-suffering good humor Zak put into their trips to the art gallery. Tonight, though, with the stress of the afternoon still thrumming through her system, dealing with the *Creature from the Black Lagoon* was almost more than she could handle.

The only thing she could handle even less, it seemed, was disappointing her son. She glanced at Zak's face, his eyes wide as he chewed at one ragged fingernail.

Not the face of a sleepy child. No reprieve from that quarter. Ellie sighed, resigned.

Just when you thought it was safe to go back in the water, she thought, making a face as her eyes shifted to the green-finned monster making its way across the television screen.

"All *right!*" Zak murmured in ecstasy as he waited for the creature to sink its flippers into its unsuspecting prey—a lone woman paddling about the water, oblivious to the danger gliding nearer, ever nearer.

She deserved to be eaten, Ellie thought grimly. Any woman stupid enough to swim in monster-infested lagoons deserved to be creature chow.

Easy enough for you to say, a voice whispered inside her. *But what if the "monster" has eyes so blue you could drown in them, and a body hot enough to melt a polar ice cap?*

Ellie slid a finger into the neckband of the oversized Shakespeare T-shirt that was her favorite nightgown and pulled it away from her suddenly overheated skin.

Danger. If the word had been emblazoned across Ryder Sloan's forehead in red neon, the threat could not have been any clearer.

Why, then, did she feel so infernally tempted—to go for a swim?

"Most likely a darn crowded pool," she muttered, visualizing Sloan surrounded by a bevy of voluptuous bikini-clad admirers. "No. More like a hot tub."

"A hot what, Ma?" Zak's inquiry made Ellie flush as guiltily as if the boy could see the lurid picture she had been imagining.

"N-nothing, Zak," she stammered, then recovered with remarkable aplomb. "I mean, I was wondering if you wanted a—a hot tub of popcorn."

Zak's freckled nose wrinkled in puzzlement; eyes far too shrewd for a seven-year-old peered out at her as he lifted the bowl she had given him when the movie began—a bowl still half-full of crisp white kernels. "Popcorn's not like coffee, Mom. It tastes just as good cold."

Ellie's cheeks burned, and she cursed herself inwardly. "Well, how about a drink then? You must want *some*thing." The boy looked hopefully at the container on the carriage-seat table, the glass bottle drained of Astro-Ice Cooler minutes before.

"How 'bout another bottle of—"

"Sure. No problem. I'll be back in a sec." Ellie was babbling. She knew it. And when she saw her son's stunned grin, she wanted to crawl beneath the carpet.

MacCrea household rule number one—she could hear her own voice mock her—*one* bottle of Astro-Ice a night....

But at the moment, she would have served the kid an eight-course meal of Twinkies and Sweet Tarts if it meant escape. She jumped up from the couch and hurried into the kitchen. Ellie had always considered herself on a lofty plane—men's minds, not their bodies, intrigued her. While other junior-high-school girls had been dreaming of winning the latest star-date contest in the most recent teen magazine and traveling to Hollywood, she had been dreaming of traveling back in time. Back to medieval England to prove once and for all that

Richard III had not murdered the two little princes in the Tower.

But she was older now. Wiser. Experienced enough to realize that, like most men, Richard had probably done whatever he had to in order to get his way. Daniel certainly had.

Ellie opened the refrigerator and pulled an Astro-Ice from the wire shelf, thumping the bottle onto the counter with unwarranted vehemence. But it was not her ex-husband's face that rose up to taunt her, rather it was the image of Ryder Sloan's thick, dark hair, that smile that could disarm a nuclear submarine.

He had wanted something, too, when he had come to the apartment that afternoon—had wanted publicity, and maybe a rush from the hero-worship that had been in Zak's eyes. Why then did she keep deluding herself that there had been a vulnerability in Ryder Sloan... lurking around the corners of that sexy-as-hell mouth and beneath eyelashes obnoxiously thick for someone who looked so unrelentingly masculine?

A throne, a baseball bat—what difference did it make? A little testosterone in the bloodstream seemed to give the possessor license to trample whoever stood in his path.

Daniel had taught her that—with a vengeance—the day he had walked out of her life. *You're smothering me, Ell. You, the kid, the house. A white picket fence and a thirty-year mortgage aren't my style.*

Ellie had looked around the house Daniel had bull-dozed her into agreeing to buy two years before—even though she had known it would stretch their already-tight budget to the breaking point. A showplace, all sprawling cedar and sleek glass with white carpeting, it had been worlds away from the cozy Victorianesque refuge she had dreamed of.

She had remembered the day he had breezed in from a chance meeting with a college classmate who had proudly displayed pictures of a newborn daughter. That very night, Daniel had urged Ellie to throw away her prescription for birth control pills. A baby...he had whispered to her as they made love. He wanted a baby—her baby, their baby....

He had seemed so sure of himself—willing to go after what he wanted without counting the cost. Ellie had envied him that. God knew, she couldn't even buy a sweater on sale without conducting a congressional investigation of every other store in the mall.

And yet, envy had faded into sharp disillusionment as she realized that it was not decisiveness Daniel displayed. Rather, he had more the abandon of a spoiled child rummaging beneath a Christmas tree, gorging himself with presents, then casting them aside.

But then, one could sell a house, quit a job, divorce a wife. The only thing Ellie hadn't suspected was that one could throw away a child.

Even now, years later, the pain of it sawed inside her, jagged, relentless, filling her with waves of hurt, disbelief and fury. She looked across the breakfast bar to where Zak sat in his Batman pajamas, his red hair tousled as he stuck the tip of his tongue into the gap where his front tooth had been.

And she hated Daniel for walking away from something that was so infinitely precious.

"Mom! The commercial's almost over." Zak's voice broke through her thoughts. "Hurry up or you'll miss it when the creature catches that dumb girl."

Shaking off the unwanted memories, Ellie scooped up the bottle and hurried in with a forced smile. "I wouldn't want to miss that," she said, plunking the drink down on a coaster.

Zak grinned knowingly. "Yeah. You *love* this stuff," he said in his spookiest voice. "The monster sneakin' up on her...."

It was abominable for a seven-year-old to be so amused by his mother's cowardice.

"Cut it out, kiddo, or I'll ground you until you're twenty," Ellie said as the eerie "stalking" music began to give her the creeps.

She took her post at the other end of the couch, hating the heightening suspense as the camera zoomed in yet again on the woman, the tension building as she waited for the creature to attack.

She dug her fingernails into her palms and tried to think of her grocery list or the essays she had to correct, but her too-vivid imagination already had *her* paddling about in that infernal lagoon ... she could feel the cool water, see the ripples as she splashed ... she could sense something lurking ... evil ....

Creak.

The sudden sound from behind her sent her heart leaping to her throat. She wheeled, peering over the back of the couch. The fire escape door was dead-bolted as always, its window reflecting the neon sign of the Chinese restaurant across the street.

But there, silhouetted in the pink-and-green glow, was the shadowy outline of a man's face.

Ellie stifled a scream as the figure pressed closer to the pane of glass, as if to look inside.

"Zakary—" she croaked, grabbing for the phone. "Get out of—"

But her warning was lost as a gentle rap sounded on the door and a muffled voice called, "Zak? Ellie?"

A burglar on a first-name basis? Ellie thought numbly.

At that moment, the glow from the television spilled past her to the window, revealing white teeth in a devastating grin.

"Ryder!" Zak bounded off the couch, elated as he dashed toward the door. "It's Ryder, Mom!"

"What the...?" Ellie gasped, fumbling to hang up the receiver, midway through dialing the police. Ryder Sloan, perched on her fire escape like some comic book hero? In the middle of the night? Why? Had he forgotten his cape?

Raking back disheveled hair, Ellie hurried over to the doorway and unfastened the lock. She threw the door open, spilling in hot night air, the sounds of the city and the overwhelming power of Ryder Sloan's smile.

"Do you make a habit of sneaking around people's fire escapes in the middle of the night, Mr. Sloan," Ellie snapped, "or should Zak and I consider ourselves privileged?"

For an instant, Ellie thought his grin faltered, but any such thought vanished as he winked at Zak over the mountain of flat cardboard boxes balanced in deliciously muscled arms. "Scared her, huh, sport?"

"We were watchin' the *Creature Feature*," Zak informed him with a sage nod. "She gets all creepily when it's on. I *love* to jump at her and yell 'boo.'"

Ryder chuckled. "It's a wonder you've made it to your seventh birthday—" he began, then, as if suddenly struck with what he had just said, and the power that offhand comment might have in the household of a critically ill child, Ryder stopped and cleared his throat.

"Mom always says she's gonna ground me 'till I'm twenty," Zak said, breezily unaware of the undercurrents zinging through the room. "But she never does it for more than ten minutes."

"Zakary!" Ellie exclaimed, wondering how many shades of red it was possible to turn in a matter of a few moments.

"Well, you don't! I watch on my clock, an'—"

"Hey, sport, we better take care of this stuff before it gets cold," Ryder broke in, extending the boxes toward

Zak. "I stopped at Nazzereno's on my way over, grabbed some—"

"Pizza!" Zak shrieked with delight. "Mom! Ryder brought pizza!"

Ellie tried to ignore the stab of guilt Zak's ecstasies spawned in her. With Zak's restricted diet, pizza had become a rare treat. And there was nothing her son loved more.

"What kind is it?" Zak badgered eagerly. "Pepperoni? Sausage? I hope it's not those little fishy things— nanchovies—"

"Zak," Ellie started to caution him, but he was already trailing after Ryder to the kitchen.

"I'm not sure what kind there is," Ryder's voice drifted back, a little sheepishly. Ellie, who had followed in their wake, leaned against the wall, unbelieving, as Ryder shifted four—no *five*—large pizza boxes onto the table.

"Are you insane?" she asked. "There's enough there to feed Zak's whole class."

Sloan shrugged, angular cheekbones darkening. "I wasn't sure which was Zak's favorite, so I just told them to give me one of each kind of pizza seven-year-old boys liked."

"One of every kind..." Ellie shook her head. "You could've called, Mr. Sloan. Asked before you spent a fortune."

"Don't worry. I can afford it." Ryder gave a gratified smile at Zak's whoop as he uncovered a double-cheese.

"My favorite!" Zak enthused, slipping two pieces onto a blue stoneware plate. "Hey, Rye, they were talkin' 'bout the game tomorrow on the news before *Creature* started. Said you were gonna drag the Angels to a pennant, kickin' and screamin' if you had to. How—"

"Zak," Ellie interrupted, her lips thinning in irritation at the man standing in her kitchen, like some beneficent monarch descending from his throne. "Why don't you take your pizza into the living room. I'd like to speak to Mr. Sloan alone for a moment."

"Aw, Mom!" the boy groaned, grabbing onto Sloan's arm. She took perverse pleasure in the smears of pizza sauce Zak's hands left on Ryder's pristine team jacket.

If the man noticed, he never showed it. Ryder only chucked the boy under the chin, saying in a conspiratorial voice that made Ellie want to slap him, "Go on, slugger. I'll clear this with the coach, here, and then come in and take a look at this monster that has her so jittery."

Zak giggled. "My Mom *did* coach one year. But she—"

"Mr. Sloan is not interested in my coaching, Zak. *Believe* me," Ellie said, her face burning as she remembered that disastrous season. She had spent the entire summer poring over books about baseball—the language more foreign to her than the old English of the poem Beowulf.

As if recognizing the warning glint in her eyes, Zak grabbed his plate and headed for the living room to gorge himself on monsters and mozzarella.

Silence descended like cold rain, and Ellie chafed beneath it. Her lips tightened in irritation as she glared at Sloan, this man who could breeze in, careless, casting about largess.

"You coached baseball?"

"Peewee League. It seemed all the fathers were busy that summer. But I did such a crummy job that by the next season they were practically fighting to get my position."

She waited for amused laughter, a patronizing quip. What she got was a look full of respect. "I bet you did a damn fine job, Ellie MacCrea. Zak's a lucky kid."

Ellie chewed at her bottom lip, more disconcerted by this solemn Ryder Sloan than ever. "And you, Mr. Sloan," she said in an effort to draw back from the lethal power of his charm, "are avoiding my questions."

"Questions?" He arched one dark brow.

"Yes. For starters, would you mind explaining why you showed up on my fire escape at ten o'clock at night? Without a phone call? Without any warning?"

He met her hostile gaze with an unnervingly sincere one. "I was afraid you wouldn't let me come."

"I—" Ellie wanted to protest, but found she couldn't as she considered what her reaction would have been to such a call. She wanted to hang on to her anger, wanted to zap him with another sharp rejoinder, but all she could do was smile.

"See, I knew it," Ryder said with engaging boyishness. "You would have told me to jump in the pizza sauce."

"Mr. Sloan..."

"Ryder." His voice was soft, sweet. "And I *am* sorry. I didn't mean to frighten you."

Ellie swallowed hard as something she had thought long-buried stirred inside her—something warm, wonderful. Terrifying.

Suddenly excruciatingly aware of how she must look in her baggy thigh-length shirt, with her feet bare and hair uncombed, she turned away from the lure of Ryder Sloan's eyes and crossed to the refrigerator, ostensibly to pull out two colas. "If you didn't intend to scare me, you might have come to the front door like a normal person. Looking out on a dark fire escape and seeing a man isn't my idea of a fun time—even when I'm *not* being coerced into watching monster movies."

She turned back toward him in time to catch the fleeting sheepishness that crossed those drop-dead-gorgeous features. Ryder reached out, taking the soft drink from her hand. Their fingers brushed for just a heartbeat. But then, Ellie thought as a thrill shot through her, how long did someone have to touch a live wire to light up like a Christmas tree?

"There were some people out in front of your building."

Ellie shook herself in an effort to clear her head. "What?"

"That was why I came up the fire escape. I was afraid . . . well, after this afternoon, I didn't want you to think . . ." With a sigh of disgust, Ryder raked his fingers through his hair. "I don't know. It's just that all the way home I kept thinking about you . . . thinking about Zak. All those reporters, photographers, circling like vultures. I'm used to having my face splashed all over the papers. Cripes, I hardly notice the cameras anymore. But it must have been . . . ugly for you, having all that craziness out on the lawn, when all you wanted was for me to spend a few minutes with your little boy."

"Ryder, you don't owe Zak or me anything," Ellie said, distinctly uncomfortable. "You were terrific. That is, once we dragged you away from your adoring throng." She couldn't stifle a rueful smile.

"I wanted to be. Terrific, I mean. For Zak. I can still remember what it felt like to be a kid and think— dream—I'd grow up to be like Mickey Mantle or—" Ryder glanced at the little boy munching on pizza in front of the TV. "I said the wrong thing again, didn't I?"

Sensing his discomfort, Ellie laid a hand on his arm. "It's okay. If I freaked at every slip of the tongue someone made regarding Zak's illness, I'd be a basket case. Believe me, Sloan. I've heard worse."

"It's just that, I don't know," Ryder paced over to examine a crayon drawing of a baseball diamond Zak had taped on the refrigerator door. "I guess I always wanted to be at least half as great as kids like Zak think I am, you know?"

Ellie stared at the broad shoulders beneath the Angels logo, disturbed to see them just a little slumped as Ryder jammed his hands in his pockets. It was a gesture wrenchingly like one of Zak's. And it tugged at her heart more than she would have believed possible.

"So, coach." Ryder turned, his face still shaded with a seriousness at odds with the cocky superstar who had grinned out from Zak's baseball cards. "Do I get to stay for a while, or would you rather I made my excuses and headed to the dugout?"

It was there again. That blasted vulnerability. That sweetness, that strength, that made Ellie want to curl her fingers into his. Comfort him, and be comforted.

Comfort Ryder Sloan? she jeered at herself inwardly. For what? Being one of the wealthiest players ever to pick up a bat?

"I may be a shrew, but I'm not unreasonable," she said, glancing away. "Zak would love to spend more time with you."

"And what about you?" The words were low, alluring.

It took all of Ellie's willpower to shrug with feigned nonchalance. "I have some essays to correct. If you can endure the *Creature from the Black Lagoon* in my stead, I'd be eternally grateful."

Did disappointment flit across Ryder's features? Ellie was sure she imagined it. He flashed her a game smile.

"Consider yourself rescued from the monster's clutches, ma'am."

Picking up a wedge of pizza, minus a plate, he strode into the living room and plopped down next to Zak.

Ellie tried to convince herself that she was glad to have escaped both the movie and the man. She tried to block out the sounds of laughter and teasing as she dragged out the sheaf of papers from her briefcase.

From the time she had been in kindergarten, she had had the power of intense concentration—the ability to blot out the shrieks of an entire pep rally if she were in the middle of reading *Jane Eyre*. But Jed Giovetti's paper on The Age of Enlightenment seemed even more confusing than usual tonight—punctuated, as it was, by the sounds of Ryder's monster imitations and Zakary's nonstop chatter.

She chewed at the end of her red pen, feeling oddly abandoned and ill-used, sitting there, alone. *That shows you just how idiotic you're behaving, Ellie MacCrea,* she scolded herself. *A gorgeous-looking guy comes to see Zak, and you're drooling over him like a high school cheerleader.*

Clamping her teeth down hard on the pen, she forced herself to turn to the next essay. "Temptation," it was aptly titled, "The World of the Victorian Underground."

The last essay was graded and stacked neatly in a pile when she finally raised tired eyes from her work. Strains from the "Star-Spangled Banner" were drifting in from the television as the station signed off for the night.

Ellie glanced at the clock above the sink, stunned at the time. Midnight. In all the time she'd been teaching it had never taken her so much time to grade such a little bundle of assignments. Zak should have been in bed long ago. And after a two-hour dose of monsters and mayhem, Ryder's mind must have turned into jelly. She stood up, her muscles stiff from sitting in one position for so long, and was suddenly aware of a blanket of unnatural quiet.

Tiptoeing to the kitchen doorway, she looked into the living room beyond. The sight that met her eyes made her pause, her throat oddly tight.

Ryder sat dozing on the couch, stocking feet stretched out onto the coach-seat that served as a coffee table. A sleeping Zak was curled up on his lap. It was as if he somehow belonged there, Ellie thought numbly. Ryder's arms curved with disconcerting tenderness around Zak's small frame. The man's square, stubble-shadowed chin rested softly on top of the child's head, Ryder's absurdly thick lashes dark crescents upon his cheekbones.

An album of photographs lay open across Zak's lap, his Pee-wee league T-shirt—obviously rummaged from the bottom of his drawer—crumpled at the edge of the couch.

Ellie winced as she glimpsed a picture of her with Zak as an infant, a beaming Daniel looking down at them, bursting with paternal pride. Before he realized that babies woke up in the middle of the night. Before he realized that they couldn't stick Zak in a kennel like a cocker spaniel, to be boarded while the two of them jetted off to ski in Colorado.

Feeling painfully exposed, Ellie crossed to the television set and flicked it off. When she turned toward the couch again, it was to see Ryder's eyes fluttering open, his gaze disoriented as he looked at her. After a moment, his lips tugged into a sleepy smile, and Ellie knew she would remember forever the way his arm tightened around Zak.

"Guess we were both monstered out," Ryder murmured, stroking the boy's pale cheek.

"I guess so." Flushing, Ellie went to slip the album from Zak's limp fingers, shutting the book with a haste that betrayed her.

She felt Ryder's eyes on her as she slid the volume back into its place, and she chafed beneath the knowledge that he must have thumbed through countless pictures—a chronicle of Ellie MacCrea's stupidity. It was all there—the naive bride, the elegant house, and the man who had made a fool of her. Had it not been for the precious pictures of Zakary, threaded through the pages, she would have burned the thing years ago.

Bracing herself, she turned and reached out her arms. "Here, I'll take Zak," she said, moving to scoop the child up.

"No," Ryder said hastily. "I mean, I'll carry him...if you don't mind."

She must have looked as surprised as she felt, but she only nodded. "His bedroom is this way." She switched on the hall light and led Ryder down the corridor. She grinned in spite of herself when she led him into what she called Zak's Chamber of Horrors. "Look out for the mine fields," she warned, stepping over the toys scattered across the carpet.

Ryder chuckled, easing past her as he started to lower Zak onto the bed.

"Wait!"

Ryder froze at her command, then grinned as she shook out Zak's baseball bedspread. Monsters and super-heroes of every description tumbled to the carpet, mingled incongruously with a stuffed dog that looked like it had been run over by a cement truck.

"During the day this unassuming bed undergoes a miraculous transformation into the planet Zariah," Ellie explained in a whisper. "That is, when it's not Angels Stadium."

Ryder set Zak down onto the mussed sheets with a tenderness that astonished her, then stepped back to let her pull up the covers.

"Who is this guy? He looks like the planet exploded on him."

Ellie glanced over her shoulder to see the stuffed dog in Sloan's large hand. "That's Fluffles." She took the dog and ran a hand wistfully over its mangy plush coat. Zak's attachment to the toy never failed to twist something inside her—the stuffed dog had been Daniel's last present to him. She tucked it carefully in the crook of Zak's arm.

"He's a great little guy." Ryder's voice was quiet, soothing, like warm brandy. "Real smart, too. He loves you very much."

Ellie tossed back her hair, resolved not to go all weepy in front of a man who was practically a stranger. "I love him, too." Dropping a kiss on Zak's forehead, she padded from the room.

After a moment, Ryder followed. In the living room once more, awkwardness descended, as if, without the buffer of Zakary, there was nothing for them to say, nothing for them to do. Ellie laced her fingers in front of her, feeling for all the world like a gawky urchin in front of this man who, despite his rumpled state, looked like some model for a Hunk of the Month calendar. Mr. February—let me warm up your winter....

She expected him to make some move to leave, but he stood there, letting the silence between them stretch out until it was unbearable. Ellie had to fill it. "Can I...can I get you some tea? Something...?" She bustled over to the cupboard, digging around inside.

"Always plying me with drinks. Milk. Tea." Was there amusement in his voice? She wanted to kill him. "Tell me, Ellie MacCrea—are you trying to keep my mouth full so you won't have to talk to me?" His eyes were gently teasing, the corner of his lips quirking in a way that made Ellie want to lean forward, trace them with her tongue.

Where in heaven's name had that come from?

"Ellie, why don't you like me?" The question was so sudden, so sincere, Ellie almost dropped the teapot she was holding.

She whirled to face him. "I—I don't know you well enough to *dis*like you. I mean, you've been wonderful with Zak—this afternoon, and then tonight—"

"But I make you damned nervous."

"Yes. I mean, no. I mean, I guess what makes me jittery is that I don't—don't know what you want. Why you're here."

"Do I have to want anything?"

"Mr. Sloan, I'm sure you're a very nice man, but..."

"You trust me about as much as you would a shark in a feeding frenzy, right?"

Ellie started to stammer a reply, but Ryder's voice cut her off. "Why, Ellie? You hate baseball? You have something against guys who drive Porsches? Or is it that you don't like the way I look?"

Was he joking? She moistened her lips; her palms were damp. If he looked any better he'd incite a riot. He seemed to overpower the small kitchen, overwhelm her, the combination of raw sensuality and compassion more potent than anything she had ever known.

"You look . . . just fine. It's just that . . . what are you *doing* here?" she asked a little desperately.

"The truth?" He walked toward her. "When I got to my place this evening, I couldn't stop thinking. About Zak. About you. I realized I hadn't—hadn't even asked what was wrong with him. Whether he'll . . . when he'll get well."

"The doctors don't know." It was hard, so hard for Ellie to admit that—admit to even the possibility of losing Zak forever. "Zak's kidneys have been systematically failing for almost two years now. We hoped that with medication, we could check the degeneration. But . . ." Ellie stopped and shook her head.

"There must be something they can do."

"He's on dialysis three times a week now. And we're on the list for a transplant. But Zak's tissue type is rare."

"Yours doesn't match."

It was a statement, not a question. Ellie was grateful for that.

"No. The most horrible moment in my life was when the doctors told me I wouldn't be able to help Zak." She lowered her face, blinking back tears.

She heard the soft sound of Ryder moving toward her, felt the strength of callused, warm hands cupping her chin, lifting it upward. Her curtain of hair spilled back from her cheeks, leaving her vulnerable to his gaze. His thumb smoothed the delicate skin of her throat, a low groan rumbled in his chest.

"Oh, Ellie..." he murmured, his other arm curving around her waist, pulling her against the hard wall of his chest. "I'm so sorry."

It was good to lean against him, to feel his fingers slide through her hair. She could feel the steady beat of his heart against her cheek, the play of his muscles, warm beneath his shirt. His lips rested against the crown of her head, his breath stirring her hair.

It had been so long. So long since she had allowed herself to lean on anyone.

She wanted to stay there forever.

She straightened and pulled away.

"So," she said, turning away from him. "Now you know about Zak. We go to the hospital, we talk to the doctors, and we pray for a miracle."

"How...do you manage?" Ryder knew he was out of line, but he could still feel the fragility of her, the strength of her, imprinted against him. He wanted to pull her back into his arms and drive away the shadows that left her so haunted. So sad. But how did one wrestle with fate? How did one snatch up a miracle?

Yet, looking into Ellie MacCrea's wide gray eyes almost made him believe in them.

"Manage?" Ellie stiffened, her knuckles whitening where they grasped the handle of the teapot. "I don't. Waiting is hell."

There was a world of hurt in those words. Ryder jammed his hands in his pockets to keep from reaching out to her. Instinctively he knew Ellie MacCrea would loathe anything smacking of pity.

But it wasn't pity he felt for this woman, her narrow feet bare on worn linoleum, the soft cloth of her T-shirt skimming slender thighs. There was something about her that crept under his skin—something in the elegant curve of cheeks unblemished by makeup, hair that smelled subtly of honey. Ryder's jaw clenched as he lost himself in the clear, light gray of her eyes.

He knew if he stayed another moment he would kiss her.

He knew if he kissed her, she'd never see him again.

Defenses. Ryder had plenty of his own.

"I think I'd better go now."

She didn't try to stop him. Ryder grabbed the team jacket he had slung over a chair. "Ellie..."

He dug into a pocket, pulling out an envelope. "I was wondering if...well, if Zak would be well enough to go to an Angels game. Tomorrow, maybe..."

"Fridays are gruesome around here." She seemed almost relieved. "I have to tutor, Zak has his treatment. He's always exhausted afterward. It's very kind of you, Ryder, but—"

"Are Saturdays gruesome, too?" He tried to keep it light, but there was the tiniest threading of panic coiling inside him at the thought that she might be closing him out. "It's an afternoon game, so he won't even be up late. And I could show him the locker room—introduce him to some of the players."

"Zak would be in heaven. But—"

"I'll even send someone to drive you to the stadium. You won't have to fight the parking."

Her lips quivered, then curved into a wry smile. "Persistent, aren't you, Sloan?"

"Notoriously. I get what I want, Ellie."

The words were so quiet, Ellie shivered. Alarm bells were clanging inside her. But what had her father always said? God hates a coward.

"Okay, Sloan. You can add Zak to your adoring throng." There was a challenge in the pugnacious tilt of her chin. "I'll survive a day at the baseball diamond somehow. Maybe I'll bring that treatise on eighteenth-century English literature I've been wanting to read for so long."

He crossed to the door, one large hand on the knob. He glanced back over his broad shoulder. His eyes were twinkling, starred by tiny white creases at their corners from squinting against the sun. "If you can read in the middle of Angels Stadium on a Saturday, lady, more power to you."

"I have tremendous willpower, Sloan," Ellie affirmed, with more confidence than she felt.

"We'll see about that." He smiled. A devil's smile. An angel's smile.

And then he was gone.

Chapter Four

Ellie jammed her sunglasses up the bridge of a nose slippery with sun block, wishing that the mirrored lenses could somehow cover her whole face as she jostled through the Saturday afternoon crowd at Angels Stadium. She trailed after the uniformed driver who had swept up to her building in a stretch limo half an hour ago. The dignified man guided her past the bleacher seats, toward the boxes directly above the team's dugout.

Ellie grimaced with wry humor. Why not seat them on the blasted pitcher's mound, so everyone could gape at them? She sighed, pulling her embroidered Indian-cotton-gauze blouse away from sweat-sticky skin. She should have known Sloan would pull something like this—maneuver two innocent tickets to a ball game into the event of the century.

From the moment the limo had pulled up to the curb, she had felt more conspicuous than she had ever felt in her life. The whole neighborhood seemed to be craning out their windows, whistling and cat-calling and waving to Zak, while the beaming little boy—garbed in full Angels regalia—had bounced on saddle-tan leather seats and played with the buttons that opened and shut the well-stocked bar concealed by a burl-oak panel.

Ellie had cursed herself, cursed Ryder Sloan, wishing she'd had the sense to at least refuse his offer of the car. But when Zak had gone into ecstasies, finding, amongst the bottles of champagne, a full stock of Astro-Ice Cooler, Ellie had felt an unexpected tightness in her throat. And long before she had poured the soda into its accompanying squeeze bottle adorned with an Angels logo, Ellie had resigned herself to reveling in this day Sloan had obviously taken a great deal of time to plan for her son.

"Mom, look down there!"

Ellie was jerked back to the present when Zak almost wrenched her arm from its socket as he pointed a bandaged finger toward a cagelike structure below. "It's Ryder! He's takin' batting practice!" As if the man was the world's most powerful magnet, Zak jerked on Ellie's fingers, dragging her down the steps to where the area near the batting cage was thronged with enthusiastic fans.

Ellie strained on tiptoe as she followed Zak, just able to make out broad shoulders encased in a white uniform, pin-striped in blue. His blue baseball cap pushed at a jaunty angle above dark, deliciously wind-tousled hair, Ryder bandied quips with a dozen women leaning over the three-foot retaining wall that separated them from the team—or more accurately, from what Ellie figured was the most adorable tush in the National League.

Ellie felt an almost irrepressible urge to go up to one particularly well-endowed blonde, whose attributes were being held up by a straining strip of hot-pink cloth, and remind the woman that there were children present.

"Mmm, Rye." The woman's throaty voice carried over the din of the crowd as Sloan waited for his turn opposite the pitcher. "Love that bat, sugar. What say you show me how you use it after the game?"

Sloan was about to reply when those blindingly-blue eyes caught on Ellie—she suffered an occupational hazard by having the reddest hair in three states. She saw something soften in his gaze, the generic grin he had flashed the other woman warming, somehow growing sweeter, more...blast it, sexy, as he looked up at Ellie.

"Sorry, sweetheart," he called out to the blowsy woman, "already got a date."

"Sloan!" Ellie started to protest, her face flaming as a barrage of feminine faces turned to stare at her like she'd just won the lottery.

When Ryder gave her a bone-melting wink, she almost felt like she had. Pink Halter's lips pursed into a good-natured pout, and eyes sporting lashes weighted with a year's worth of mascara rounded in confusion as she gave Ellie the once-over. "I don't know what you've got, honey," the woman said, "but you oughta bottle it, if it got you a date with that bod. All I want is ten minutes in a closet with 'im."

Her friends giggled.

"I don't! I mean, I'm not..." Ellie figured it was impossible to die of embarrassment, or she would be ready for a casket fitting. "Mr. Sloan and—and I..." She was an English teacher for God's sake. Why did it suddenly seem like a foreign language?

But at that moment a willowy model-type swished up, stealing the show as certainly as Sloan had. Ellie would have been grateful as the woman's perfect lips curved in a smile, except for the condescending words that rolled out in the newcomer's sultry voice.

"Don't worry, you haven't lost your touch," she said to Pink Halter. "The only thing she's got that you don't is this." The woman tugged at Zak's baseball cap.

The little boy glanced up, and the woman gave him a smile. "My name's Tara Lane," she said through the ripple of the other women's laughter. Ellie couldn't help but stare.

Deep purple eyes that had adorned countless advertisements for eye shadow flicked up to Ellie with a casual interest that was belied by the tiniest crease between winged brows.

"I'm a friend of Ryder's," Tara said, smoothing a crimson-silk tank top over breasts that had obviously never nursed a crying baby. "An *intimate* friend."

Ellie felt the sting of something that couldn't be jealousy as she looked at the woman whose name had been linked with politicians, millionaires and, more pointedly of late, Ryder Sloan.

A hot lump of envy lodged in Ellie's chest, thoughts of Tara's carefree, exciting life making her feel even drabber than usual. Irritated with herself, she turned her gaze back to where Ryder was taking his practice swings and wondered if he'd mind her borrowing the bat just long enough to smear dirt on Tara Lane's perfectly creased white shorts.

Ellie clenched her teeth, wondering why the dismissive light in Tara's eyes, and those of the other women, should bother her so much. God knew, she'd never thought herself to be any man's wild-night dream, but there was something about their assessment of her that rankled.

The crack of wood on leather snapped Ellie's attention back to home plate. Appreciative whistles rose from the onlookers as Sloan knocked a baseball into the next century. Well-defined muscles rippled beneath his jersey; his tall, rangy form contained all the lean grace of a world-class runner; his shoulders held the strength of the

Olympic gymnasts she and Zak had watched on television some time ago.

No wonder the man had half the females in Atlanta straining to get a glimpse of him. Everything about Sloan was designed to make feminine mouths water.

Ellie shook herself, aware she'd been daydreaming, as Tara's voice again intruded. "The guy's terminally gorgeous, isn't he?"

Ellie winced, aware that she'd been caught ogling as shamelessly as the rest of them.

"I mean, look at him." Tara laughed. "Pure perfection. It's annoying. The man doesn't have to do a thing to look like that except throw himself in a shower and wash his hair. Drags on whatever he grabs first out of his drawer, and always comes out looking like he just walked out of a jeans ad."

One of the groupies—a teenager in strategically ripped jeans and a tube top—giggled. "What I want to know, Tara, is if he looks that good *out* of his jeans."

Ellie felt a strange curling sense of discomfort, embarrassment at their banter. Not for herself, but strangely, for the man who now stood talking to the batting coach about his swings. Everything she'd ever seen of Ryder had indicated he reveled in the adulation he received. And yet, oddly, there was something about Tara and the other women—their open drooling, as if he were a piece of merchandise, to be handled and examined, inanimate, without feelings—that made her irritable on Ryder's behalf. That gave her an odd urge to protect him from something she sensed must subtly hurt him, the man who had fallen asleep in her living room two nights before.

She raked slender fingers through her tumbled mass of hair, remembering the feel of his callused hands against her skin, the way he had held her, gently, against the hard wall of his chest and rested his lips on her hair. Tenderness... Did any of these women—even Tara

Lane—know how much of that emotion Sloan possessed? Ellie doubted it, doubted they would even want that warm, flowing gentleness from the man who dominated their fantasies.

No, they would want Ryder Sloan, the hard-driven, blatantly sensual athlete, with a body seemingly hewn out of stone and a sex drive to rival Lothario. They'd want his mouth, his hands, his laughter, his groans of pleasure, but Ellie doubted they'd want that soft, sleepy smile that had been on Ryder's lips when he had tucked Zakary into bed two nights before. That disturbingly vulnerable, uncertain light that had been in eyes as blue as a midsummer sky.

At that moment, Ryder left the coach, his gaze searching the crowd until it lighted on her and Zak. Sloan jogged over to the wall. Passing by countless outstretched hands that waved pens, and programs and baseballs to be autographed, he came straight to Zak. Leaning over the brick barrier, Ryder tugged the Angels cap low over the child's nose.

"Hey, slugger. Ellie." Sloan's gaze flicked to Ellie, and her heart melted just a little before the crowd welled around them in a suffocating wave, the cacophony of scores of voices quelling all chance of a conversation. Ellie saw Ryder grimace in wry good humor, then, in one fluid movement, his hands reached across the wall that separated them, clasping Zak around the waist and swinging him down onto the edge of the field.

Instinctively Ellie leaned toward them, but when Ryder turned to her, arms outstretched, she would have backed away, if the people behind her had not pressed so close, cutting off any chance of escape.

Whistles and teasing quips echoed around her as Sloan's hands closed around her rib cage, whisking her over the barrier as easily as he had Zakary moments before.

But this time, his hands lingered, warm even through the layer of batting gloves that encased them, as he slowly slid her down, a bare whisper from his body.

Not close enough to be objectionable, or even suggestive, but close enough for Ellie to feel the hard-muscled power of him, to smell his lemony-clean hair, feel the pre-game adrenaline surging through him in a rush that was blatantly masculine, devastatingly sensual. She had read of warriors returning to their women after the heat of battle, had read of how passions fueled by matching skills in combat had spilled over into their beds. For an instant, she allowed herself the foolishness of imagining Ryder thus, his eyes glowing with triumph, his mouth on hers, hot and demanding and wonderful.

It was Zak's voice that drove the dizzy dreams from her eyes, made her step away from Ryder as if he could somehow see the imaginings she had conjured.

"Wow, Ryder!" Zak bubbled. "Bet that ball you hit still hasn't landed."

"The trick is to do that in the game, when it counts, kid." Ryder laughed. Then his mouth softened, and Ellie detected a rare solemnity misting his eyes. "I'm gonna win this one for you, Zak."

Ellie's heart flip-flopped in her chest, her eyes blurring at the sincerity, the sweetness in that deep voice, and she couldn't stop from imagining Ryder's dark hair set against the glinting silver of a helmet, a knight's lance in his hand, as if he were some champion out to do combat.

"Don't trust him, kid," Tara's call shattered such alluring fancies. "He said he was going to win one for me once, and they were shut out, 14-zip."

"Tara." Ryder's eyes snapped up to the beautiful brunette who now perched on the edge of the wall. An expression of genuine surprise, and a kind of resigned displeasure, creased his brow, but without being openly rude, it seemed, there was nothing he could do save haul her down as well.

"Glad to see me?" she asked, twining her arms around his neck in a way that made Ellie want to retch. The woman's voice dropped—low enough to be suggestive, loud enough to be certain Ellie could hear every word. "I was so disappointed when you said you had to sleep last night. I had much more...er...exciting plans. Maybe after the game?"

Ellie noted a flush stealing beneath Ryder's tan. His lips firmed in irritation, and not a little unease, as he grasped the model's gold-bangled wrists and put her away from him. "Tara, I want you to meet Zakary and Ellie MacCrea." A trace of annoyance roughened his voice. "They're my guests today."

"Your...oh." The woman gave a knowing glance. "The little boy who's got...who's sick? And you must be his *mommy?*"

The woman was positively gloating with triumph as she accented the word. Ellie stiffened, nodding her assent.

"Is your husband saving your seats?" Tara inquired. "Or did you send him off to get hot dogs already?"

"For God's sake, Tara—" Ryder growled, in disgust, but Zak's face was already clouding.

"My dad's not here," the child said, slowly. "I don't know where he is."

"We're divorced." Ellie tried to keep her voice matter-of-fact, despite the temptation to wring the woman's neck. To her credit, Tara appeared taken aback, genuine dartings of unease in those magnificent eyes.

"Oh. I'm sorry." Her hands fluttered to her breast. "Rye never told me." Tara gave Sloan a killing glare. Ellie wondered just how much Ryder did tell her—how much he whispered to her in their tumbled bed, his voice husky, drowsy, delicious with remembered lovemaking.

Ellie grimaced inwardly, remembering how she'd felt the night before last, as if she needed to keep Sloan at a distance, to quell the dangerous attraction that had seemed to be stirring in both of them. The whole thing seemed ludicrous here in the light of day. Raucous fans swarmed as near as possible, one of the most beautiful women in the world hovered there beside him—every word, every movement, all but screaming ownership.

She glanced away, something shriveling inside her, something she hadn't even known existed. Hope.

Eyes strangely blurred shifted to see the other players strolling in the direction of what must be the locker rooms, their exit giving Ellie a blessed escape.

"I think we'd better get up to our seats," she said.

Ryder glanced over one shoulder at the retreating backs of his teammates. Ellie sensed that he was torn. He swore under his breath.

Though Tara hung back, as if she wanted to get the last word with him, Ryder turned to face her, plunking the woman onto the wall with a few curt words Ellie couldn't hear. Then he swung Zak up, letting the boy sit on the ledge for a moment as he turned to Ellie.

She gritted her teeth against the pull of those eyes that snapped with life, a vitality, an optimism, she knew she could never share.

"After the game I'll come and get Zak, show him around the clubhouse and introduce him to the players," he said. "And then...then, Ellie, we need to talk."

Ellie turned her gaze away, her throat feeling oddly tight. "After the game, Ryder, there'll be nothing left to say. Except maybe thank you. For all you did for Zak today."

"Damn it, Ellie, I—"

"Sloan, you gonna stand out there all day gettin' women's phone numbers, or you gonna play ball?" A man Ellie recognized from Zak's baseball cards as Alex Craig bellowed, unbuckling his catcher's chest-guard.

Ryder raised a hand in acknowledgement to his friend, then turned back to Ellie. "I told the driver to get you anything you want from the concession stand—food, pop, T-shirts...whatever."

"Sloan, I can pay for a can of soda for God's sake. You don't have to—"

"I want to," was all he said. He lifted her up on to the wall, then he turned and loped off the field. The sunshine glinted gold streaks in the dark brown of his hair, and gave his skin a burnished glow, as if the sun from a score of summers, thick with baseball, still clung to him.

Ellie watched him until he disappeared beneath the arch that led to the locker rooms.

"Mom, am I gonna get to go with Rye? Am I gonna get to meet the other guys?" Zak asked, his eyes so hopeful, Ellie couldn't have denied him that pleasure if a hundred Tara Lanes had barred the way.

"I guess so, sweetie."

"I like Ryder. I like him a lot."

Ellie swallowed hard. Lifting the Angels cap from his head, she ruffled her son's russet curls. "I like him, too, Zakary," she said.

Maybe far too much.

Chapter Five

The afternoon sun melted in a shimmering line along the rim of the stadium as Ellie stared at the place where Ryder and an ecstatic Zakary had disappeared into the clubhouse twenty minutes before. Fans, sated with an Angels' victory, still threaded their way out to where their cars awaited, crammed in various parking ramps surrounding the stadium.

Time and time again Ellie heard voices rising above the din, raving on about the plays of the afternoon. Diehard fans dissected every pitch, every out, while exulting over the generous helping of home runs they'd been served up with their hot dogs—courtesy of Ryder Sloan.

He had been dazzling.

With the athletic grace of a dancer, he had dived to make spectacular catches, impossible throws. And his bat had been so lethal, Ellie could almost feel the sweat dampening the opposing pitcher's palms every time Sloan had stepped up to the plate.

His grin would have done a highwayman proud. Pure devilment. Arrogance, sweetened with a beguiling touch of boyishness.

He played the crowd like a master—and they loved him for it. Despite the sprinkling of Pink Halter types, there were hundreds of fans who obviously held a great affection for one they saw as a hero—as if somehow Ryder Sloan belonged to them, his reflected glory warming mundane lives of job, school, housework and endless, blazing summers.

Lives like Ellie's own.

She shifted on the hard seat, hating the hollow feeling in her chest. She was glad, now, that she had come here. These hours at the ball park had crushed whatever tenuous fantasies she had been unable to quell regarding Ryder.

Reality had slammed into her with a jolt, driving away the images of how right he had looked cuddling the sleeping Zak on her couch, how endearingly awkward he'd been, standing on her fire escape, his arms overloaded with pizza.

He'd appeared so entrancingly touchable then. Warm. Real. Strength shining in those blue eyes.

But it had only been an illusion. One she dared not indulge in again. Even if she were foolish enough to succumb to Sloan's megawatt charm, or the strange, almost wistful expression on those handsome features whenever he looked at her, it would be hopeless. There could never be anything between them. Anything real. Anything lasting. Not that Ellie believed in forevers anymore.

She grimaced, remembering the time she had captured a lightning bug while visiting her grandparents' farm in Illinois. Elated with her prize, she had locked it away in a dark-glass jar. When she had opened it the next day, the lightning bug was dead, a small, brown corpse amidst the grass she had put in for its bed.

Her grandmother had told her that the insect had suffocated because she had forgotten to punch holes in the jar's lid, but Ellie had always been certain that it had died because it could no longer shine.

She drew in a deep, surprisingly painful, breath. Even though she'd only known Ryder a brief time, she knew he'd been born to shine—center stage. If it hadn't been on a baseball diamond, it would've been somewhere else—playing the star of some sensual television detective show, or maybe the hottest new heartthrob on the big screen.

It wasn't Sloan's fault. But it wasn't hers, either, that she'd been born to be burrowed in a cozy chair on a night with thunder growling, her nose stuffed in a book that carried her back to an era of masquerade balls and gallant cavaliers and ladies who risked their hearts on a dangerous rogue's smile. She had indulged in dreams ever since she could remember, fantasies that were buried so deep in a misty realm of the impossible that she had been safe.

Ellie was jarred back to the present as she saw two figures emerge from the clubhouse—the lean, broad-shouldered man running backward to catch a baseball tossed by the red-haired boy. Regret and resolve twisted in Ellie's chest, bittersweet as she watched them zigzag their way across the field toward her.

Zak had an oversized baseball glove on his hand, and his thin form was swallowed up in a striped Angels jersey that reached to his ankles. When he turned his back to her, Ellie could see the bold blue lettering across it: SLOAN, 32.

She swallowed hard as she watched Zak throw a ball to Ryder, the child laughing with glee as the man feigned a spectacular catch, rolling over and over on the ground before coming up with the ball triumphantly in his hand.

They were close enough now for Ellie to see that Ryder was freshly showered and shaved, his damp hair skim-

ming the collar of an ice-blue shirt, faded black jeans
clinging to his long legs. There was a grass stain on one
shoulder, but somehow it only made him look more ap-
pealing as he scooped Zak up in his arms and ran over
to where Ellie sat.

Ryder settled Zak on the wall, the child fairly explod-
ing with excitement.

"Mom! Mom, did you see Ryder catch that? Did you
see me throw the ball? All the Angels signed it, an' Ben
Mitchell gave me his old glove, an' I got the shirt Ryder
wore last year when he got four home runs against the
evil Thunder, an' this was the best day of my whole
life!"

Ellie tried to speak, but for a moment, couldn't
squeeze the words past the lump in her throat. "That's
terrific, munchkin," she finally managed.

"Kid's got an arm like a rocket," Ryder's voice broke
in. "Told Mitchell he'd better watch his butt."

Ellie's eyes flashed to Ryder's face and what she saw
there made her heartbeat accelerate, her palms tingle
with the need to reach out and touch him. He was soaring, triumph rippling off of him in waves. His eyes
burned with excitement beneath dark-fringed lashes, his
whole body exuding a masculinity, a heat, that fired Ellie's blood, made it race more wildly than she had ever
dreamed possible.

Hunger. Danger. Promise. They clashed beneath
Sloan's civilized facade, beckoning her.

"Mom, Ryder told the driver t' leave. We get to go
home in Rye's Porsche." For once, even Zak's prattle
couldn't drive back the tide of awareness swirling around
her. The thought of being trapped in the intimate confines of the sports car with Ryder sent a rush of anticipation, of dread, through her.

"I hope you don't mind," Ryder said, his fingertips
tapping a staccato on an iron rail. "I need to move fast
after a game." Sensation prickled at the tender swell of

her lips as that burning blue gaze flicked down to them
in an almost physical caress.

Ellie all but sprang from her seat, busying herself
gathering the paraphernalia Zakary had left scattered
around the box. His squeeze bottle skittered off the edge
of a seat, rolling beneath. She dove for it, grateful for a
moment to compose herself. But at the same instant,
Ryder moved to retrieve Zak's treasure, accidently
bumping into Ellie with a force that made them both lose
their balance.

Ryder caught her in his arms to steady her, and Ellie
felt raw jolts of something she dared not name zing
through her.

His body was so solid, smelling of soap, and sensuality and victory. It was as if his skin hummed with it—an
electric charge just beneath its tanned surface. Ellie
wondered fleetingly what it would be like to strip away
the veneer of clothes and run her palms over those unyielding planes and angles, what it would be like to
plumb the depths of the emotion rampant in Ryder
Sloan's eyes.

She shook herself inwardly, aware that he was still
holding her, his breath just a touch irregular as it wisped,
hot, across her cheek, his lips parted, mouth enticingly
near.

With a tiny, choked sound, Ellie drew back from the
precipice, trying to infuse her voice with a composure
she wondered if she would ever feel again.

"You can let go now, Sloan."

"Can I?" Low, throaty, his voice sent a shiver rippling through her, his thumbs skimming mesmerizing
circles on the sensitive flesh of the inside of her arm.

Ellie had shared Daniel MacCrea's bed for years, but
never, even in the heat of lovemaking, had she experienced anything even remotely as sensual as the delicate
tracings of Ryder's callused thumb. It was as if he were

savoring her, the texture of her skin, the pulse beat, erratic beneath his touch.

Their eyes locked, and she saw hunger leap into Sloan's gaze. For an instant, he leaned toward her—that raw animal power a bare whisper from her racing heart, then he glanced to where Zak was hanging over the rail, flinging leftover popcorn at a wayward ant.

With a rueful grin, Ryder jammed his hands into the pockets of his jeans with the expression of a child in a china store, determined to be good.

But there was nothing childlike in the heat that still simmered in Sloan's cerulean eyes. Or the promise.

Unnerved, Ellie hastily scooped the rest of Zak's prizes into an oversized tote adorned by a medieval print of a portion of *Le Morte D'Arthur.*

She glanced around one last time with the practiced eye of a mother who has made far too many return trips to retrieve forgotten baseball cards, action figures and comic books.

"I think we're ready now."

She started at Ryder's low groan. "We're more than ready, Ellie."

Her cheeks burned at the double entendre, and she all but ran out of the box, Zak in tow. Within moments Ryder was leaning over the side of his gleaming black Porsche, unfastening the cover protecting the interior of the 911 Carrera. Ellie grimaced. Sloan would want to have his face bared to the sun, the wind whipping through that thick, dark hair.

As he folded the cover and stowed it in the trunk, she eyed the leather seats he'd exposed askance. "Ah, Sloan, in case you hadn't noticed, there are only two seats in your car. And there are three of us."

"No!" He feigned shock, mocking her by looking at the interior of the car, then at his fingers, ticking them off one by one as if counting while Zakary dissolved into gales of laughter. "There *are* only two seats. Maybe we could use Zak as a hood ornament. You wouldn't mind riding on the front of the car, would you, slugger?''

''I'd hang on real tight, Mom,'' Zak said, reveling in the joke.

''Forget it, both of you. Ryder, Zak has to be seat-belted in, or—''

''MacCrea household rule number two,'' Zak said, shaking his head with a long-suffering moan. ''Mothers. She still thinks I'm a baby.''

Ryder nodded sympathetically, then turned to reach back behind the two seats.

''Ryder, I mean it. I—''

''Chill out, Mom,'' Sloan said with a laugh as he tugged on something. ''We've got it covered.'' A panel swung up, forming two more seats in the impossibly small space behind the leather backs of the other ones.

''All *right!*'' Zak said, his sweaty fingers leaving prints on the car's glossy surface as he leaned over to feel the leather.

''Any more objections?'' Ryder asked with an inno-cence that irritated her.

''Mom, can I sit in the back?'' Zak entreated.

''No!'' Ellie said with a sharpness that surprised her. ''I—I'll sit back there.'' *As far away as possible from Ryder Sloan.*

Ryder shot her a glance that made her squirm, those blue eyes conveying to her that he understood exactly why she was intent on cramming herself into the small space. For a moment she expected him to argue, but he only turned to the grumbling Zakary.

''There's a CD player up front,'' Ryder told the boy. ''You can put in any song you want. I might even let you help shift.''

Zak's eyes widened as he examined the stick shift. ''Really?''

''Yeah. I'll tell you when.''

The thought of her seven-year-old son fooling with such an expensive car gave Ellie palpitations. "Ryder, that's very nice of you ... but I don't think ... I mean, I probably couldn't afford to replace the floor mats on this thing, let alone the transmission."

Ryder rolled his eyes skyward, groaning in unison with Zakary. *"Mothers!"*

Sloan opened the door, then took the tote from her hands and tucked it on the car's floor. As if inspired by the poem on the bag, he mimicked an English accent. "Your carriage awaits, milady."

Grinding her teeth, Ellie scooted inside, deciding that the sooner she quit arguing, the sooner she'd be home. She would just close her eyes and think about tutoring assignments for next week, totally block out Ryder's presence for the duration of the ride. Before she knew it, this upsetting, irritating, wonderful time with Ryder Sloan would be over. She could forget about the way his hair skimmed the corded muscles of his neck. She could forget the way he moved, the way his eyes crinkled at the corners when he smiled.

It would be a relief to get their lives back to normal.

Then why did she suddenly feel so empty?

She sobered as Ryder swung the car out onto the road, the miles whipping by as, true to his promise, he taught Zak the shifting pattern. She had sought escape in the back seat of the Porsche, but found instead an even more exquisite form of torture. Zakary's laughter drifted on the wind, high and sweet in counterpoint to Ryder's deep chuckles.

It seemed Sloan had the musical tastes of a seven-year-old, because Zak took the greatest delight in playing selection after selection from a rock group he adored.

Unfortunately the music fit, the pulsing beat melding with the drone of the expensive sports car's engine. And as for Ellie's closing her eyes—it was impossible with

Ryder's broad shoulders so near, the wind tugging back his dark hair until wisps of it tantalized her cheeks.

She had angled herself sideways for comfort, and from her vantage point, could see a delectable slice of that ruggedly handsome face, the jut of that stubborn, square jaw, softened by the laugh-lines carved at the side of his mouth.

Blast the man, it wasn't fair. Wasn't fair that he was so gorgeous, so sexy, and so...so sweet. He made her want things that were impossible.

Contentment to her was looking at Zak's worn-out sneakers, seeing in them a summer's worth of running and jumping and climbing trees. It was a crayoned birthday card, or breakfast in bed—chocolate cake, milk, and pretzels, served on Mother's Day by her grinning son. It had nothing to do with million-dollar endorsement contracts, jet-set parties or fans slavering over autographs in airport terminals.

There was no room in Ryder Sloan's world for her. And, despite the fact that he'd obviously enjoyed his brief respite in hers, he was as unsuited to dealing with grocery shopping and middle-of-the-night treks to the pharmacy for medicine as she was to riding in this luxurious car.

She was stung by a sudden sense of hurt at the realization of how quickly she and Zakary would fade from Ryder's life, until they were only a hazy memory of a goodwill offering he'd been involved in—doubtless one of many.

Maybe once in a while, Ryder would think of them—maybe he'd check on Zak's progress, dash off a couple of tickets to a game. But in a few weeks there'd no doubt be another cause in need of Sloan's attention, a charitable one, or more likely, some financial dealing.

The music and laughter from the front of the car drifted away, making Ellie feel as if the Porsche's sides were closing in on her, insulating her in a brittle shell she alone could see.

And she only wanted the day to be over, wanted to be waking up a week from now when this unexpected ache had eased.

She was suddenly aware of the silence—the music fading, her tumbled hair wisping around her face in the wind's absence as Ryder brought the Porsche to a stop at the curb.

The apartment building loomed above them, the paint just a little weatherbeaten, the flowers drooping, dispirited in the heat. Zak hit the sidewalk running, racing, no doubt to tell his precious Mr. Allison about the wonders of the day. It was as if the boy had complete faith that Ryder would be there when he returned. As if Zak expected Ryder to be there always.

Ellie winced at the thought of her child's reaction once he knew that he was wrong.

She felt raw with the pain of it, as she clambered out of the car, pointedly ignoring the hand Ryder had extended to help her. She saw his grin waver, then disappear, his brow furrowing in confusion as he reached in and retrieved her tote.

"I can take that," Ellie snapped, aware that the edge of her temper had crept into her voice.

"Humor me," he said, shouldering the bag.

With a muttered curse, Ellie stalked up to the building, wishing that the blast of coolness from the air conditioner could diminish the strange heat inside her, the bubbling of anger, the sense of injustice, the suffocating hopelessness.

She knew Ryder was following her, could sense him there as she let herself in the apartment door.

Zakary's voice drifted faintly from the direction of Mr. Allison's, only serving to fuel the unreasonable sense of resentment she suddenly felt for the man now slinging her things onto the couch.

Like a footman in an eighteenth-century novel, Ellie braced herself against the doorjamb—allowing Ryder no margin for doubting that she expected him to leave.

"I want to thank you for everything you did for Zak today. He'll always remember it."

"I will, too." Ryder looked patently confused at the drastic change in her, his eyes clouding. "Dammit, Ellie, did I do something wrong again? Say something? I mean, if you didn't want Zak to shift the car, you should've said—"

"Like it would've mattered? The two of you seemed to have everything decided beforehand. And mothers, after all, everyone knows what wet blankets they are." Tears burned behind Ellie's eyelids, and she hated herself for them.

"You're a terrific mother. But you're a woman, too. Sometimes I think you forget that."

His words stung. Ellie forced a bitter laugh. "What do you do? Read pop psychology magazines in hotel lobbies? You've known me three days!"

"I know you well enough," Ryder asserted stubbornly, stalking over to where she stood. He towered over her, and there was something about the set of his lips and the spark in his eyes that disconcerted her. "I know you well enough to see that you pour everything that you have, everything that you are, into that little boy. That you've given away so many pieces of Ellie MacCrea that sometimes you wonder if there's anything left."

"That's ridiculous! Just because I don't fawn all over you like that *thing* in the pink halter top doesn't mean I've . . . how did you put it? *Forgotten I'm a woman?* In case you hadn't noticed, Zakary only has one parent— *me.* He's sick, and he's scared."

Ryder flinched, but held his ground. "Zakary isn't half as scared as you are. And there's a lot more to your fear than hospitals and dialysis machines."

"What are you implying?" Two spots on her cheeks seemed afire.

"You're afraid of me."

She forced her gaze to rake a dismissive path down his body, her lips curling in defensive scorn. "Sloan, it would be darn embarrassing to be afraid of a man who runs around playing little boy games all day—even when he does get paid an obscene amount of money to do it. As far as I'm concerned, you can take your ball and bat and go play in somebody else's yard. I had my fill of little boys in men's bodies when I lived with my ex-husband."

None of the pictures in the tabloids, or on the glossy surfaces of baseball cards, had ever captured the image of Ryder Sloan angry. In that moment Ellie knew why— he would've given small children nightmares.

His eyes darkened to indigo between his narrowed lids. The mouth that had been so sensitive, so sensual, tightened into a line that made her think of Oliver Cromwell—when the Lord Protector had been about to witness the lopping off of Charles I's head.

She tried to take a step back, but the hardwood jamb would allow her no escape.

"So that's it." He was angry. Worse, still, he was hurt. It was his pain that cinched, crushing, around her heart. "You think I'm like that bastard who deserted you and Zak."

"Ryder, to be honest, I don't know *what* you're like. These past days have been terrific. You've been so generous, it's been like a dream for Zak. But it's time for Zak and I to go back to the *real* world now. And it's time for you to go play Peter Pan."

"Peter—what the blazes?"

"The classic children's story—the boy who'd never grow up."

"I read the damn story. Believe it or not, I'm actually semiliterate. I can read, add, subtract—it's necessary in order to balance my *obscene* profits."

Images of the day flitted through Ellie's mind, shame washing through her at the thought of Ryder's many kindnesses, and her reaction to them. "Ryder," she said. "If I hurt you—"

"Hurt me?" he gave a harsh laugh. "Hell, no. You didn't hurt me. Everyone knows jocks don't have feelings."

She swallowed hard, the unmasked pain in his features lashing at her conscience. "Ryder—"

"You've made it real clear how you feel about me, Ellie. About what I do for a living. It's inexcusable, the salaries jocks draw—for what? Do we contribute to world peace? Preserve the environment?"

His voice was thick with hurt, and Ellie felt as if she had struck him. "You don't like games, do you, Ellie?" he said, bracing his arms on either side of her. "Don't like men who play them. But how do you feel about scared little girls, hiding from real life?"

Ellie's heart slammed against her ribs. "That's enough. I don't need—"

"Need? You sure as hell do, lady. And I'm going to show you how much."

Ellie's breath hissed out in denial as Ryder's hands delved into the tumbled waves of her hair, his mouth covering hers with devastating power. Hot, hard, his lips moved over hers, the unyielding plane of his chest pinning her against the wall. The muscled ridges of his thighs pressed against her bare legs, the rough material of his jeans impossibly erotic as his tongue traced the crease of her tight-pressed lips.

"Ellie...ah, Ellie, don't fight this...." Ryder pleaded. "Feels...feels so right..."

She could feel his heart thundering, his breath catching in his throat. He was trembling, those strong, sure hands shaking as they roved hungrily over her hair, her shoulders, her waist.

Her lips parted in a gasp that was half pleasure, half protest, as his thumbs skimmed the undersides of her breasts. Ryder pressed his advantage, deepening the kiss, his tongue gaining entry to her mouth.

Ellie knew a fleeting sense of relief at the strong arms bracing her upright, as her knees melted away beneath the sensual magic of Ryder's kiss.

He was good.

So good at this.

She had known he would be.

With a moan, she surrendered, threading her own fingers back into that thick mass of hair. Warm satin, it slipped through her fingers. Sensations pooled inside her, drowning her.

Heat. Raw, pulsating power. Yet tempered with the most heart-wrenching undercurrent of tenderness.

Her eyes burned with tears as Ryder filled an emptiness inside her she hadn't even known existed. An emptiness that would yawn deeper still when he vanished from her life.

His palms skimmed up to cup her cheeks as his kiss gentled, dissolving into a wonder so beautiful Ellie couldn't stand the pain of it.

By force of will, she dragged the tattered remnants of her defenses around her, knowing that if she allowed him to insinuate himself any deeper into her soul there would be no haven left to her.

"Rye . . . Rye, stop," she said, low, insistent, pressing against his chest. "I can't do this…not here…not now. I just can't—"

As if the desperation in her voice pierced through the haze of need, Ryder drew away from her, looking down into her face with eyes wide with astonishment, and some other emotion that scared Ellie to death.

His breath was still ragged. This man who had supposedly bedded scores of beautiful women was as shaken as Ellie herself had been. Shaken by a single kiss. The knowledge flooded her with a kind of wild triumph, and with a pure, bounding terror.

"R-Ryder, I—"

"Don't, Ellie. Don't say anything." He leaned his forehead against hers, sucking in a shuddery breath. "For once just listen. I want to be there for you and Zak."

Ellie felt a stab of something akin to hope, a shivery, silvery sensation that shook her to her core.

"The medical costs must be staggering," Ryder went on, his words chipping away at the fragile emotion. "I don't know how you've made it on your own this far."

Money. This was about money, not time, not love, Ellie thought with a suffocating wave of cynicism. *Million-dollar ball player casting largess to the lowlings beneath him.*

She broke away from him. Crossing her arms over her chest, she chafed at her overheated skin with her palms. "We don't need your charity, Sloan."

"Cripes sake, Ellie! Stop it! I care about Zak. Care about you. I've got more money than I'll ever spend. Why shouldn't I do something worthwhile with it if I want to?"

"Because I won't let you!" Ellie raged, with sudden fury. "Because I won't stand by and watch you storm into our lives, make me care about you, make Zak depend on you. It took me two years to clean up the mess Daniel made of Zak's life. I'm not going to go through that again."

"I'm not Daniel."

"No. You're worse. You're Ryder Sloan. Hotshot third baseman. Have you stopped to think where this would lead if I were ever foolish enough to let things get out of hand? What would Zak do while you were jetting all over the country posing with sports cars and endorsing tennis shoes? He'd be waiting again . . . hoping for the phone to ring, waiting for a man he adores to show him the least little bit of attention. I can't do that to him, Ryder.''

''You think I'd hurt Zak?''

''You wouldn't mean to, but you would. You couldn't help it. If there ever was another man in Zak's life, he'd have to be stable. Dependable. Someone he could count on, even when it wasn't convenient.''

''Maybe I could be that someone, Ellie.'' His voice was low.

She couldn't quell a choked little laugh. ''Oh, Ryder.''

''I'm just saying that *maybe* I could. I don't know. This is happening damn fast for me, too, you know.'' He paced away from her, leaning one arm against the wall as he gazed out over the fire escape. ''Hell, maybe you're right. I wouldn't be good for Zak. I'm on the road most of the summer. And God knows, I've been on my own a long time. I don't know.''

He made a fist, tapping it gently against his lips, his face more solemn than Ellie had ever seen it. ''I just know I want to try.''

He looked so vulnerable, so sincere, Ellie wanted to go to him, slip her arms around that narrow waist. She held her hands rigid at her sides. The words she spoke were the most difficult she'd said since the day she'd told Zakary his kidneys were failing. ''Zak and I can't afford to take that risk, Ryder. I'm sorry.''

She saw his shoulders stiffen, his lips parting to speak, but at that moment there was a commotion in the hall, Zakary's voice carrying to them through the open door.

''Mom? Ryder? I told Mr. Allison—'' The child charged through the door, then froze on the threshold, glancing from Ryder to Ellie as if he had already sensed the tension in the air.

Ellie winced as she saw darts of worry pierce the excitement in her son's eyes. "I told Mr. Allison 'bout goin' to the locker room," Zak said, but his words had lost their gloss of untarnished ecstasy. "I told him I was gonna invite Ryder to my birthday party an' stuff an' he said Mrs. Allison'd bake me a cake that looked like Rye's rookie card. She paints stuff on 'em with frosting... the cake, not the baseball card, an'..."

He faltered, came to a stop. How many times had Ellie seen that uncertainty on the little boy's face? How could it still hurt her as badly as it ever had?

"Ryder is a very busy man, munchkin," Ellie struggled to explain, "I don't think—"

"I'll have to check the schedule, slugger," Ryder's voice broke in. He brushed past her to hunker down in front of the crestfallen little boy. "I may be out of town."

"But I saw Billy Prescott on the way an' told him—"

"I want to come, kid, I really do. Wouldn't miss it for the world."

Ellie seethed inwardly, her blood boiling at Ryder's carelessly flung promise. "Ryder, I don't think—"

"Your problem is you think too damn much," Ryder snapped at her, levering himself to his feet. "Maybe it's time you started *feeling* for a change. This isn't over, Ellie. Not by a long shot." He paced over to lance her with a steamy glare. "When I get back from this road series, we're going to finish what we started."

Ellie's whole body burned with the memory of his fevered kisses. "It's over, Ryder," she said with more authority than she felt.

"Ah, no, Ellie," he said, his voice laced with that dangerous, sexy tone that made her skin prickle with awareness. "This is only the beginning."

Chapter Six

Ryder pushed open the locker-room door, and the Philadelphia night closed around him in a thick muggy blanket.

Enemy territory.

He kneaded the stiffening muscles of his neck and glanced around the stadium where he'd played his first major league ball game. But even the memory of the home run that had launched his Rookie of the Year totals failed to lighten his mood. His thoughts dwelt, instead, on the game whose statistics were even now being inked onto tomorrow's sports page.

He'd made an error. Granted, a small one that hadn't cost them the game, but that had only been because catcher Alex Craig had managed to pull it out of the dirt, keeping what would have been the winning run on third base. It wasn't the first time Alex had pulled Ryder's butt out of a sling, though sportswriters rarely gave the steady-playing Craig the credit he deserved. But it was the first time Ryder had screwed up because his mind hadn't been on the game.

No, his mind had been hundreds of miles away in Ellie MacCrea's living room, lost in the frightened gray depths of her eyes.

Ryder walked over to board the sleek bus waiting to take the team back to the hotel, but as he fielded greetings from his teammates, he was remembering how Ellie had felt in his arms, how she had tasted, smelled.

Clean, wholesome, so damn good.

It had been a long time since he'd kissed a woman like Ellie—if he ever had. Even the girls he'd dated in high school had been years older in experience. They'd lavished attention on him—and God knew, he'd enjoyed it. He'd thrown himself into the role of heartbreaker jock as if trying to prove something—that maybe he was worth loving.

But the affairs had been a kind of game on both sides. One that had left him even more empty than before. It wasn't that he hadn't had chances to grab on to something better, more lasting, in those years. He'd just been so enamored of his hard-won place in the spotlight that he'd refused to try.

He settled into his accustomed seat at the back of the bus, away from the lively banter of his teammates. The air conditioning dried the faint film of sweat on his face, and he leaned back against the headrest, letting the vent blow welcome coolness over his heated skin.

He closed his eyes, wincing at a sudden, unwelcome memory. Lindsey Hender had been his lab partner in chemistry, a shy, quietly pretty kind of girl with a sweet smile and adoration in eyes she'd never muddied up with makeup. She hadn't given a damn about team championships or grand slam homers. Instead, they'd talked about everything from Vietnam to world hunger, and she'd listened to his opinions, then argued with him, openly, intelligently.

By the time he'd made it through the class, he'd felt a warmth for her that had been special. He'd always meant to ask her out. Just to talk. But that had been when model-gorgeous cheerleader Stacey Mattingly had been pursuing him with especial flair, and Lindsey had faded back into the woodwork at school, brushing past him in the halls with a kind of wistful smile that had made him feel guilty as hell.

She'd been the only girl Ryder had ever really hurt. And when he'd gone to a class reunion years later, seeing Lindsey and her husband sporting a walletful of pictures of their kids had wrapped a quiet kind of ache around his heart.

He rubbed his eyes, his mouth setting in a grim line as Lindsey's wheat-gold hair melted into the red curls of Ellie MacCrea, soft green eyes dissolving into wide, sensitive gray ones. He'd been an arrogant jerk in high school, too stupid to appreciate what Lindsey had offered, but he was worlds wiser now. A dozen Stacey Mattinglys and twelve years as the golden boy at third base hadn't filled the void inside him.

Ellie MacCrea could.

"Hell, Sloan," he muttered to himself. "Why knock your head against a wall? Every time you try to get close to her, she looks at you like you kicked her puppy."

"Puppy?" The familiar voice of Alex Craig startled Ryder as the man plunked himself down on the seat beside him. "You gettin' a puppy, Rye?"

Ryder felt his cheeks burn, and he sat up, wondering how much of his muttered lament Craig had heard. "No. Just talking to myself."

"Hmm." Craig eyed him, and Ryder squirmed at the intuitive light in the other man's eyes. "Talkin' to yourself. Sleeping on a play. Off night, huh?"

"I guess you could say that. Maybe 'off series' would be better."

"Everybody has 'em." Craig shrugged, but the watchfulness in his gaze didn't waver. "Even the legendary Philly slayer, Ryder Sloan. Makes you human, Rye. Otherwise the rest of us'd have to hate you." There was a friendly teasing in Alex's voice, one of the things that had kept Ryder's ego from getting too big in the years since he and Alex had come up from the minors together. "You'll kill 'em tomorrow, man."

"Not unless I can get my mind back on the game."

The bus shifted into motion, the low hum of the engine obscuring their words from the rest of the team. Ryder raked his fingers through his still-damp hair, aware of Craig scratching at his chin, puzzled.

"Never known your brain to be on vacation when you're on the bag, Rye. Not even when...well, when everything was falling apart our rookie year."

Falling apart...an understatement. His marriage in ashes, while his career soared. Yet even so, he'd been able to leave Marla and their problems outside the baseball field, shedding them, like his team jacket, before he took his position, then dragging them back on as soon as the ninth inning was over.

"Anything you want to talk about?" Alex asked. "I mean, if it's none of my business, just say so. I just thought...well, you haven't seemed like yourself ever since we left Atlanta. Even Gina's worried about you."

Ryder thought of Alex's pretty, heavily pregnant wife, with her sharp wit and a heart as big as the state of Texas. She'd been destined to marry a ball player, with her gruff, no-nonsense toughness, softened by an angelic smile. Gina Craig had fussed over Ryder with the zest of an Italian mother for years now, bullying him, teasing him, worrying about him in a way that had made him love her like a sister.

Three times Ryder had flown home with Alex, pacing the hospital waiting room while Gina gave birth.

He was ready to get plane ticket number four, whenever Gina was ready.

He gave a wry, weary smile. "I thought that mental telepathy stuff was garbage, until I met you and Gina. Spock's mind-meld has nothing on you two."

"Called her from the locker room to check on Bozo the Clown," Alex said, referring to the coming baby by the affectionate nickname the Craigs had given each of their offspring in turn before birth. "She said the baby's fine, but Ryder stinks. Her words, exactly."

Ryder laughed, shaking his head.

"She says she still loves you, anyway, but to get your act together. Wanted to know what the problem was. Said, at least she knew it couldn't be a woman. Never saw you worry about one of them, yet."

Ryder sighed, toying with the drawstring of the sweatpants he'd dragged on after the game. "There's a first time for everything, I guess."

Alex grew quiet, and Ryder could feel his friend watching him. After a moment, Craig cleared his throat. "Tara?" he asked, a dubious tone in his voice. "I guess I never thought it was that serious between you."

"It's not. In fact, we won't be seeing each other at all anymore. I broke things off for good after the last home game." Ryder remembered the surprisingly tepid scene when Tara had stopped by his penthouse, after he'd left Ellie's. He'd still been raw from the kiss he and Ellie had shared. He'd still been hurt and aching and needing. When he'd told Tara how he felt, honestly, openly, she'd raised her perfect eyebrows in amazement and amusement. With a little laugh that had been edged with only the faintest of regret, she had warned him to be careful. That women like Ellie MacCrea didn't play games, and that that was all a man like Ryder knew how to do.

"You split up?" Alex's voice brought Ryder back to the present. "Gina'll be glad to hear that. Not that Tara isn't real nice, and God knows, she's a knockout, but…"

Caught in the web of his own words, Alex let the sentence dangle in the air. "Well, you know how Gina is. She's just never forgiven her for the time we were all at that party, and Tara disappeared with that Broadway director guy."

Ryder warmed, remembering Gina Craig's indignation on his behalf. He hadn't much cared where Tara had gone off to—there were no commitments between them. Still, Gina's outrage had endeared her to Ryder. His ears still burned from the lecture she'd given him about "wasting himself" on a woman with all the personality of a department store mannequin.

"So, is this babe who's making you crazy some kind of top secret? You gonna tell me her name, or do I have to wait for Gina to worm it out of you?"

Ryder crossed his ankle over one knee and tapped his fingers against the side of his running shoe. "Remember the kid I brought to the stadium the other day?"

"Cute little redheaded guy. He was sick or something, wasn't he? Damn shame."

"Yeah. Well, the woman who has been throwing off my game is his mother."

Craig let fly a low whistle.

"She's divorced from a real creep who deserted her and the kid," Ryder went on. "Been hurt like hell. And as for me . . . well, let's just say she's not impressed with the old Sloan razzle-dazzle. Doesn't give a damn about Porsches, hates the media, and thinks jocks have sweat socks for brains. Only thing is, I think . . . I think I may be falling for her."

"Whoa, Rye. I'm glad for you. Really I am. But you gotta be careful, here. If she's got a kid, and they've both already been through hell, it might not be such a great idea for you to . . . well, plunge into this thing the way you usually do. You'd have to be sure. Damn sure, before—"

"I'm sure." The words were spoken with a quiet conviction that made Alex Craig gape.

"Hot damn and hallelujah! Millions of women all across the nation'll be wearing black arm bands in mourning! Wait 'til I tell Gina! She'll go into labor on the spot!"

"Don't start planning the bachelor party now, bud. I kissed the hell out of her before I left, and I don't know if she'll even speak to me again. Like I said, she's not particularly impressed with me at the moment."

"Be the best thing in the world for you, Rye! A woman who'll make you take out the garbage like the rest of us poor slobs. I love it!" Craig laughed, clapping Ryder on the shoulder, as if already offering wedding congratulations. "So when do we get to meet... what's her name?"

"Ellie."

"Ellie Sloan. Sounds terrific."

"Damn it, Alex, this thing's already way out of control without you flying into left field. She thinks I've got all the emotional depth of a rain puddle."

"Then show her different. Call her. Ask her over to our house for dinner. Gina'll be happy to tell her all your darkest secrets."

Ryder groaned. "That's all I need—Gina telling her some 'poor little rich boy' sob story."

"She'd be more likely to tell her how you make donations for every hit and stolen base you get. Let alone what you shell out to those family shelters for every home run. And you make a helluva lot of home runs, man."

"That's exactly what I *don't* want Gina to tell her." Ryder's cheeks heated and he looked away. "If it hadn't been for the two of you dragging me along to that benefit a few years back, I never would have—"

"Gotten involved? Like hell. You're the biggest sucker for stuff like that I ever met. If you'd just let word of it leak to the press, you probably wouldn't be having these problems with your lady now. Cripes, Rye, if I just read your press clippings like everyone else, I'd think you were a real arrogant, penthouse-type jerk with an attitude problem, too."

Ryder dragged his hand through his hair, a laugh rumbling deep in his chest. "I am a real bastard on paper, aren't I?"

"Yep. And if you want to break through your Pet of the Month image, you're gonna have to give Ellie some time, let her see you when you're not neck-deep in groupies and sportswriters. Ravioli at our house would be the perfect way to start. Ellie's kid—Zak, wasn't it?— he can play with Tony and Will, and you and Ellie and Gina and I can hang out and eat garlic bread. It'll be great."

Ryder closed his eyes, his mind filling with images of the Craig's cheery kitchen.... The massive, scarred-oak table Gina had bought at an auction, then insisted on restoring herself, the marble rolling pin her great grandmother had brought from Italy. There was always the faintest hint of garlic in the air, a scent Ryder had long since begun to equate with the feeling of belonging he always had while sandwiched between eight-year-old Tony and two-year-old Mia at the Craig family table.

He'd never brought Tara or any of his other dates along on his sojourns to Alex and Gina's. The women always seemed to be in the way of important things, like pitching a few to Will, or coloring with Tony, or building block towers for Mia to knock down. But picturing Ellie and Zak in that setting made something warm squeeze around Ryder's heart.

"All right," he said at last. "You win. We'll come to dinner, as long as you and Gina promise you won't make homemade ravioli. She shouldn't be bending over that rolling pin so long. How about if I bring steaks and you and I can see how badly we can burn 'em?"

"Fine with me. Gina'll squawk, but I'm used to it."

Ryder braced himself as the bus slowed outside the hotel where the team had been put up for the three-night stand of games.

Alex bent down to retrieve the jacket that had slipped off the bus's seat. "So, you wanna go get something to eat? A couple of guys know this place with linguini to die for."

"No," Ryder said, anticipation already making his fingers tingle. "I'm going to head up and see if I can get ahold of Ellie."

"The woman's already taking precedence over your stomach. Sloan, you're a goner."

Ryder's lips quirked. "I guess so. Ain't it great?"

Alex's grin was warm, his eyes dark with emotion, but his voice was gruff as he strode down the aisle. "Yeah, Rye. Yeah, it is."

Ryder made his way out of the bus, pausing only long enough to lift one hand in a wave toward his departing teammates. He hurried into the hotel lobby, its forest of mirrors and gigantic silk-floral arrangements nothing but a blur as he all but jogged to a waiting elevator.

His heart was thumping like a kid calling his first girl, and it felt wonderful, but not as wonderful as the conversation Ryder was already playing in his head. He could hear her voice, forthright, but with just a touch of smokiness to make it sexy.

She'd be surprised, but would she still be mad at him? Maybe. But maybe she'd had time to think, too. Maybe she'd started to miss him just a little. His kiss might have worn her down, night after night, the way the memory of her mouth under his had eaten away at him.

He mentally shook himself, an abashed grin tugging at his lips as he almost bumped into a formidable tourist in an orange-and-pink muumuu as he charged out of the elevator. Murmuring his excuses, he hurried to his room, sliding the coded card into the lock.

Flicking on the light, he waded through Alex's discarded belongings and, shoving his roommate's shoes off of the desk chair, plunked himself down. His gaze turned briefly to the picture of Gina and the kids Alex had set on every desktop of every hotel room they'd shared in the past years. Maybe, soon, Ryder would have a picture of his own to set beside Craig's.

He sucked in a deep breath and picked up the phone. When the line began to ring, Ryder's fingers clenched around the receiver, and he chewed at the corner of his lip.

Once. Twice. Ten times the phone buzzed. He was just about to hang up when there was the clatter of the receiver being snatched up in a hurry, Ellie's breathless voice coming over the line.

She only said hello, but in that instant Ryder had a gut-clenching feeling that something was wrong.

"Ellie? It's Ryder. What's the matter? Is Zak okay?"

"Contrary to popular belief, my son is just fine." If it was possible to suffer deep-freeze through a phone line, Ryder's fingers should be turning blue. Even that first day when he'd arrived surrounded by admirers, Ellie's voice hadn't held such pure loathing. Ryder felt hurt well up to drown the warmth he'd felt moments before.

"Contrary to...what the blazes? Ellie, for cripe's sake, what's wrong?"

"I have nothing to say to you, Ryder. If I'd followed my instincts from the beginning, none of this would have happened in the first place."

"None of *this?* None of *what?* Dammit, Ellie, you at least owe me an explanation."

"Owe you?" She gave a sick laugh, and Ryder heard her voice catch. Something jagged twisted inside him. "Oh, no, Ryder. I'd say all debts between us are paid— with interest."

Ryder levered himself to his feet, his pacing tethered only by the phone cord. "Now just a blasted minute, Ellie. If you're mad about my kissing you, I—"

"Rest assured your prowess on that account remains untarnished," she said. "You're a terrific kisser. Maybe you should have fed *that* story to those sleazy..." She stopped for a moment, and Ryder got the sick feeling that she was crying. There were no tears in her voice when she continued. "I've said it before. This time I mean it. I never want to see you or hear from you again."

The phone went dead.

Ryder stood there, stunned, feeling as if he'd taken a line drive in the chest. For a moment, he couldn't move, then, with an oath, he fiercely redialed her number. He let it ring for a full ten minutes, knowing she was there, refusing to answer. In raw frustration, he hung up, and attempted to reach her again. This time the phone was off the hook.

He banged it down, pacing, cursing, more hurt than he'd ever been in his life. *I never want to see you again...* her words echoed in his ears. Just like that. No explanations. Nothing. Just Ellie MacCrea slamming the phone down.

Because she was afraid? Well, he was damn scared of all this, too. It wasn't like he'd set out to fall in love with her.

Nothing better to do on a Thursday afternoon, so I think I'll complicate the hell out of my life....

He stalked to the window, glaring out into the twilight. "Fine," he growled. "If that's the way she wants it, fine. God forbid she be tainted by being linked to a...how did she say it? A boy in man's clothing, like me."

Pain jolted through him—a pain he hadn't felt since he'd staggered under his parents' rejection. The walls of the room pressed in on him, making it hard to breathe.

He had to get out of here—maybe run or find a pickup game of basketball.

God knew, he was tired from the game, but from the time he'd been a kid, he'd buried his hurts beneath the layer of exhaustion he'd gained by pushing himself past his physical limits. Running, playing racquetball, whacking baseballs at the local batting cage.

Scooping up the coded card for the door lock, he jammed it into the pocket of his sweats and stormed out the door.

Within minutes, he was racing down pavement still heated from the burning sun. He plunged through pools of light from street lamps, oblivious to the people on the streets. He fought desperately, determinedly, to encase himself in the safe world of straining muscles, thundering heartbeat and sweat, where he'd always been able to forget everything that pained him.

But with every stride, Ellie's face danced before him, her eyes filled with tears, her voice catching, then freezing, like a little girl, trying very hard to hide her hurt.

What had gone wrong? With her? With them? He'd known she'd been wary, had good reason to be. But she'd responded in their kiss. Not just with animal attraction—he'd experienced enough of that to know the difference. There had been a melting of walls between them, a melding of hopes and fears and dreams that had shaken him to his very soul.

And she had felt it, too.

But it hadn't mattered to her. Not enough to take the risk. Not for him.

The certainty wrenched inside Ryder and he slowed his pace, suddenly aware of the exhaustion vibrating through his whole body. Sucking in a deep breath, he braced his hands against his knees and leaned back against the rough-board wall of a newsstand. His legs trembled, his skin was slick with sweat as he drew burning gulps of air into aching lungs.

I never want to see or hear from you again…never…

"Why, dammit?" he grated aloud. "Ellie, why?"

He buried his face in one callused palm and swallowed hard.

"Mister? Hey, mister, you okay?" a deep voice intruded.

Ryder shut away his roiling emotions and raised his head to look into the concerned face of a middle-aged man in work-stained coveralls.

"Yeah. I'm fine. Just overextended myself a little."

"More'n a little by the look of you. You sure—hey, don't I know you? You're a ball player with Atlanta."

Ryder forced a wan smile. "Third base."

"Well, I'll be." The man's jowls wobbled as he grinned. "I'm a Phillies fan myself, but I've watched you rough up our pitchers enough to recognize that mug of yours. My grandson's an Angels fan. Black sheep of the family." The man clapped Ryder on the shoulder with a laugh. "Thinks you walk on water."

Ryder squirmed inwardly, feeling the usual surge of inadequacy in the shadow of such hero-worship. "I appreciate the support."

"Well, I'm inclined to agree with the boy, what with the way you were so good to that little guy in Atlanta, taking him to the ball game and all. Nothing more sad than a sickly child. No sir."

Ryder winced inwardly. He'd expected coverage of his time with Zakary MacCrea in the area surrounding Atlanta, but *Philadelphia?* "It was no big deal," he said stiffly.

"You know," the workman continued, "the wife and I have been trying to figure out what to get our grandson for his birthday. He's at that age where they want toys but think they're too old to ask for 'em. He sure would go crazy over an autograph from Ryder Sloan, though."

The man's eyes were hopeful, his face honest and weathered by years of hard labor. Ryder straightened. "Be happy to, but I didn't bring a pen...."

"Take mine." The man fished in his shirt pocket, dragging out one with a chewed tip. "Even got something you can sign on. A picture..."

He dug into the minicooler that obviously served as his lunchbox and withdrew a much-read wad of newsprint. Ryder glanced at the lurid red-and-blue banner at the top of one of the most infamous rag-sheets in the country.

"Just a minute," the man muttered, flattening the crumpled paper against his paunch. "There we are," he said at last, apparently satisfied that he'd smoothed it enough. "Sign here." He extended the paper to Ryder, jabbing one finger triumphantly at a somewhat fuzzy color photo. The Angels field was a blur of emerald backdrop, splashed with the image of Ryder carrying a laughing Zakary in his arms.

But it was the bold headline above the story that drove like a fist into Ryder's belly, sickening him, making him break out in a horrible chill sweat.

"My God," Ryder whispered. "Oh my God."

Ryder Sloan Grants Dying Child Last Wish.

Chapter Seven

Ellie glanced at her watch and shut the freshman comp text with a weary sigh. It was time. Time to call Zak away from his crowd of friends in the apartment playground and carry him off to the world of gleaming machinery, jabbing needles and uniformed doctors she prayed the other boys would never know.

Dialysis. It was keeping Zak alive and she was grateful. Heaven only knew how much. But it had become more difficult, week after week, to take Zak in where he knew he'd be hurting—to a place of secrets, where physicians grew increasingly grim and the nurses' smiles more brittle.

How often lately had Ellie ached for someone to talk to about fears that seemed to cinch tighter, ever tighter, around her. A need she'd never felt—or at least never acknowledged—before Ryder Sloan had slammed like a perfectly timed fastball into her life.

She got stiffly to her feet and crossed to the window cut in the fire escape door. Beyond it, the sky was a sweep of iridescent blue, spangled with cotton candy clouds that drifted temptingly out of reach.

It wasn't fair. Wasn't fair that the sky should be the same color as Ryder's eyes. Wasn't fair that she could hear his voice on the phone line, pleading for some explanation over and over again. Desperation. It had been thick in his voice. Almost as thick as the hurt. It was irritating that it should gnaw at her so. Guilt as pure and sharp as any she'd ever known shot through her.

Because of him, her child's face had been splashed across a tabloid whose sensationalism made her skin crawl. She still remembered the horrible drowning feeling she'd had, standing at the grocery store checkout and casually glancing over to see the glaring headline.

Dying Child...

Even now her hands shook, her stomach turned, as the image of those words rose before her. Her most secret terror, her most devastating fears, ripped out and paraded before people who slavered over others' misfortunes. She could see them, tsk-tsking over Zakary's picture, lauding Ryder to the high heavens. But worse—*far* worse—had been the knowledge that Zakary's friends, even Zak himself, might well see the headline.

And believe it.

"How could Ryder have let that happen?" she muttered to herself, feeling again the fearsome rage that had been seething inside her from that moment in the grocery store on. "How could he?"

But he hadn't 'let' anything happen. He had done nothing to court the media this time. It just shadowed him constantly, always there, always waiting for anything that smacked of a story. And sick little Zakary MacCrea, being swept around the city by the baseball player he adored, was the stuff Movies of the Week were made of.

The only thing that could be more appropriately maudlin in such an undertaking would be if the divorced mother of the child fell in love...

"Absolutely not," Ellie said aloud, as if the words held the power to make it so. "I'd never do such an irresponsible, dim-witted thing."

Then why do you dream about him every night? Why is he the last thing you think of before you sleep? The first thing you think of when you wake? Why is it that you keep slipping into Zakary's room when he's asleep to look at the rookie card with Ryder grinning that cocky, drop-dead gorgeous grin?

"Because I'm a masochist, that's why. Maybe I should black out one of his teeth...draw a wart on his nose. Maybe then I could forget the way he looks, the way he feels...."

But would she ever be able to forget the rough-velvet sound of his voice, so sincere, so concerned, a steady mooring in a sea of uncertainty? Would she be able to drive away the image of Zak cradled in those hard-muscled arms, Ryder's dauntingly masculine chin pillowed gently on Zakary's hair?

If he'd been anyone else—any man save a baseball superstar with a swath of mistresses Hugh Hefner would have envied, she would have given this feeling between them a chance, wouldn't she? It couldn't be that she was afraid...afraid of trusting her instincts, of making a wrong choice again.

She was just being wise, careful...*stupid,* a voice inside her whispered. Ryder was the stuff of which fantasies were made. "Well, the fantasy is over. It's back to reality. Even Sloan had to get the message when I didn't answer the phone." She flinched inwardly at the memory of how many times the phone had rung, and even when she'd left it off the hook, she could almost feel Ryder's anger and hurt half a country away, knew he was dialing and redialing, until in fury and frustration he stopped trying.

Had he stormed out of his hotel room then? To seek comfort with one of his feminine following? Even without his baseball notoriety, a man with Ryder's looks would be able to find romantic companionship by flashing a woman even the slightest hint of his sexy smile.

She felt a sting of guilt. No, she wasn't being fair. Ryder had been hurt. It had been in every nuance of his voice. And no matter what the media proclaimed, she knew that he was far more sensitive than the shallow, glitzy image projected on television and in newsprint.

She had resolved to be painfully honest with him regarding her feelings. The least she could give in return was the same ruthless honesty with herself. He was hurting. She was hurting him. But it was a necessary pain, a quick, clean severing of the ties that had unexpectedly sprung up between them. For her emotional survival, Zakary's as well.

She tried to quell the sense of loss that tugged at her heart, but at that moment a soft rap at the door roused her from her thoughts.

Assuming that Zak had accidently flicked the lock when he'd gone out to play, she crossed to the door. "Coming, sweetie, it's about time for us to go—" She twisted the knob, vaguely surprised to find it unlocked, then pushed the door wide. "Zak, I—oh."

The last word was a tiny choked sound as her gaze locked on rumpled brown hair, eyes swept with dark shadows, a jaw whose two-days' growth of stubble only served to accentuate its clean, virile line.

"Ryder."

"You going to slam the door on me, Ellie?" His words were quiet, his face vulnerable. The combination was devastating.

"Yes...I mean, no. I mean, I—I asked you not to—"

"To what? Care about you? Care about Zak? It's too late. I already do."

Ellie turned away, unable to bear the solemnity in his face any longer. "I know that you do," she said quietly, at last. "But it won't work between us, Ryder. I've told you the reasons I can't risk it. If you don't understand them, or agree with them, fine. But if you really want what is best for Zakary and—and for me, you'll respect my wishes."

"Because of this?" Ryder reached into the back pocket of his jeans. Even before she saw the crumpled newsprint, she knew what he held. "You believe I had something to do with this?"

"Of course not. But don't you see? That doesn't change the damage it's done."

Ryder walked over to the carriage-seat table and picked up one of Zak's toys. His long fingers smoothed over the shiny plastic super-hero. Ellie winced at the sight of Ryder's broad, beautifully formed shoulders slumping just a whisper, as if she'd heaped on some burden too heavy to carry. Guilt, where there was none.

"Did Zak...see the article?"

"No." Ellie flushed, twisting her hands. "I've been trying to think of a way to tell him, but every time I start I just can't." She turned and walked away to the wall where a collage of Zak's pictures from babyhood to his last gap-toothed school photo were hung. "I don't know how to explain it, Ryder, but there is something about seeing words in print that makes them seem so real. I don't want Zak to believe..."

"Come on, Ellie, this is the magazine that has twelve-year-old girls giving birth to alien babies. Give Zak a little credit. He's a bright kid. Let me talk to him about this before one of his friends tells him."

"Ryder, I don't think—"

"A stranger showed it to me on a street corner," he broke in, a bitter edge to his voice. "I felt like someone had kicked me in the face."

Ellie flinched at the raw pain in those words.

But Ryder pushed on, relentless. "Is that what you want for Zak? You may want to wrap him in cotton batting and keep him safe forever—hell, I don't blame you. I want to, myself. But we can't do that, Ellie, and you know it. Even if I'm not around, there'll be times Zak—sick *or* well—is going to have to take some bumps."

"It's not your decision to make," Ellie bit out, bristling. "You're not his father."

"No, his father's out climbing Kilimanjaro or hang gliding off the pyramids or something. I'm just the guy who wants to be around to take Zak to Little League and sit up with him when he has nightmares. I'm just the man who wants to love Zak's mother."

Ellie's knees turned rubbery at the sound of those words—such sweet, sweet words—coming from Ryder's beautifully formed mouth. Sincere, intense, he made her want to hope. But even as she felt herself drawn toward him, common sense reasserted itself. "Ryder, my ex-husband knew me for five years before we were married, and he never really loved me. You've known me a matter of what? Two weeks? You'll have to excuse me if I don't buy in to claims of undying passion. I don't mean to be cruel, but your track record romantically has been about as high as your batting average."

"You believe everything you read, Ellie?" Sarcasm dripped from the voice that could be so warm. She had the grace to flush.

"Look," he said, "I'm not particularly proud of the image the media has painted of me. I'm a commodity to them, like stocks and bonds. They use me to—"

"To the tune of millions of dollars."

A muscle in his jaw twitched in barely checked anger. "Yeah, that's right. It's been damn lucrative to let them use me. But maybe I just never gave enough of a damn about anything to make them stop."

The words were lost in the slamming of the front door as Zak charged through it, the child's whoop of delight making both adults wheel around.

"Rye! Rye, you came back!" Zak shouted, flinging his arms around Ryder's lean hips. "I knew you would! And just in time for my birthday. It's only a week away!"

Strong tanned fingers caressed Zak's cheek for a heartbeat before Ryder gave way to the much more satisfying greeting of swooping Zak up in his arms and turning the squealing boy upside down. "Birthday? Who said anything about a birthday? All that cake and ice cream and presents—yuck!"

"You like ice cream! Everybody does!" Zak cried as Ryder righted him. "And you don't have to give me a present."

"Too late, slugger, already got you one. 'Course, if you don't want it . . ."

"I want it! I want it! What'd you get me, Rye? Can I open it early?"

"Zakary!" Ellie's voice was sharper than she intended, but the sight of her son in Ryder's arms raked up a maelstrom of confusion, longing, frustration. "The only thing you can do is scrub your face and hands, put on a clean T-shirt and head out to the hospital."

"Aw, Mom!" One glance at Zak's crestfallen face pushed her guilt meter to the danger stage. "But Ryder just got here, and—"

"'Fraid Mom's the boss on this one, kid," Ryder said, setting the child back on his feet. Relief at the prospect of escaping Ryder was just beginning to uncoil the tension around Ellie's shoulders when her gaze snagged with blue eyes, blazing with defiance, a mouth set with a stubbornness that made her start to sweat.

"But, Zak, before you go," Ryder said, hunkering down before the boy, "I wanted to show you something." He withdrew the paper from his pocket. "You know how people write about me sometimes, in the papers and sports magazines and such?"

"Yeah. You were in *KidSport* a couple a months ago. The poster in the middle."

"Right." How could Ryder look so calm, when all Ellie wanted to do was scream? "You know, they got everything right in that article except one thing."

"I know what it was! They said you were traded to the Angels from Philadelphia, but you weren't. It was Chicago!"

"You got it. Sometimes magazines—like that one— make little mistakes when they don't mean to. But sometimes magazines can make big mistakes—on purpose—because they think that more people will want to buy their magazines if they make things sound more exciting, or scary or dangerous than they really are."

"I saw a story once about somethin' like that. It was about a baboon takin' care of a baby in the rain forest for a jillion years until its mom found it. The baby, not the baboon. Mom said that was just a silly story someone made up."

"Your Mom's a pretty smart lady."

"Ryder, I don't appreciate—" Ellie began, but Ryder cut her off.

"Zak, someone has written a story about me and you."

"Radical! Hey, Mom, did you hear that?"

"Whoa, slugger, there's a problem. Some of the story is true, but some of it is not."

"They get your batting average wrong or somethin'? Or did they spell my name with a *CH* in the middle 'stead of a *K?* I don't care if . . ."

"I care about what this magazine got wrong, Zakary," Ryder said, his face solemn. "I care very much. And so does your Mom. It's important to both of us that you know that what this magazine says is not true."

The boy glanced from Ryder to Ellie, nonplussed. "Oh. Okay. Do I, like, get to see it?"

Ellie's stomach clenched, and she stepped toward them, her lip caught between her teeth. "No," she said as firmly as she could muster. "Ryder, I will not—"

She touched the edge of the paper, but Ryder deftly whisked it out of her hand, flipping to the front page with a speed that stunned her. Garish colors splashed Ryder's and Zakary's faces across the page, the headline screaming out at Ellie. She wanted to snatch the paper away from Ryder, hide it from Zak, but it was too late. The little boy was looking down, a crease marring his forehead as he scanned the bold black lettering.

He paled, his lip trembling. "Mom . . ." The little quaver in his voice tore at Ellie's heart. "Mom, I'm not . . . not . . ."

"You're not dying, Zakary, any more than I got traded from Philadelphia." Ryder met Zakary's eyes squarely. Whatever the little boy saw there braced his faith in his mother and the tall man before him. Fear and uncertainty flip-sided into indignation.

"Those liars! Those stinkin' liars!"

"That's about it, Zak," Ryder agreed. "The way I figure is that if they had to use us in a story, the least they could have done was stick us on Mars or make us capture killer alligators stalking the White House."

"Yeah, what a rip-off," Zak said. "What a crummy thing to do."

"I think so, too. I've already sent a letter to the people who wrote this telling them that I'll never give them another interview because of the lies they told. And I told them that if they ever use you in a story like that again, I'll sue the hell out of them."

Ellie might have winced at Ryder's language in front of the boy were it not for the feral light in those blue eyes, the curve of his mouth so pugnacious she could imagine the savage fury his letter must have held. She could almost see the pond slime of an editor who had printed the story quaking in his loafers. She hoped he shook so hard the pennies popped out.

"It's too bad that story lied," Zak was saying, examining the picture of him and Ryder with great interest, now that he'd dismissed the frightening headline above it. "It's awesome to get your picture in the paper. And to get it with you, Rye... You know, I wanted a picture of me with you a bunch, 'case my friends didn't believe I know you and all. Could I get my scissors and cut this thing out or are you saving it for your scrapbook or something?"

Ryder chuckled. "I'm saving the page in my scrapbook for the story on the killer alligators. If you want this picture, it's all yours."

"Hey, I know what'd be even better than showin' my friends the picture," Zak said brightly, turning hopeful eyes on the man whose arms were still looped loosely around him. "I could take you up to the hospital, like show and tell. All the kids would think it was bad, and you could sign autographs and stuff, and make 'em not think how much it hurts when they stick needles in."

"Zakary—"

"Ryder doesn't have anything to do or he wouldn't 'a come over, right, Rye?" the boy pleaded.

"You got it, slugger."

Ellie looked into eyes so blue you could drown in them, into that sexy face that hid such surprising sensitivity. Even if she had wanted to refuse, how could she, when the faces of all the kids in Zak's ward rose up to haunt her? Kids who would be in ecstasy just to see an Angels game would be crazed with happiness when they saw the real live Ryder Sloan.

And she didn't want to refuse. Not when she felt as if Ryder had lifted a two-hundred-pound weight off her chest. She wanted to thank him. Wanted to apologize for her anger. But she couldn't get the words past the lump of gratitude in her throat.

"Ryder..." she managed at last.

"Sorry, Ellie, I don't have any commercials to make or any jet-set parties to attend," Ryder said in a hard voice, steering Zak toward the bathroom. "Can't think of anything I'd rather do than go along with the two of you."

Super-heroes and circus animals sprawled in vivid abandon across the walls of the pediatric urological ward, the waiting room brimming with fathers and mothers, grandparents and raucous brothers and sisters of the other child-patients. Whole crazy-quilts of love, patched together by the families to keep their sick children warm.

Always before, Ellie and Zak had been alone here. And though he'd never mentioned the lack, she caught him, sometimes, looking wistfully at some father reading a story aloud while the dialysis machine hummed, or a grandfather holding a small patient's hand while parents were off conferring with the doctors.

She'd seen Zak brave, resigned, rebellious and heart-wrenchingly scared in Dr. Jim Tyler's domain. But she'd never before seen the child like this—bubbling with excitement as he explained the steps of the treatment he was receiving to an attentive Ryder Sloan.

Just the knowledge that Ryder's presence was relieving some of the stress of this single treatment would have been enough to make Ellie glad he was there, but when she saw the expressions Ryder hid from Zakary—the empathy, the helplessness, the...*love*—it touched her so deeply she knew she would never be the same.

"Mrs. MacCrea?" An imp of a nurse, whose Irish heritage shone in her rosy cheekbones and red hair, addressed Ellie, eyes twinkling as she gestured toward Ryder's lean form a dozen yards away. "I think you should bottle that guy and stick him under the pillow of every kid who has to come to Atlanta General. Be the best cure in the world for 'em. Of course, if you had an extra, you could stick one under *my* pillow, too. For medicinal purposes only, you understand."

The genuine warmth in the nurse drew a smile from Ellie in spite of herself. "The man's a disease. Trust me."

"You mean, he—" the nurse stared, aghast "—he has..."

"No! No!" Ellie said quickly, imagining lurid headlines spawned by her own careless words. "I mean that once you catch him, you can't get rid of him."

"Infect me. Puh-leeze!" the nurse said. Looking heartily relieved, she gave a sigh that would have done a teenager proud. Ellie recalled her irritation with Pink Halter at the ball park two weeks before, but the nurse's reaction was so good-humored and open, she couldn't muster an ounce of disgust. Instead, she found herself laughing just a little.

"Believe me, you don't know what you're asking for," she said.

The nurse grinned, flashing the modest diamond engagement ring on her finger. "I'm asking for trouble. Charlie's jealous as anything already. Anyway, I didn't come over here to enjoy the scenery. Dr. Jim would like to see you."

Ellie had been summoned into the doctor's office many times in the past two years to discuss anything from Zak's illness to how her tutoring was progressing. But she never faced the prospect of entering Tyler's warm brown-and-gold office without a sinking sensation in the pit of her stomach.

She crossed to where Ryder was ensconced at Zak's side. The hand that had won eight straight Gold Glove awards was resting lightly on the boy's shoulder, while those blue eyes watched with a protective light as Zak was hooked up to the machine that was saving his life.

Ellie saw Ryder flinch as the tubes were connected to Zakary, the compressed line of Sloan's lips whitening just a whisper. She remembered her own reaction, the first time she had watched Zak being linked to the dialysis machine, remembered the clawing denial that had raked inside her, her anger at God, at Daniel, but most of all at herself as she had tried to find someone, anyone, to blame Zak's misfortune on. She'd been hard-pressed to hide her feelings from her son. But she had managed to, for his sake.

Ryder did as well. Whenever Zak turned his eyes toward Ryder, all the child saw was his idol's easy smile.

"Ready for lift-off, commander?" Ryder asked when the nurse set the machine whirring.

Zak gave Ryder a brave nod, jumping with great relish into the game. "Yep. The Algernon Alien Army is attacking the planet Homeworkia. I'm gonna go there an' help 'em trash the place."

Ryder laughed, but Ellie saw him glance down at tubes that carried Zakary's blood to be filtered of toxins.

"Ryder," she said softly. He glanced up, and she saw he was a little green. "Dr. Tyler wants to see me for a minute. If you and Zak could manage without me..."

"No problem. Zak and I have a planet to total." His brow puckered. "There's not...um...anything wrong?"

Ellie tried to infuse confidence she didn't feel into her voice. "I'm sure it's nothing. Periodically the doctor likes to review Zak's files with me, and..."

"And look at her legs," Zak offered with a candor that made Ellie's face flame. "Dr. Jim was gonna take her to a movie an' stuff, but Mom always said no."

"Zak..." Ellie started to protest, then stopped, knowing it was futile to deny it. When Zakary knew he was right, the child was tenacious as a bulldog, and, truth be told, Jim Tyler had expressed a romantic interest in her about a year and a half ago.

Though she genuinely liked the young doctor, she'd given him the same firm rebuffs she had given Ryder. The difference had been that Jim had been gentleman enough to bow out, gracefully.

She started, suddenly aware that Ryder's eyes had darkened to that dangerous hue that had snapped at her from beneath his lashes a heartbeat before he had kissed her. Possessiveness and jealousy glinted from those impossibly blue depths before he shuttered it away.

"A doctor, huh?" Ryder said with just a touch of bitterness. "Stable. Reliable. Neck-deep in a humanitarian profession. What's wrong, Ell? Does he have a Cyrano de Bergerac nose?"

Zak giggled, obviously acquainted with the classic story of the long-nosed cavalier. "Dr. Jim doesn't have a banana nose! But he can't even hit a slow pitch softball. Saw him an' the other doctors when they played the radio station guys to raise money for some new machines and stuff." Zak rolled his eyes. "Pretty sad, Rye."

"There are more important things in life than hitting a ball with a stick, Zakary!" Ellie knew the words stung, but couldn't help herself, the tension coiling in her belly fraying her self-control. She turned away, trying to blot out the image of Zak's stunned face, and Ryder's, grim with hurt, as she hurried down the gleaming tile hallway.

She paused for just a moment to steady herself before knocking on the door whose raised steel lettering proclaimed James Tyler, M.D.

"Come on in." Jim's soothing voice came through the door. From the moment Ellie had met the lean, blond doctor, there had been something in that voice that had inspired confidence in her. She pushed open the door and entered. Jim's soft gray eyes peered up at her from behind the lenses of clear-rimmed glasses.

He stood and came around the desk, taking her hand. "Ellie. How are things going?"

"Fine. I mean, I think they're fine. You tell me." She tried to keep her voice light, as if her mood alone could ward off any bad news. But her unease filtered into her tone until it was strained even to her own ears.

"Sit down."

She hated it when he said that. Her heart raced as she sank into a blue leather chair. "Jim, is there something . . . something wrong?"

"Ellie, the news regarding Zak . . . I'm afraid it's not good."

Ryder checked his watch for the two-hundredth time, his gaze flicking yet again to the hallway where Ellie had disappeared an hour ago. For the first twenty minutes he had wallowed in the acid sting of hurt, her words a raking echo of his parents' scorn for the career that had been his whole life.

Then he had made a lateral move into jealousy, thoughts of Ellie in a room with the respectable, sickeningly responsible doctor who had the hots for her spawning the gnawing, biting emotion. It had roiled inside him the whole time he joked with the tiny patients in the ward and fended off the flirtations of a leggy receptionist with a tanning-booth tan.

But as the hands on his watch neared the hour mark, he'd gotten a crawling sensation of unease in the pit of his stomach. A sensation that had deepened with each movement of the minute hand around the watch face until he felt more edgy than a rookie pitcher on a twelve-game losing streak.

He bit at his fingernail, the childhood habit a sure sign he was losing it. Where the hell was she?

He glanced down the hallway again, straining to catch a glimpse of Ellie.

Something was wrong. He knew it. Knew it with the same gut-instinct that made him hit the dirt when a bullet of a pitch was rocketing toward his head.

The certainty made him sick to his stomach and more than a little shaky, and the banter he'd been trying to keep up with Zakary and his friends grew increasingly more disjointed, until Ryder finally climbed out of the chair where he'd kept his vigil.

He flexed fingers stiff from scrawling autographs on everything from casts to baseball cards to the hospital's paper towels. "Listen, guys, I'm gonna stretch my legs for a little while. Gotta find out if Zak's Mom got poisoned in the hospital cafeteria or something."

The kids giggled, their horror stories regarding the notorious Atlanta General cuisine having filled whatever conversation hadn't been taken up by tales of RBIs and stolen bases.

"Mrs. MacCrea wasn't in the hospital cafeteria," a latecomer named Jake volunteered in a piping voice. "When they brought me back from X ray, I saw her sittin' in the little garden. I yelled hi to her, but she must not've heard me, 'cause she didn't even turn around."

Ryder's stomach lurched. He peered down into Zak's face, and the love and pain and savage terror that welled up inside Ryder stunned him.

Let him be all right... for God's sake, don't take him away....

"Rye, you okay?" Zakary's voice. Worried. Ryder noted the crease between silky auburn brows. Zak's eyes looked up at him with such innocence and trust, Ryder's hands knotted into fists.

"Yeah, slugger, I'm fine. You think you can hold down the space station without me for a little while?"

"No problem. I'm kinda tired, anyway. Tell Mom I wanna go home."

"I will, Zak." Ryder brushed back a lock of dark red hair from a forehead that was far too pale. He could see the faint blue threadings of veins beneath Zak's skin. Cerebrally, Ryder knew it was in large part because the boy was so fair complected, but now, it seemed almost a jeering reminder of how fragile life was, how tentative a hold on it this child had. Ryder's hand lingered against the warm softness of Zakary's face another precious moment. Then he straightened and drew away.

"Don't get captured by aliens while I'm away." He kept his tone light. Zak's grin was only a little weary.

"Copy, Rogue Leader."

"By the way, where is this garden where your Mom's being held prisoner?"

"Just down that hall an' to the right—no, left... I don't remember. Just look for a big door."

Ryder grimaced and resisted the temptation to ruffle the boy's curls as he thought of the endless maze of corridors and doorways that made up the hospital.

Not wanting to offend Zak, he merely started out in the direction the boy had pointed. Surprisingly the garden exit was easy to find. It lay adjacent to the hospital chapel, two welcoming islands of hope—one serene with dark wood and glowing candles, the other with tapers of cascading roses lit by the golden sun.

Even if the boy, Jake, hadn't told Ryder that Ellie was there, he would have known it. He could feel her, all her pain, all her fear, as if it were burrowing deep into his own chest. As deep as the love he was beginning to feel for her.

Ryder hesitated at the glass double doors and peered through them at the lone figure sitting on the stone bench. Her face was buried in her hands, her loose hair afire in the sunshine.

She looked so lost, as fragile as her son.

He pushed open the door, and walked through it, closing it behind him as quietly as possible. He stood there, his palms against the sun-heated glass, helplessness ripping through his gut.

After a moment he crossed to where she sat, his shadow falling across her. "Ellie?" He said her name quietly, not touching her, though his fingers ached to.

For a moment he thought she hadn't heard him, but then she raised her face to his, a choked sob rising in her throat as she reached out her arms to him. In a heartbeat Ryder had gathered her against him, her tears dampening his shoulder, her body feeling so slight, so tremulous, he feared he would crush her.

"I w-wanted you so much... to see you... talk—talk about everything, but you were—were with Zak, and I couldn't—"

"I'm here now," he murmured into her hair.

"Oh, Ryder, I can't... can't lose him. He's all that I have...."

"You have me, Ellie." Ryder's throat constricted.

Her arms tightened around him, and he felt the first bittersweet surge of hope, the knowledge that she did care for him, need him, even if she didn't want to.

"I'm not going to let anything happen to Zak," he said fiercely, stroking her hair. "I haven't even gotten to take him to the park, or watch one of his games, or... damn it, there's so much I want to do with him."

"But don't you see? Zak won't be able to do any of that soon. Jim says he's getting weaker, that without a transplant—" A sob wracked through her, piercing deep into Ryder's heart. "How could God have been so cruel, Ryder? Why couldn't I be the one to give a kidney to my little boy? I feel so—so helpless, watching him get sicker and sicker... and not being able to help him."

Gently Ryder eased her down onto the stone bench, then sat beside her, cradling her in his arms. "There must be something we can do. Some other hospital or doctor that can help Zak if this one can't. I'll charter a damn plane, fly the two of you there before morning, Ellie.''

"It wouldn't matter. Not without a donor... without someone who matches Zakary's tissue type." There was a wild kind of pain in her eyes, and he cupped her face in his hands, stroking her cheeks with the pads of his thumbs as if to smooth away the grief carved in her features.

"All this time..." she choked out, "all this time I've been hoping, praying for a miracle. A miracle! That Zak would get a kidney somehow. But my miracle would have been some other parent's tragedy, Ryder. A—a car accident, or... Do you know what it's been like waiting for some other child to die?" Her voice broke, and she clung to him, shattered. "But now... now it might be Zak who... sweet God, Ryder, I can't..."

"We're not going to lose him, Ellie. And we're not going to wait any longer, either. If you can't give Zak a kidney, your ex-husband will damn well have to."

"Daniel?"

"I'll drag him to the hospital myself. Hell, I'll pay the guy whatever it takes...."

"You'd have to find him first. I've done everything I can to locate him—sent letters through his lawyers, his friends, I even begged his bank to tell Daniel about Zak's illness when they wired him money."

Ryder tried to swallow his rage on her behalf. "He never contacted you?"

"I'm not even sure the messages reached him. Daniel's careless, but he's not a monster. For all our differences, I don't think he could stand back and let his own child die. If we could just find him, Ryder. Beg him to... to help Zak, there might be a chance."

Ryder looked down into that tear-streaked face that had known so much pain, the summer-storm eyes with spiky dark lashes, holding what seemed the first real whisperings of hope.

"I'll find him for you, Ellie," Ryder said, the words more solemn than any vow he'd ever taken.

Chapter Eight

The hotel room desktop was a study in desperation. Its elegant walnut surface was littered with scrawled notes, ragged envelopes and phone numbers from a dozen far-flung countries. Maps were tacked on foil-papered walls and spread across tables, lines in red marker tracing the swath of macho adventures Daniel MacCrea had cut across three continents. Mountain climbing in Tibet, sailing, solo, in the Pacific ocean, exploring deep in the wilds of the Amazon. It seemed Daniel MacCrea had been everywhere, done everything—except bother to find out that his son might be dying.

Ryder swore, crumpling up a letter hot off the type-writer of a private investigator in Zimbabwe, another promising lead disintegrating into yet another blind alley. Where the hell could that selfish bastard MacCrea be?

Had he finally fallen off a cliff somewhere, been buried in an avalanche or been devoured by crocodiles? No,

Ryder wouldn't even think it. The possibility was too real, the repercussions too painful.

Ryder slammed the balled-up letter into the trash and snatched up a marker. Gripping the cap between his teeth, he yanked it open, drawing a black line at the end of one of the numerous snaking trails. Jamming the lid back on the marker he all but crushed it in his hand, then, with an oath, hurled it at the headboard of the bed where he'd spent the three sleepless nights of this road trip.

"That's not the pitch I called for." Alex Craig's muffled voice came from beneath the mound of covers on the other double bed. Ryder felt a twinge of guilt as his friend emerged from the blankets, levering himself to a sitting position. Huge smudges darkened the skin beneath Craig's eyes, lines of weariness bracketed his mouth. Alex looked like hell. Ryder knew his own mirrored image would be far worse.

Craig squinted balefully at the travel alarm perched on the only corner of the nightstand not cluttered with papers and notes. "Five a.m. You getting up, or going to bed? No, let me guess—you're going for the record in the *Guinness* book for the number of hours a person can go without sleep. You might want to wait 'til the season's over, buddy, 'cause you've still got a helluva lot of games to play." Craig gave an eloquent yawn. "And so, by the way, have I."

"Dammit, Alex, this isn't a blasted game," Ryder snapped. "I have to find that scum ex-husband of Ellie's. Help Zak, or—"

"I know, Rye. I know. I just don't think you're going to do them any good when you're this strung out. Hell, I've never seen you like this. I'm getting worried."

"Well, don't be. I can take a hell of a lot more than a few sleepless nights."

"Yeah, but can you take your heart getting all twisted up like this? Can you take the way that kid's sickness is grinding away at you? You're not God, Ryder, no matter what the sportswriters say. You're doing your best, man.''

''What if it's not enough?'' Ryder stalked to the desk, slamming his fist down on the mass of papers. ''I promised Ellie I'd find MacCrea for her. I promised her, Alex. And she... the way she looked at me, all trusting... I love her, and I love her kid. And I'm scared as hell I'm going to fail them both.''

Ryder kicked the chair out from under the desk and sank down into it, burying his face in his hands. ''Dammit, Alex, it should have been easy—to find this guy, bring him back. I've had Byron working on it nonstop for days, hired a blasted army of private investigators. And I don't even know how many television appeals and newspaper interviews I've done. But all I ever find are trails that are cold. All I ever get are messages saying, yeah, Daniel MacCrea was here awhile back, but who the devil knows where the crazy bastard went off to now.''

There was the muffled creak of Alex getting up, then padding across the floor on bare feet. ''Rye, I know this is tough. I can't imagine what it'd be like to have one of my kids that sick. But you gotta know that this thing is beyond your control. Even if you do find Zak's father, things might not work out. If Ellie's not the kid's tissue type, there's no guarantee MacCrea is, either. And even if he is, you can't be sure the guy'll be willing to have himself cut open.''

''Oh, he'll give Zak the kidney,'' Ryder snarled, eyes narrowed. ''And Zak will be fine.'' His voice dropped low, his mind filling with images of the little boy's freckled face, tousled red hair, and eyes full of blind adoration. ''Alex, he has to be.'' Ryder's chest ached. He'd never known loving someone could hurt so damn much.

Craig started to speak, stopped, clapping Ryder on the shoulder. ''It'll all work out somehow,'' the catcher said softly. "I know it will. But in the meantime, man, you're going to have to start taking better care of yourself. We're going back to Atlanta tomorrow. Do you want Ellie to see you looking like this?"

"I don't give a damn what I look like."

"That may be, Rye, but let me tell you this. One look at you in this condition is going to scare the devil out of Ellie. You're the only hope she's got right now. And you look like the last man clinging to a sinking ship."

Ryder grimaced, remembering his reflection in the mirror the last time he'd shaved—yesterday, or was it the day before? He'd looked like he'd just played a triple-header with the devil and lost.

He sighed, leaning his head back, fighting the clutching sensation that had been balled in his chest these past days. "How am I going to face her, Alex, with no news? No leads?"

"She might be hoping for news, but I doubt she expects any this early. If it was going to be easy to find the guy, don't you think she would have flushed him out by now? I mean, I've never met your lady, but if Tony were in that kind of danger, you'd better believe Gina would make herself crazy trying to find me."

"I guess so. I just…she's been through so much, I just want this over with for her. Just want to fix it so I can see her smile again."

Alex cleared his throat and finger-combed his sandy hair. "Anyway you look at it, Rye, this thing is going to take time. Finding Zak's dad, setting up surgery, Zak's recovery afterward. And no matter how careful you are, it might not work at all."

"It's going to work, dammit—" Ryder raged.

"Okay, well, say you're right. Everything works out just as planned. Terrific. But it's still going to take a little while. I was just thinking that you should leave all this *Magnum, P.I.,* stuff to Byron and the investigators you hired. You're probably just getting in their way, anyhow. And while you're waiting for things to fall into place, you can take the time Zakary has now. Make it special. Didn't you get the boy a present or something when we were in Philadelphia?"

"Yeah. For his birthday."

"Well, even a kid that's healthy has only one eighth birthday, friend. We're going back for that ten-game home stand tomorrow. There's a lot you could do in ten days." Alex grinned. "Consider yourself the kid's fairy godfather, except instead of a wand, you've got a Louisville Slugger."

Ryder looked at his friend, a slow smile spreading over his face. "No wonder the pitchers let you do their thinking for them, Alex. You're a genius."

"I've been telling you that for years. Now can we both get some doggone sleep?"

A light rain speckled night-cooled sidewalks, the dusky gray morning broken only by the lamp of an occasional early riser. Ryder closed the door of the airport limo and slung his bags over one shoulder as he dealt the driver his fare.

The man scratched at a grizzled salt-and-pepper beard, and looked up at the modest apartment building with a puzzled expression. "Guess them stories ya hear about million-dollar contracts are a bunch'a hogwash, huh?"

Ryder winked at the man, a smile creasing his face. "Believe me, penthouses aren't what they're cracked up to be."

The driver laughed as he pocketed Ryder's generous tip. "There's folks in this town that wouldn't mind if you all got a billion-dollar contract if you won 'em a division championship. You bring the pennant on home this year, Mr. Sloan. Ya hear?"

Ryder promised to try, then turned, taking the steps to Ellie's building two stairs at a time, his heart pounding with anticipation as he shed the ache of loneliness that had dogged him throughout the road trip to San Francisco.

Between him and the enthusiastic Gina Craig, half of Atlanta must be buzzing with news of the plans the two had labored over the past twenty-four hours. A dozen calls to make arrangements, bribes, browbeatings and countless cajolings helping convince various businesses to humor the obviously eccentric but beloved third baseman of the Atlanta Angels.

It had been a slapdash affair, a race with the clock, but for once it seemed the fates smiled on Zak, things falling into place with a serendipitous perfection that amazed and delighted Ryder. He only hoped Zak had half as much fun indulging in what was planned for him as Ryder had had arranging it all.

He stopped outside Ellie's door, grinning at the grapevine heart that she had hung there. It was woven through with silk flowers, and a small teddy bear was tucked amongst some green vines. Pearls and lace and ribbon had been looped artistically throughout the arrangement, but the effect was lost because upon the bear's furry head, Zakary had tucked one of the miniature plastic baseball caps you could get ice cream in at the stadium. With a grin, Ryder tugged the bear's cap down over shoe-button eyes.

Lowering his bags to the floor, he listened for a moment, the slumberous silence within making him hesitate. They were obviously still sleeping, Zak tucked into his rumpled baseball sheets, monsters and superhero figures and that dog, Fluffles, tucked under his little chin. And Ellie . . . she would be in the bed where she'd slept alone these past few years, her hair tossed across the pillow, her slender arms and legs warm in sleep.

He hated to wake her . . . no, he *wanted* to wake her, with slow, lingering kisses, and hands stroking her. He wanted to wake her every morning, wanted to watch her sleep after he'd loved her all night long.

He'd never wanted anything the way he wanted Ellie. Never needed anything the way he needed her. It was terrifying. Wonderful.

Like coming home.

He rapped on the door, faintly, wanting just a few minutes alone with her before Zakary awoke. After a moment he heard muffled sounds of someone coming to the door, heard her gasp as she looked through the peephole. She fumbled with the safety chain, awkward in her haste to get it off, and Ryder felt a surge of pleasure that she was as eager to see him as he was to see her.

The door flew open, and an in instant she flung herself full-length against him, her body warm beneath the age-worn T-shirt, her hands clinging to him, eager, as a choked laugh came from her throat. "Ryder...wh-what are you doing here? Is there any news?"

"Only this." He twined tumbled red-silk hair around his fingers, heat seeping down into his loins, making him hard with wanting. A low growl sounded in his chest as his mouth covered hers. No searching, tentative kiss was this—rather it was hunger, need, its sweetness sharpened by a tang of desperation. "Ellie, I missed you so much."

She didn't say anything, but her body told him the secrets that she couldn't. She nestled against him, her arms clutching tight around his lean waist, her face buried against his chest. She smelled of honey and lemonade and sunshine, the subtle fragrance that was Ellie's own.

Ryder pressed a kiss to the top of her head, breathing in the scent of her hair. "If I'd known I was going to get a reception like this, I would have skipped out on the team two days ago."

"If I'd known you'd come back sooner, I would have told you." She turned her face up to look into his eyes. Her eyelids were still heavy with sleep, the gray of her irises shadowed with dreams. He wondered if they'd been dreams about him. Heaven knew, she'd been haunting what little sleep he'd been managing to catch, haunting it with that elusive smile, that petal-soft skin, those eyes that made him want to make sweet, sweet love to her and drive away her sadness.

"I heard someone's got a birthday today," Ryder said, tracing her cheek with one fingertip.

A faint smile darted about Ellie's lips. "We should stick a bow on top of your head and make you a present. All Zak has talked about is whether or not you'd be coming."

Ryder remembered the day he'd taken Zakary to the Angels clubhouse. They had been touring the place when the boy had confided his disappointment in his last birthday. His father had written a letter promising to come for his party. Zak had waited and hoped for weeks, but MacCrea hadn't even bothered to mail the kid a postcard.

There had been so much hurt in that piping little voice, its tone undercut with silent questions, pleadings—*why? Doesn't he love me? Doesn't he want me? I've been a good boy...*

Ryder had asked himself those questions a thousand times during the years he had wandered about the magnificent Sloan mansion, more a stranger there than any of the servants.

Ryder shut away memories that were too painful, memories he'd never shared with another person. Forcing a smile, he delved into the pocket of his jacket, extracting a small box. Though the elegant foil wrapping was torn in one corner and the glinting gold bow crumpled, it was still evident it had come from one of those intimidating stores where most people only ogle the wares through windows, under the watchful eyes of clerks with the dignity of nineteenth-century butlers.

"A present for Zak?" Ellie asked, dubiously eyeing the embossed foil seal.

"No. Something for you. Kind of a badge of honor or something for doing such a terrific job raising that kid of yours."

"Ryder, you shouldn't have." Her eyes went dark, glistening as she took the small parcel from his fingers.

"Don't tell me what to do, woman," Ryder said, cuffing her gently on the chin. "I'll spoil the hell out of you and Zak if I feel like it. Now open it, and at least pretend you like it. I looked all over creation for that thing."

Her fingers were trembling as she slowly tugged at the ribbon, as if to savor it, prolong the enjoyment. Ryder wondered how long it had been since Ellie had had any present, except the treasured crayoned drawings Zak had affixed to the refrigerator.

When she got to the royal-blue velvet box, she cradled it in her palm a long moment, then carefully opened the lid. The first watery rays of sunlight trickled over the object pillowed on rich velvet, setting gold that had existed over a hundred and fifty years alight with a mellow glow. Twined roses and ivy wreathed a delicately carved cameo pin; the artist had portrayed a woman in a Grecian gown feeding a swan from one outstretched hand.

Ellie's lips formed a silent circle, and a tear escaped to slide down one cheek.

"It reminded me of you," Ryder said thickly, jamming his hands in his jacket pockets. "Soft and classy and old-fashioned. I thought it'd look real pretty on that blouse you wore the day I met you. The Victorian one with all those tiny buttons."

She gave him a wobbly smile, her eyes so bright, Ryder's chest ached. "It's the most beautiful thing I've ever seen. Every time I wear it, I'll think of you."

The pain in Ryder's chest deepened at her bitter-sweet, wistful words. It was as if she expected to keep the cameo tucked away in a box with her memory of him when she was alone again.

He wanted to drag her into his arms, kiss her until even she couldn't deny they belonged together. But as he looked at her, so fragile despite that fierce inner strength, he knew he didn't dare rush her, or he might lose her forever. Time. She needed time. Trouble was, he'd never been as good at patience as he was at baseball.

He tore his gaze away from those storm-soft eyes. "Well, you've got your present. Isn't it time we woke up the birthday kid and give him one of his?"

Ellie closed the cameo safely back in its box and lay it on the carriage-seat table. "We don't usually open until later." She gestured toward the small pile of brightly wrapped packages in the corner.

Ryder feigned a wounded expression. "I thought I was supposed to be the present."

She smiled, and it was like the first ray of sun piercing the dark. Stealing a neon bow from one of the gifts, she brushed back the thick fall of his hair and stuck the ribbon on his forehead. Her fingers lingered, the feel of them making Ryder suddenly damned uncomfortable in his tight, faded jeans.

"What every eight-year-old boy wants for his birthday this year," she teased.

"What about their mothers?"

"Mothers can be real picky, you know," she said, her brow puckering as she slid her hand down the side of his face, the corded muscles of his neck. Her fingers hesitated to draw patterns on the pale blue cotton of his shirt. "I don't know about anyone else, but I examine things I'm going to...um...consume very carefully."

He had thought she was driving him mad a moment ago, but as her fingertips abraded his rigid nipple through the fabric of his shirt, he felt so hot he was melting.

For a moment Ryder couldn't breathe. Ellie, solemn, had been beautiful, but Ellie laughing, smiling, loving him with her eyes, was dangerous as hell. His heart couldn't take much more of this.

"Do I pass the squeeze test?" he asked, trying to conceal the desire ripping through him.

"Sloan, if they sold you in the produce aisle, women would be killing each other to do their grocery shopping."

"I don't much care about women—plural. What about one woman in particular?"

"I have real trouble making decisions. How about if you ask me tomorrow."

Ryder grabbed her, his own laugh rumbling out. "How about if I tickle the heck out of you 'till you tell me?" His fingers played up and down her ribs, and she laughed so hard she shook.

"Stop! R-Ryder, I can't stand it...." He released her, still holding her in his arms. "H-how did you know I was...ticklish?" she gasped out.

"Never trust a red-haired seven-year-old. They tell your darkest secrets every time."

"*Eight.*" A sleepy voice came from the direction of Zak's bedroom. "I'm an *eight*-year-old. And...*Rye?*" Zak squealed the name, as if jolted awake by lightning.

In a heartbeat the spindly boy ran out, his cartoon character pajamas askew, his stuffed dog tucked under one arm. With a cry of pure delight, the child hurled himself at Ryder and was swept high in strong arms.

Despite his joy in holding the little boy, Ryder couldn't blot out the glimpse he had caught of that small, freckled face. A face even more pallid than when Ryder had left three days ago.

"Whatcha got that thing stuck on you for?" Zak asked, tugging off the bow still affixed to Ryder's skin.

"I told you I got you a birthday present," Ryder said. "I'm yours for the whole day."

"You're...what?"

"Got the whole day planned, so you'd better go get dressed. Got a lot to do."

"All right!" Zak started to tug away, but Ryder held him.

"There's just one thing—you need something to wear to the ball, Cinderella."

"Oh, gag! We aren't going to some wimpy dance, Rye...?"

"Ball*park,* slugger."

"But there isn't a game today," Zak protested. "I looked on the schedule."

"Watch it, kid. It's rude to argue with fairy godfathers. There's some stuff going on at Angels Stadium I want you to see. Some people I want you to meet. Good friends of mine. The Craigs."

"Craig? You mean the catcher? His batting average stinks—"

"Try not to remind him. He'll be impossible to live with. Now, shut your face. I've got something I want you to put on." Ryder went quickly to the door and dragged in one of his bags. He dug in a zippered pocket and tugged out a soft, crumpled package.

Zakary fell on it like a ravening wolf, tearing it open with unbridled glee. A miniature of Ryder's baseball uniform spilled out, complete even to the baseball mitt and batting gloves he wore.

"Look on the back," Ryder directed.

Speechless, the little boy turned the striped jersey over. MACCREA arched in bold blue lettering above the number 00.

"For me?" Zakary shook his head, disbelieving. "You got this for me?"

"Well, I really got it for myself, but the blasted thing shrunk...."

"Thank you! Rye, thank you!" Zakary flung himself into Ryder's arms. Ryder cuddled the ecstatic little boy close against him, his own eyes blurring. "If I never had another birthday as long as I live, I wouldn't even care! This is going to be the best one I've ever had!"

Ryder grinned over the boy's tumbled curls, his eyes catching Ellie's. The soft gray beneath her lashes was touched, yet haunted once again. As if reflecting on Zakary's careless words.

. . . If I never had another birthday . . .

Ryder's arms tightened around the boy, as if he could somehow protect him from the doctors and their predictions of doom.

Whatever happened in the future, Ryder resolved grimly, today he'd make certain that every one of Zakary's wishes would come true.

Chapter Nine

The wind whipped through Ellie's hair as Ryder wheeled the Porsche down Wakefield Avenue, the throbbing beat of a rock station blaring through the radio. Zak was singing along in a gritty Rod Stewartesque voice, his face beaming with happiness as he clutched his treasured batting gloves against the front of his Angels jersey.

Time and time again, the little boy had tried to pry information out of Ryder, wanting to know where they were going, what they were going to do. But aside from the vaguest hints, framed by wide, insufferably smug grins, Ryder had been more secretive than James Bond on a mission.

Ellie had loved him for it. Loved leaning back in the rich leather seats, listening to Zak plead and Ryder tease. From the day Daniel had left, she'd felt guilty because Zak would be missing out on this kind of bantering, this child adoration for a man who would adore Zakary right back.

But she knew even if Daniel had stayed, Zakary would never have experienced the kind of attention he was getting from Ryder Sloan. The kinship of spirit, the understanding of what it was like to be newly eight years old, with a million dreams from moon landings to winning international skateboard championships still tantalizingly within reach.

Ryder guided the car around a turn and Angels Stadium rose out of the mass of surrounding buildings, grand turn-of-the century residences cut up now into apartments for eccentrics with six-figure incomes.

The gates that were usually thronged with fans were deserted except for a family of tourists taking pictures below the huge Angels sign, and a few scraggly looking boys hitting bottletops with sticks. Only the parking lot reserved for players was filled with a dozen or so cars. Jaguars, Corvettes, Mercedes-Benzes.

One top-of-the-line van was parked in the middle, the automobile seeming out of place with its bike rack and assorted images of popular cartoon characters stuck to the windows. Ryder pulled in next to it and parked. He glanced down at the van's scuffed fender and grinned. "Tony must've been taking driving lessons again."

"Tony?" Ellie echoed.

"Gina and Alex's oldest. Last year he decided to move the van so he and Will could play basketball in the driveway. Unfortunately he couldn't find the brakes."

Ellie pressed a hand to her chest, thinking of the numerous stunts Zakary had pulled, and the possible dire consequences. But obviously Tony Craig's prank had all turned out for the best, or Ryder wouldn't be telling the tale with that glint of amusement in his eyes.

"He must've given his mother heart failure," Ellie said.

"Tony? With great regularity," Ryder said, laughing as he climbed out of the Porsche. "But that time it was Gina who gave the neighbors heart failure. She'd hopped into the shower for a minute while their youngest, Mia, was taking a nap. Gina was just getting out when she saw the van rolling down the drive. Ran out in nothing but a bath towel. Thought Alex would die laughing when she told him over the phone."

"Over the phone?"

"Yeah. We were in Cincinnati that week...or was it San Diego? No, it was Cincinnati, because we called for Will's birthday."

It was as if rain clouds had suddenly edged their way across the sky, blotting out the promise of a perfect day. Ellie got out of the car, Zak clambering to the pavement in her wake. The pure pleasure she had felt on the ride to the stadium diminished into a kind of painful resignation as she looked at the grinning cartoon characters on the van.

She wondered how often the children's father piled them all into the vehicle for an ice cream cone, or took them to the movies. He'd obviously missed one of his kids' birthdays. How many school programs or Little League games or Sundays at the park had Alex Craig missed because he was on the road? How many times during the summer had he been able to tuck his kids into bed and read them a story?

Or did it even matter to him? Lord knew, Ellie had seen few men who were genuinely involved with their kids—even men who worked nine to five three blocks from their home. Occasional outings when it was convenient was about all most fathers could bear. Vignettes of familial bliss in which they bore their offspring about as if expecting to be decorated for parental bravery, flashed in Ellie's mind.

"Ellie? Something wrong?" Ryder's voice broke in. She looked up into troubled blue eyes.

"Your friend . . . Alex. He must be gone a lot."

"Yeah, it's rough." Ryder's eyes darkened, his voice taking on an almost defensive tone. "But he's home all winter, and during the team's home stands. And sometimes Gina and the kids come along when we're on the road."

Ellie tried to imagine three small children crammed into a hotel room five states away from their toy boxes. It was the stuff nightmares were made of.

As if aware of the direction of her thoughts, Ryder rubbed one hand along his jaw. "We'd better go in. We're already a little late."

"Late?" Zak piped up. "Late for what?"

Ryder tugged at a lock of red hair. "You'll see, sport. C'mon."

They walked to a door cut in the stadium's red brick side and entered. A security guard gave a nod of greeting. "Morning, Ryder."

Ryder waved. "How you doing, Fred?"

"Passable, passable." Fred glanced down at Zak. "Hear you have a birthday, son."

"I'm eight."

"Well, you have a good one, now."

Raising one hand in goodbye, Ryder led them deeper into the stadium's confines. Concession and souvenir stands were empty, the cool cement area a yawning tunnel filled only with silence. Footsteps echoed as Ryder led them through a passageway toward the block of sunshine that shone from above. A muffled sound drifted down the corridor, followed by a quiet shushing sound, then the light tap of running tennis shoes.

When he was almost to the top landing, Ryder hesitated, going down on one knee on the concrete. "Have to tie my shoe," he said, fiddling with the laces. "Zak, go on ahead."

The boy darted past him to the landing in the midst of the stands. A roar greeted him, shouts of "happy birthday" and "surprise" rippling on the hot summer air. Zak froze, and one of the batting gloves clutched in his fingers dropped to the floor.

Ellie bent to retrieve it, then felt as if she, too, was rooted to the spot as the panorama below spilled out before her. A gigantic balloon billowed rainbow silk above a gondola in the middle of the field, and a banner attached to the basket read Happy Birthday Zak. A long table covered with birthday paraphernalia stretched along the first-base line, and hundreds of helium balloons were tied to the backs of the chairs.

A cake was in the center of the table. Ellie gaped at it, remembering how Zakary had chattered about getting one made in the image of Ryder's rookie baseball card. This cake was exactly as the little boy had wished it to be, except that instead of Ryder's cocky grin and dark hair, it was Zak's own face that stared out above the Angels logo.

And ranged around the far side of the table stood the whole baseball team, women who must be their wives and a scattering of children interspersed among the players.

Ellie glanced back to see Ryder, hands on Zakary's shoulders and a smile on his lips, looking down at the child's awe-filled features.

"Happy birthday, slugger." Did she imagine it, or was there a thickness in the voice that was smooth as warmed whiskey?

"Rye! Oh, Rye!" Zakary spun around and wrapped his arms around Ryder's thighs. Ryder stroked the child's hair, holding him close, and Ellie thought she had never seen anything so beautiful as Ryder's dark head bent over Zakary's red one; Zak's thin arms clinging to Ryder's lean-muscled frame.

They stood there long minutes, and Ellie had a strange feeling as if she, somehow, were the one who was intruding. But at that second, Ryder reached out his other arm and drew her into the circle of that warmth, holding her tight against his side.

"I hope you don't mind," he said, looking at her solemnly. "I wanted this year to be special. Our first one together."

His words were like heaven, like hell, Ellie's mind whirling with hope and terror, resignation and . . . could it be love?

It welled up deep inside her, and the certainty made her chest tighten until it burned, made her hands quake.

"How could I mind?" she managed, just as Zakary was beset by a wiry boy about his own age. Huge dark eyes that melted with innocence were belied by the pure devilment in the child's grin as he regarded Zak from beneath a fall of wavy raven hair. A smaller version of the boy was hot on the older one's heels, only the fact that he was tugging along a curly, dark-haired imp in a frilly pink dress preventing him from keeping up with what must be his older brother.

"Tony! Tony, no fair! He cut again, Ma!" the younger boy squawked. But before whichever of the women present who was "Ma" could come in to referee, Ryder moved into the breach, swinging the little girl onto his shoulders, tweaking the one named Tony on the nose, and all the while teasing the younger boy out of a fit of the sulks with as much skill as if he had done so a hundred times.

"Watch it, you barbarians, or I'll feed your cake to the sharks," Ryder threatened.

But Tony was unperturbed, staring at Zakary with undisguised interest. "You the kid who's sick?"

Ellie winced. The younger boy, whom she deduced must be Will Craig, hissed at Tony to be quiet. But Zak met Tony's gaze levelly.

"Yeah. I'm sick."

"I had stitches once. Hospitals stink."

"Yeah."

"So, you gonna stand here all day, or do you wanna get a ride on that balloon?"

Zak looked up at Ellie for permission.

"It's perfectly safe," Ryder interjected softly. "The thing will be tethered to the ground the whole time."

But what if the lines break? What if Tony decides to take the balloon for a spin? What if the gas in the thing catches fire and it explodes?

Ellie forced down the nervousness bubbling up inside her. Dear heaven, it was bad enough that she was falling in love with the man. But this... to *trust* him, even a little, made prickles of pure terror race down her spine.

She steadied herself, then nodded. "Go ahead, Zak. If Ryder says it's safe..."

With a whoop of triumph, Tony Craig bolted down the stairs, Will an arm's length behind him. Zak started after them, but his failing health had already taken its toll on the legs that had once raced about so tirelessly.

Will glanced behind them, then slowed, jogging back to keep pace with Zakary. "Tony always has to be first. He thinks he's some big track star or somethin'. But Ryder says that when I get bigger I'm going to beat Tony's..." As if suddenly aware of the adults within hearing range, Will flashed Ryder a grin. "Beat Tony's cookies," the boy finished with infinite satisfaction.

Ellie saw Ryder wink. His big hands engulfed the tiny ones of the moppet still perched on his shoulders, the little girl kicking at his chest with miniscule patent leather shoes. "Wye! Wydo!" the child babbled happily. "Pwesents for me?"

"Not this time, baby," Ryder said, deftly tumbling the little girl over his head and into his arms. "These presents are for Zak's birthday."

The tiny pink lip thrust out, quivering. "Did you fordot me?"

Ryder buried his face in the child's plump belly, tickling her. "Of course I didn't forget you, sweetheart.

There's a present with your name on it in my bag, but you'll have to wait 'til after the party."

"Potty?"

"Watch it, Sloan, that's a dangerous word." A petite woman with waist-length dark hair emerged from the crowd. A wedding ring glinted on slender fingers that were pillowed gently over the swell of her advanced pregnancy. "Mia usually says it two seconds before the floodgates open."

Ellie expected Ryder to thrust the child into its mother's arms, but instead he perched the little girl on one hip. "I'll take her down to the restroom quick, just in case," he said to the woman. "By the way, Gina, this is Ellie. Take care of her for me."

Without another word, he turned, hurrying away with the two-year-old in his arms.

Ellie watched him, nonplussed, then turned to the woman who stood beside her. Lips glossed in pale coral tipped in an affectionate smile, but the smile faded perceptibly when Gina's dark eyes fixed again on Ellie's face.

"I've heard a lot about you," she said. "You're all Rye talks about."

"He's been very kind." Ellie watched Ryder's broad shoulders disappear.

Gina laughed. "That's Rye for you. Especially when there's a kid involved. Sick kids, abused kids, kids who are just in trouble. Whatever their problem is, Ryder is always there to listen."

Ellie fumbled with the cameo she'd pinned at the collar of the Victorian blouse Ryder had liked so much, feeling as if all the brightness had gone out of the day. The time he had spent with Zak had seemed so special, unique. But was it really just Ryder's way to involve himself so deeply in such causes? In the lives of such children?

"Ryder...ah, does this all the time?" Despite the admiration she felt for him, she couldn't keep the edge of disappointment from her voice.

Gina tossed her thick tresses over one slender shoulder, her eyes warming. "Ryder's been neck-deep in kids ever since I met him. But this much I can tell you. I've never heard him talk about one of their mothers."

Ellie wavered, uncertain what to say beneath the forthright appraisal in Gina's brown eyes.

"He's a good man. I hope you know how lucky you are."

"Luck?" Ryder's voice echoed through the cavernous passage as he and little Mia emerged through the arch. "There was no luck about it. This kid's got this bathroom stuff under control. She's a genius."

"Geen-sis!" Mia echoed. Gina reached out her arms, taking the beaming child. "Well, come on, genius, let's go down and drive your brothers insane, shall we?"

The girl crowed with delight as Gina started down the steps. A few feet from the bottom, the woman stopped, her eyes holding Ellie's for a long moment. "It was nice to meet you, Ellie. You might just be good enough for our Ryder after all."

"Gina! For cripes sake!" Ryder yelped, his face turning bright red.

"Just wait, Sloan," Gina teased. "After the party, I'm going to tell her all your most intimate secrets. Like about that time you . . . oh, never mind. I think I'll just keep you in suspense."

With that she went down to join the others, leaving Ryder and Ellie suddenly, strangely, very much alone, in spite of the crowd of well-wishers thronging the field.

"Ellie...about Gina. It's her mission in life to torment me. Don't believe a word she says."

"She said I was lucky." Ellie leaned back against the iron rail and looked up into Ryder's golden-tanned face. Fingers of the breeze threaded through his sun-streaked dark hair, the longish silky strands brushing against his high cheekbones and strong, square jaw.

"Funny," she said, "from the time I was small, I always thought luck was something other girls had—along with pretty clothes and straight teeth, and handwriting that looked like copperplate." Ellie reached up one palm to gently cup his face.

"You coveted your neighbor's braces, huh?" Ryder said with an indulgent smile.

"I was an awkward kid with red hair, and with the fatal flaw of being the smartest girl in the class. I wanted so much for everyone to like me."

Ryder's smile turned bittersweet. "I would've been happy enough if my parents had..." He stopped, but Ellie saw the hurt in his eyes, some pain too raw to touch even now. She knew about pain like that, knew enough not to press him. But she skimmed her knuckles back into his warm-satin hair, her heart squeezing tight with love for him.

She saw Ryder swallow hard, a shudder working through him. "So what...what happened? When you were a kid?" he asked.

"There wasn't any fairy-tale ending, if that's what you're asking. When the other kids were off playing, I'd spend a lot of time by myself, reading and making up stories in my head. There was this tree in our yard. An oak tree, all twisted, and so tall it made me dizzy to look down from the top branches. I climbed up it every night in the summer, because from there I could see the whole sky. I would watch for falling stars, hour after hour, and make wishes... I wanted to be a princess, or have a jillion dollars, or be prettier than Peggy Sue Wallart. And once, once, I was even so terrible that I wished Sister Lourdine would fall down the fire chute out our classroom window. I didn't want her to get hurt, you understand. I just wanted to see her slide down, her habit flying."

Ryder smiled at her, tender. "Did you ever get your wishes?"

"No. When I was eleven, I quit climbing the tree. I kicked it whenever I ran past, I was so disappointed that none of my dreams had come true. I figured I was just unlucky. That I must've done something terrible so that the stars wouldn't listen. But now . . . now I want to believe, Ryder. In you. In this." She skimmed her thumb over the velvety curve of his lower lip. "I want to so much. Ryder, help me try."

Disaster reigned in the Craig family living room, enough toys to stock the Christmas shelves at Santa's workshop blanketing the plush country-blue carpet. A tent Ryder had constructed of bed sheets strung across chairs dragged in from the dining room still stood in one corner. Stuffed animals ranged around it in a most convincing facsimile of a jungle.

The natives had been restless that night when they had been caravaned away from the birthday party, but since neither Tony nor Will could bear the thought of being separated from their newfound friend, and Zak felt the same way, Gina had insisted that the lot of them descend upon the Craig house for dinner.

It had been relaxing, refreshing, wonderful, to sit in Gina's cozy kitchen, laughing and talking while Zak and the other children stalked headhunters in the Amazon. And when it finally grew quiet in the living room, it had felt so right for Ryder to slip his hand into hers, drawing her out to see how Zak and the other boys had fallen asleep, sprawled inside the blanket tent, Zakary snuggled close to a lifelike stuffed gorilla.

"If we were headhunters, these guys would be wall decorations," Ryder said quietly, reaching into the tent to tuck a blanket snugly around the three children. "Want some help lugging your two into their bedrooms, Alex?"

Alex Craig chuckled, rubbing the back of his neck with one hand. "I don't know, Rye. They look so peaceful I hate to disturb 'em. Funny how angelic kids look when they're sleeping." Alex eased his oldest son's bare foot beneath the blanket edge. "Especially when they're a regular demolition squad when they're awake."

Gina leaned back against her husband, and Ellie's heart twisted as Alex's broad palm caressed the swell of the new life the two of them had created.

"My maxim has always been let sleeping children snooze," Gina said, cupping her hand over her husband's.

"Well, we'll just slip Zak out—" Ryder began.

"Oh, no, don't!" Gina protested. "He looks so adorable all snuggled in there. The poor little guy is exhausted. Why don't you leave him here until morning?"

"I couldn't impose. . . ." Ellie said, doubtfully.

"Don't be ridiculous! Will and Tony will be in ecstasy when they wake up and find Zak here. They can help Alex make pancakes in the morning and the boys can show Zak the treehouse Alex built them. I'm sure Tony has some old jeans that will fit Zak."

Ellie chewed at the corner of her lip. "Zak would love it, I'm sure. But I . . ." she flushed. "I've never left him alone overnight."

Gina slipped one slender arm around her and gave her a bracing hug. "He'd hardly be alone, crammed between my two little Indians. And Alex and I would watch him really close."

Ellie hesitated. "There is just so much medicine to keep track of. I'd hate to put you to the trouble—"

"Believe me, with three kids we've forced more than our share of prescriptions down their throats," Alex said in the tone of someone who had often had the dubious honor of dispensing medicine to reluctant small patients.

"We could give him whatever he needs," Gina encouraged. "And we'd call the minute there was any trouble."

Ellie couldn't help but smile. "I know you would."

"C'mon, Mom, please, let us keep him," Alex urged. "You try and drag him out of the middle of our two kids, and they'll wake up, and then they'll be crazed because Zak's going home, and they'll have a fit, and Gina and I won't get a wink of sleep all night. You don't want that on your conscience, now do you?"

"Besides," Gina said. "I think you and Rye could use a little time alone."

Ellie met Ryder's gaze for an instant, knowing instinctively where the night would lead if she left her child tucked safely under the Craigs' care. Ryder knew it, too. She could see it in those cerulean eyes, in the curve of that devastatingly sexy, impossibly vulnerable, mouth.

"Ellie, if you're not comfortable leaving him, it's okay," Ryder interjected quietly. "We can load him up in the Porsche and—"

"No." Ellie reached out and took Ryder's hand. His breath caught, and his fingers tightened around hers, trembling just a little. "If Gina and Alex really don't mind . . . let him stay."

Chapter Ten

The Porsche engine purred as Ryder wheeled it along the streets of the city, the night parade of theatergoers and elegant diners, a-sparkle with diamonds, sweeping in and out of limousines and hotel lobbies. He released the wheel with one hand, wiping his sweaty palm on his thigh, but before he'd even gripped the steering wheel again, he felt the slickness returning, the tension building inside him more powerful than anything he'd ever known.

He glanced over at the woman beside him, so quiet, her face translucent in the pools of street lamps they passed. She was so beautiful, so fragile, the high lace collar of her blouse skimming the soft curve of her chin. She'd pinned his cameo there, at the hollow of her throat. And all Ryder could think of was unfastening the golden clasp, slipping each tiny pearl button through its loop to bare the skin beneath it.

Ellie, I need you so much, he thought silently. *Let this be right for you.*

He'd been uncertain when they'd left Alex and Gina's, hadn't known what to say to her, what to do. So he'd kissed her, softly, savoring the feel of her lips trembling under his.

"Do you want me to take you home?" He'd squeezed the words through a throat constricted with need.

"No." She'd said it quickly, looking uncomfortable, shy. "I'd—I'd rather go somewhere else...to your place."

So he'd driven, heading toward his penthouse, dreaming of Ellie in his wide, empty bed.

He pulled into the parking garage, guiding the vehicle to a smooth stop, his heart hammering against his ribs. He killed the engine, staring straight ahead, not trusting himself to look at her. "Ellie, are you sure?"

"Is anyone ever really sure about anything?" Her voice was soft, a little sad. "I only know I want to be with you, Ryder. Tonight. I don't want to think about anything else."

"Ellie, I don't want to hurt you."

"I know." She reached up, tucking a wisp of dark hair behind his ear. Ryder wanted to gather her in his arms, wanted to steal away all her fears with his kisses, but he got out of the car and walked around to swing her door open. She put her hand in his, and his fingers curled around it, protectively, all sensation seeming to be centered where their palms brushed, melded.

Hand in hand, they walked to the elevator, the rush of it hurtling skyward mimicking the racing of Ryder's pulse.

He'd been with other women before, had wanted to please them. But he'd never felt this desperation, this craving, to be everything a woman had ever dreamed of.

He wanted miracles for Ellie.

The elevator slid open, and Ryder led her to the door of his penthouse, unlocking it with hands suddenly unsteady. Flicking on the lights recessed in the ceiling, he stepped back to allow her entry. She gasped softly as she walked in, her slim hand reaching out to skim over the surface of a glistening ebony table.

"It's beautiful. So shiny and new." A tiny smile quirked her lips. "All your furniture matches."

"A decorator did the whole thing. Until it was finished, I'd never realized how a room so full of things could feel so empty." Restless, he paced over to the stereo and flicked it on. The melting voice of James Taylor drifted into the room, whispering of fire and rain and yesterdays.

Ryder stood and watched as Ellie slid open the glass doors, stepping out onto the balcony that looked out over the Atlanta skyline. The fabric of her blouse was all but sheer, a lacy camisole just visible beneath it. The slightest stirring of a breeze cupped the material around her breasts, allowing him a shadowy glimpse of nipples pushing against her bra. Her dusky rose skirt was belted softly by a mauve sash, the fabric beneath it draping about the curves of her hips in soft waves that skimmed past her knees.

No tight leather jumpsuit or slinky silk sheath could have been more alluring. Every muscle in his body throbbed with wanting her, but for the first time in his life, he was uncertain, afraid that somehow he might hurt her. And she'd already been hurt. Badly.

Cursing himself inwardly for a coward, he went to the bar. "Can I get you something? Wine or champagne?" he called. "We can sit out there, and . . . talk."

She turned and came to him, closing the door behind her. Looking up into his eyes, she said, "We both know why I'm here. Let's not . . . not pretend. . . ."

Pretend. . . How many times had he gone through the motions of making love? Being in love? Roses in green tissue paper, candlelight dinners... But there was nothing of illusion in what he felt for Ellie. It was real. Excruciatingly real. And it scared him to death.

"Ellie, I don't know what to do. Hell, I've never... never felt this way before. I don't want to ruin things between us."

"I want this, Ryder. Want you."

He froze as she took his hand and laid it between the soft swells of her breasts. Her heart beat against his palm, quick, light, irregular. Ryder groaned as he felt her breath catch at the contact.

"Ah, Ellie... Ellie..."

"Dance with me." She reached up and put her arms around his neck, her breasts brushing against his chest, her thighs skimming his as he lost himself in mist-gray eyes.

Pulling her closer, he rested his cheek on the tumbled fall of her hair. He moved to the music, Taylor's melancholy ballad about lost lovers wrapping its strains around him until his eyes drifted shut. His arms tightened around her and the melody carried him away.

Away to a place he'd never been before, a place of innocence and trusting and hope. A place where he felt love enfold him, embrace him, make him whole.

When the last notes faded into silence, he froze there, with Ellie in his arms, holding her, never wanting the night to end.

He curled one finger beneath her chin, tipping her face up so the light could wash over her features. "I love you, Ellie. I never even knew what love was until I met you."

Were there tears in her eyes? He saw her lips tremble. She didn't speak. She only reached out to touch him.

Warm, so warm, her fingers skimmed his face, as if she were learning him by heart. Cheekbones, jaw, the hollow above his chin. She ran one finger down the bridge of his nose and let her thumb slide back and forth across his lips, his breath heating her skin, moistening it.

From the time he'd been a kid, women had been drawn to him. Mothers and grandmothers at his Little League games had fawned over him, the older sisters of his friends had used him to practice kissing on. And the number of girls that had hung around his high school locker had always made his teammates jealous as hell.

He'd enjoyed their adulation—who the devil wouldn't have? But he had never given a damn about his appearance, had never been able to see the dangerous attraction he posed. Now, for the first time, he was glad he looked the way he did, because each butterfly-light touch of Ellie's hand against his face brought that sweet, heavy heat into her wide gray eyes.

"It's not fair," she murmured, flattening her hand against his cheek, sliding her fingers down the cords of his neck. "It's not fair for you to look like this, feel like this, so hot and hard. So good. You should be cold inside, always looking in the mirror. But your eyes are the warmest blue I've ever seen. Like summer."

Raw pleasure squeezed Ryder in its fist, Ellie's hushed admission peeling away the layers of image that had surrounded him so long, giving him some small hope that Ellie might be able to delve into the reality of the man beneath. The Ryder Sloan who was a stranger to interviewers and reporters and television screens. Maybe a stranger even to himself.

He rubbed his palms up and down her waist, feeling the layers of fabric shift beneath his hands, her ribs delicate ridges, tempting him. He wanted to scrape his teeth along their curves, so lightly it made her moan.

His voice was hoarse as he stroked her, kneading her flesh with gentle hands. "Ellie, I was never warm," he breathed against the pulse point of her throat. "Never, until you."

She smoothed her hands over the expanse of his shoulders, as if testing their strength. Her eyes darkened. "I didn't want this in my life, Ryder."

"I know."

"I was so sure."

His thumbs whispered across the underside of her breasts, and a sigh of pleasure shuddered through her. Her eyelids drooped, the thick, dark-tipped lashes on the top, mingling with those at the bottom. The gray that shone between them was hazy. Summer rain.

"I was wrong, Rye." Her fingers skimmed down to the buttons on his shirt, undoing them one by one. Ryder held himself rigid, reveling in the feel of her, the thrumming desire in his very center quickening.

Her knuckles brushed the flat plane of his stomach, and his muscles clenched, a curse tearing from his lips as he tangled his hands in her hair, his mouth fastening greedily on hers.

She welcomed him, her lips opening, her tongue making shy, mind-shatteringly sensual forays into his mouth.

He crushed her full-length against him, the pounding heat of his arousal demanding release.

Slow . . . he had to go slow. Give them both time to remember this night forever.

Gathering her up in his arms, he carried her to his bedroom, his lips never leaving hers. Her breasts pushed against his half-bared chest, the delicate material of her blouse whispering across the hair-roughened surface as he moved.

Moonlight filtered through thin gray blinds, spilling across the expanse of his bed. He laid her on it, gently, the white of her blouse glimmering in the faint light, the cameo glowing richly at her throat.

She was more beautiful than any dream he'd ever dreamed. And more fragile. Like some fairy-tale princess in a castle made of ice, locked under a wicked queen's spell. Sleeping, she'd been sleeping since Daniel MacCrea had left her. Maybe she'd been sleeping ever since she'd dreamed of dragons in that tree.

Ryder wanted to wake her.

He sank down onto the mattress beside her and bent low, brushing her eyelids, her nose, her cheeks, with his mouth. "On the road I couldn't stop thinking about you. About this. Wanting you. I couldn't sleep, the way I kept wondering what it would be like to have you in my bed. Then, when I came back and Zak got so sick, I wanted to be there for you."

"I tried not to want you. But I spent so much time trying to forget the way you laugh, the way you kiss, that all I did was think about you."

"That was only... fair." Ryder worked the delicate clasp of the cameo. "You played holy hell with my game in Philly."

The corner of Ellie's mouth curved into a tiny smile. "That error you made... it was because of me?"

Ryder drew back, surprised. "How in God's name did you know I... Zak." He answered the question himself and grinned. "Yeah. I was thinking about the way your breasts looked in this blouse. The way this lacy stuff shows through the material makes me crazy."

Ryder traced one finger over the scalloped edge beneath the meager veiling of the fabric's surface. "I was thinking about how much I wanted to taste you. Touch you with my tongue through the cloth and then strip it away from you real slow, until my mouth was on your skin... all over."

She made a tiny sound low in her throat, and he could feel her, quivering, as his fingers slipped the first tiny loop over its pearl button. There were dozens of them, so close together, they formed a glistening ridge down her middle.

He'd never suspected how sensual, erotic, the task of uncovering such closely guarded secrets could be.

He let the callused pads of his fingers dip until they touched bare skin, watched Ellie's head sink back against the pillow. Her hand was in his hair, sifting through the dark strands as he leaned near her.

He'd seen lust in a woman's eyes, seen eagerness, hunger. But he'd never seen the misty magic that was in Ellie MacCrea's eyes as she watched him.

Tenderness.

Vulnerability.

Love.

It was here, though he doubted she would admit it... even to herself.

His hand fumbled with a button, a frisson of excitement working through him as he slid the blouse aside. Her breasts were still shielded by the camisole. A wisp of ivory satin with roses woven in, it dipped low between the full mounds, the lacy garment held up by straps as thin as a violin's string. "You're beautiful."

"No I'm not. I have red hair and freckles, and...and my mouth is too wide. But you..." She traced her finger over his lips. He caught the soft tip gently between his teeth. "Do you have any idea how it makes me melt inside, just to see you smile? Do you know how tempting you look in soft denim, or in that uniform that molds itself to your legs? They're so long and sinewy. Runner's legs. Even from the first, I couldn't help wondering how they would feel under my hands."

"But you didn't want me. You tried to keep me away."

"I'm not good at this, Ryder."

"This?"

"*This.*" She gestured around the dim-lit bedroom, a flush highlighting her cheekbones. "At being with a man. Making love. Daniel was the only...well, the only one I was ever with. And I know I was a disappointment to him." Her gaze fluttered away from Ryder's, her voice dropping to the barest whisper. "I don't want to be a disappointment to you."

He stared in disbelief, his fingers falling still. "A disappointment?"

She caught her lip between her teeth, her muscles tensing beneath Ryder's hands. She shrugged. "If even a quarter of those tabloid things are true, you've been with...well, with more than your share of women. I saw at the ballpark how they look at you, like they want to...to gobble you up like one of Zak's monsters on *Creature Feature*. You've had your choice, Ryder, all these years. Whoever, whatever, you wanted."

"It bothers you? The other women? Ellie, what happened before in my life was mutual lust, pure and simple. Even with my ex-wife it was...well, like you said awhile ago...two 'beautiful people' looking at each other in the mirror." Scorn dripped from his voice.

"It's none of my business, I know. Your marriage, or—or your women. I just...I can't understand how...why you would want..."

Me.

The word hung, unspoken between them. Ellie turned her face into the pillow. Fury and tenderness ripped through Ryder, leaving him shaken.

He wanted to soothe Ellie, make love to her until she would know how desirable he found her. He wanted to find Daniel MacCrea, meet the man long enough to beat the living hell out of the bastard who had so shattered her self-esteem.

"Lord, Ellie!" His voice throbbed with need. "Feel how much I want you." He cupped his hand around hers, carried it down to lay it lightly against the frayed fly of his jeans. He was rigid beneath the worn fabric, so hard he was afraid he would explode.

"If there were problems in your marriage, it had nothing to do with you...with this." Her hand stirred against him, and he grimaced with excruciating pleasure.

"How do you know that? I haven't...we haven't..."

"I know, damn it. I can feel it whenever I touch you. And when we kiss, I . . . hell, you send me over the edge so fast, I can't even breathe." The tenderness that had enfolded them vanished and a roaring sounded in Ryder's head. There was so much hurt in her face, so much regret, disbelief.

And though she'd said nothing, he could sense that part of her reluctance to get close to him had always been her fear of this . . . lovemaking. Her dread of making herself totally vulnerable to another man and being found lacking.

Ryder bit off a curse, and then his mouth was on hers, wide, wet, his tongue probing deep, as if to sweep away the memories, the self-doubt tormenting her.

He wanted her tormented . . . but only by the fire in his hands, his mouth, the fire in her own body. Not by the egocentric inadequacies of the bastard who had once been her husband.

A man who had doubtless been as selfish in bed as he'd been in everything else.

Ryder's whole body tensed, and he resolved to give her everything he was, freely, openly, to pleasure her until she was wild with wanting, until she would forget ever having been with any man but him.

With hands suddenly rough, he tugged the camisole over her head, his fingers fumbling with the front clasp of her peach-satin bra. He nudged the cup away with his nose, breathing in the scent that clung to her skin, tasting the warmth, the silkiness.

His jaw grazed her nipple, and his loins clenched at the feel of the hard tip, tight with wanting him. With a guttural moan, he slid his mouth up the milky pale mound. His lips parted as they brushed the dainty pink of her aureole. His tongue stole out, seeking.

It flicked the straining bud, and he heard her gasp. "Ryder . . . feels so . . . so good . . ."

Her words drove him, hard. He twined his legs with hers, his mouth fixing upon her nipple with ardent fervor. He suckled, drawing the aching bud into the hot cavern of his mouth, shaping it with his lips, licking it, plucking at it as if to take nourishment there, at her breast. Not nourishment of the body, but nourishment of the soul. A soul steeped in barrenness for far too long.

Her fingers delved into his hair, her legs shifting restlessly against the straining muscles of his own.

"Sweet..." he murmured against her skin. "Taste so sweet. Knew you would." He trailed kisses across the valley between her breasts, nibbling delicately on the other straining crest. She arched against him, shuddered as his tongue stole out to soothe her.

"R-Ryder."

He tensed at the agonizingly erotic feel of her thigh moving against his throbbing hardness, her hands tugging at the cloth of his shirt.

"Rye, I want...want to feel you, too. Your skin. I want..." Her fingernails scraped against his shoulders as she tried to bare them, and Ryder's mouth paused long enough in its questing so that he could brace himself upright and shrug the garment from his body.

The coolness from the air-conditioning wisped over his back, but nothing could have eased the fevered heat possessing him, engulfing him, as Ellie flattened her palms on his chest. His breath caught as her fingertips swirled in mind-numbing patterns over the ridges of muscles and through the golden-brown dusting of hair that spanned his chest, then arrowed down toward his navel.

He fought the need to crush her to him, take her, swiftly, thoroughly, sensing in her the need to discover him in tiny, delightful stages. Her thumb whispered over the sensitive dark brown disk of his nipple, and he gritted his teeth against a moan.

The fall of her shimmering red hair brushed against his skin as she leaned toward him, the tendrils pooling above the waistband of his jeans as she bent forward to rub her petal-soft cheek ever so lightly against him.

Her breath dampened sweat-sheened skin, made his muscles contract with the need to have her open the fly of his jeans.

He slid his hand beneath the folds of her skirt, following the curve of her calf, her slender thigh, in an effort to distract himself, keep himself from rushing her, frightening her. His other hand tugged her sash free, but the fastening of her skirt was beyond his power, the simple button and zipper a mystery beyond imagining as Ellie traced kisses down the line of dark gold bisecting his stomach.

"Ellie," he said, unable to stifle a groan. "Touch me. I need you to touch me."

She glanced up at him, their eyes locking for a heartbeat. Then her fingers skimmed downward.

Slowly, so slowly, she slipped one flat metal button of his jeans through its hole, then another, and another, the fly parting to allow her access. Her hand ran over the hard length of his arousal with a torturous delicacy, learning the shape of him through the soft cotton underwear.

Ryder's muscles felt ready to snap as he arched his head back, the feel of her fingers pushing him to the brink, leaving him teetering on the edge of a chasm he'd never known existed until this moment. A sea of flame seemed to leap all around him, to lap at his skin. When she raised her face to his, he felt himself drowning. Her eyes shone, piercing him, soul deep, then she bent her head downward. A bolt of raw sensation seared through him as she hesitated for but an instant, then gently, ever so softly, pressed a kiss against the straining cotton.

Hot, moist, exquisite, the caress sent Ryder reeling. He swore, his hands locking around her upper arms, dragging her upward along his body. He was ravenous for the taste of her, his tongue plunging deep into the welcoming, wet recesses of her mouth, his hands everywhere, struggling with the zipper of her skirt.

She pushed against him, and Ryder's arms tightened, as a sudden fear stabbed through him—fear that he'd somehow startled her, frightened her with the wildness of the passion pumping through his veins. He fought for control for an instant, but then, through hazy senses, heard the rasping of a zipper, as Ellie struggled to free herself of the skirt.

Breaking away, Ryder yanked his jeans and his briefs down his legs and kicked the garments onto the floor. He turned back to Ellie, his heart beating so fast it threatened to burst from his chest. His hands were burning, aching to touch her, naked, with nothing between them. No hurt, no pain, no bitter, barren past.

Her skin was pale against the blue coverlet, every curve of her body etched in vivid relief against the dark background. Her breasts were bare, the lacy bra gone. Her trim rib cage swept down to the indentation of her waist. Ryder cupped it with his hands, smoothing them down the curves of her hips, stopping when they reached the only thing that kept her from being completely naked beneath his eyes.

A confection of peach and ivory wisped low on her hips, dipping in a dainty vee between her thighs. In all his dreams of Ellie, he'd never imagined her in such a garment, all femininity and sensuality, yet oddly, tantalizingly innocent.

He reached out and traced a circle around her navel, then smoothed his callused finger down until it snagged on the ivory lace edging.

He swallowed hard as he tested the silkiness of the fabric, heated by her skin. "I want to see all of you, Ellie. Touch all of you. Taste you."

His palm cupped over the warm mound, the tips of his fingers skimming the fragile skin of her inner thighs. There was a sweet, sweet dampness there that made him grit his teeth in an effort to control his surging need.

She wanted him. Was ready for him. More than ready. And he hadn't even touched her most intimate places, plumbed her headiest secrets.

He pressed his palm against her abdomen, sliding his fingers beneath the lacy band. Silky warm down curled around his fingertips, sending tremors through his body.

He searched lower, finding the slick, velvety petals below. With a groan, he dipped inside her. A tiny cry tore from her throat, and she arched against his hand. Her fingers were clamped on his shoulders, tight, so tight, and her lip was caught between her teeth.

With his other hand he reached up to her face, running his fingers over her lips until they parted. She nipped at his fingertip, drew it inside her mouth. "Ryder...now...I need you now."

Low, urgent, her words fed the flames inside him.

He withdrew his hand from the panties, and hooked his thumbs in the band, drawing the whisper of satin and lace down the pale columns of her thighs. Inch by delectable inch, he smoothed them downward, leaving a trail of hot, wet kisses in their wake.

The inside of her thigh, the soft flesh behind her knee, the curve of her calf, her ankle. When he slipped the garment from her feet, his lips trailing over her toes, she cried out.

Ryder kissed his way back up her body, lingering on the delights he found along the way—a tiny freckle just below her hip bone, the glisteny red down at the juncture of her thighs. Tenderly, gently, he slid his thumbs over the center of her desire, drove her higher, higher.

She writhed against the pillows, her cheeks flushed, her hands desperate in his hair, on his shoulders. He hesitated a heartbeat, trying to remember the fragile woman who had stared into his eyes on the balcony in what seemed an eternity before. The woman who had feared to disappoint him, who had feared her own response.

But that woman had vanished, leaving in her wake a temptress, wild, hungry, but so agonizingly loving, it made his chest ache.

In that instant, he wanted to give her back some small portion of that love, the most unselfish of caresses. He parted her, his lips seeking with a gentle fervor that made her stiffen, gasp.

"R-Ryder..."

Sensitized beyond belief, he could feel the cataclysm building inside her, her legs quivering against him, her body writhing. She turned her face into the pillow to keep from crying out.

"I'm not very good at this..." her hushed admission echoed through the hazing of his passion, and anger and a fierce possessiveness gripped him.

He wanted to hurl her from the brink, strip away the last layers of inhibitions ensnaring her, heal the last scars left by her bastard husband.

"R-Rye...I...I can't...can't stop it...I..."

"Shh, let it happen, Ellie. Let me take you there."

Then she was clawing at his shoulders, dragging him upward with a fierceness that stunned him, bewitched him.

Her hand was between their bodies, grasping him, guiding him. Ryder staked his arms on either side of her, staring into her desire-hazed eyes, her lips still red from his kisses.

He probed the entrance, not wanting to hurt her. But her legs were tangling around his hips, her hands clutching the hard curves of his buttocks, urging him to take her.

With a harsh groan, he drove his hips forward, imbedding himself, soul-deep in the woman he loved.

He closed his eyes, moving inside her to a primitive rhythm as old as time. Images were branded indelibly in his mind. The way she quivered beneath him, the way her eyes glowed, the way her hair spilled across his pillows. Warm, glistening, smelling of honey and hope and forevers.

"I love you, Ellie. Love you." He buried his face in her hair as he thrust, saying the words over and over, as if, somewhere deep inside him, he hoped she might believe him.

When the magic consumed her, he was just a breath behind, his own body aching, soaring, swirling into a torrent of wonder that left him stunned, and needing, and new.

He held her as she drifted down softly, to a place beyond imagining, a place where he could keep her safe, warm, where he could make things right for her, and for the little boy he'd come to adore.

He nuzzled his cheek against her, felt the stinging dampness of her tears. Her hands clung to him, as if she would never let him go. Her voice was soft, and sad, and more than a little afraid.

"I love you, Ryder." She touched his lips with her fingertips. "I don't want to, but I do."

"We'll work things out somehow, Ellie. You'll see. After Zak is well, and our lives are more settled . . . I'm not going to lose you, lady."

He cradled her in his arms, stroking her hair until her breathing slowed, deepened into the hazy dreamworld of sleep. But though he was more exhausted than he'd ever been before, Ryder stared blindly into the darkness far into the night.

It had been perfect, their lovemaking, even more beautiful than he had imagined. She had given more than he'd dreamed possible. And he . . . he'd lost himself completely in her arms.

He wanted to keep her there, in his room, protected from hospitals and doctors, and glaring hurtful headlines. He wanted to wake up with her every morning, wanted to make wild, wonderful love with her every night.

Tomorrows. They'd always been glossed with a kind of dread for him, the looming reality of the day he'd have to hang up his glove for good. The certainty that one day he would take the long walk in from third base for the last time.

There had never been anything else for him. Never been anything else in his life. He'd used baseball since he was seven years old to fill the emptiness inside him, to make people care about Ryder Sloan.

But Ellie loved *him* . . . loved him for more than his skill with a bat, for more than his million-dollar grin, more than his Porsche and his penthouse.

The question was, did she love him enough to endure the constant blaze of the spotlights? The ever-present flash of the paparazzi? Did she love him enough to endure the prying questions, and answers twisted by unscrupulous members of the media until there was only the slightest grain of truth in them?

More sobering, still, was she willing to subject Zakary to such scrutiny?

Ryder closed his eyes, his heart twisting as his mind filled with images of Angels Stadium, the roar of the crowd, the feel of the bat slamming square into a fast-ball over the middle of the plate.

Baseball.

It had been everything he'd ever wanted. His whole damn life. Now that he'd finally found something even more important, more lasting, was it possible that the game he so loved would cost him the woman who had made him whole?

Chapter Eleven

The bed was empty, and only a hollow in the pillow and the tingling whisker burns on Ellie's breasts made her certain that the night before hadn't been a dream.

She struggled to focus on her surroundings, but the carefully closed blinds left everything in a dim, twilightlike haze. The furniture was shrouded in shadow, the pictures on the wall smears of dark and light, but there was no sign of the man who had lain beside her through the night, waking her often to love her yet again.

Where was he? Off running laps or hitting baseballs or scrawling answers to the mountains of fan mail he must receive? She had wanted to awaken beside him this morning, cling to the last precious wisp of the fantasy he'd woven about her. She'd wanted to lose herself in his body one more time.

But it seemed that the world outside this lush bedroom had already intruded, the glare of reality piercing through like the slices of sunlight visible along the edges of the blinds. Regretful, resigned, Ellie pushed aside the coverlets, cool air trickling over bare skin still thrumming from the memory of Ryder's loving. The unmistakable scent of his cologne hung in the air, teasing her, tantalizing her, with the memory of how he had felt, how he had tasted, how heart-wrenchingly generous he had been with his loving.

Her whole body fired with embarrassment as her gaze caught on the outline of the pale blue shirt she'd stripped from his shoulders in such a frenzy, and the long, worn jeans she'd opened with her hands.

She swallowed hard at the memory of Ryder's groan when she had touched him through the thin layer of his underwear, when she'd kissed him....

Ellie pressed chill palms to her burning cheeks. Merciful heaven, she'd never done anything so bold before. Had never felt so daring, so comfortable, exploring a man's body.

With Daniel, sex had been a sprint to climax. His climax. As quickly and expediently as possible. There had never been that slow, torturously wonderful immersing of oneself in the other's body. There had never been that excruciatingly pleasurable feeling of descending into lava-hot waves of passion.

She'd drowned in Ryder Sloan.

In the sensations he drew from her, in his hoarse, urgent voice, in his hard, skilled hands and his sweet love words. She'd wanted to burrow deep into the haven his loving had offered, had wanted to remain in his arms forever.

But could there be forevers with a man like Ryder? A man whose life was a string of perfect summer days, with blue skies and crowds cheering? Endless summer, where he never felt the cold that crept around other people's hearts?

While she . . . she had known too many bleak winters.

Ellie drew her knees to her chest, leaning her chin on her knees as pain washed over her.

He'd told her he loved her, with such sincerity in those electric blue eyes her heart had melted. And yet, despite the jet-set life he'd led, despite the praise and adoration lavished on him, despite the scores of women who must have shared his bed, there was an innocence about him. A kind of Peter Pan boy inside the man.

One who still believed that the guys in the white hats always won, that there was always a way to slay the dragon before the princess was lost.

Ellie knew better.

And it was time for her to go back to the castle.

Depression settled over her, her limbs feeling leaden as she swung her legs over the side of the bed and pushed herself to her feet. Thick gray carpet swallowed her toes as she glanced around the room, searching for her clothes. But though Ryder's things were still scattered about, hers were nowhere to be found.

Surrendering the search, Ellie glanced around for something to wrap herself in. There was nothing save Ryder's shirt. Taking up the soft blue garment, she slipped her arms into the sleeves.

She had wanted to escape the feelings he had stirred in her. Had wanted to find him so he could take her back to her apartment, back to the reality of her life. *Away from the ball, Cinderella...*

But as the folds of his shirt fell around her, she felt an unaccountable urge to cling to him, cling to the strength in him, the optimism that she knew she could never share.

She had told him she loved him, and she did. But though their lovemaking had changed her forever, some things hadn't changed, would never change. There were walls between them that even a fairy godmother couldn't raze.

The shirt skimmed the middle of her thighs, and she buttoned it, then rolled up the long sleeves to her elbows. At the bedroom door she hesitated, listening, but beyond, the rooms were quiet.

She pushed the door open and padded out into the hallway in her bare feet. The aroma of rich coffee drifted in the air, mingled with the hot, sinful smell of something sweet baked brown in an oven. But when she poked her head in the black-and-white kitchen, Ryder was nowhere to be seen.

She wandered farther down the hall and found another door ajar. She looked through the opening and saw a richly furnished office that would have done the president of a corporation proud.

The walls were lined with bookshelves, the surfaces holding distinctive pieces of sculpture. Here and there some tribute to Ryder's skill in baseball was tucked— Gold Glove awards, certificates of appreciation from various charities, pictures of Ryder in front of a building Ellie recognized as a shelter for battered children.

Off to one side of the room a huge desk sprawled, its surface littered with papers, maps, notes. Behind the desk, Ryder sat, his hair damp from a recent shower, his long fingers riffling through a notebook. His chest was bare, and for an instant she wondered if he'd bothered to drag any clothes on when he'd arisen that morning.

The muscles she had only felt in the darkness the night before glistened in the light pouring in the windows— sinewy, taut. His body exuded the powerful aura of a professional athlete—a man who had honed physical perfection to an art form. One long bare leg was stretched out beneath the edge of the desk, a beautifully shaped foot tapping a muted staccato against the burgundy carpeting.

He was chewing on the end of a pencil, scowl lines showing between his brows. And even from an angle Ellie could see the burning intensity in his face.

She twisted the hem of his shirt, uncertain whether or not to interrupt him. But he could hardly expect her to lie around in bed all day. She needed to check on Zak, and there was Jed's tutoring session later that afternoon....

Sucking in a steadying breath, she rapped softly on the door.

He jumped as if the knock had been cannon fire, his eyes flashing up to meet hers.

"Ryder?" she said, uneasy. "I woke up and you were gone."

His cheeks darkened, and he rubbed his palm over his naked chest. Droplets still clung to the golden brown web that spanned it, the skin, usually covered by his jersey, was a lighter shade of brown than his face and arms. Ellie felt a sudden urge to trace the tan line with her lips.

"I just slipped out of bed for a minute," Ryder explained, abashed. "Thought I'd make it back before you woke up."

The knot of embarrassment and dread in Ellie's stomach tightened. She'd never experienced this "morning after" routine. Didn't know what to do, what to say.

Terrific night, Sloan. Thanks for everything...?

As if sensing her discomfort, Ryder forced a smile. His gaze slid in a lazy path from her head to her bare toes. "Lady, what you do for that shirt ought to be illegal. Maybe I should demand that you give it back so you don't give some poor guy heart failure. Me, for example."

Ellie started to tug self-consciously at the hem, but found herself smiling back in the face of the hungry alligator grin Ryder fired at her.

"C'mere, Ellie, I'm real cold all of a sudden," he said, licking his lips, a lascivious twinkle in his eyes.

"Forget it, Sloan. I'm holding this shirt hostage until you return my skirt and blouse."

He looked confused for a moment, then winked at her. "Oh, yeah. You *were* dressed when I got you up here last night. Must've slipped my mind."

Unable to resist, Ellie crossed over to him and slugged him playfully on one shoulder. It was a mistake. The feel of his hot, firm flesh against her knuckles made her knees go weak.

"Fess up, Sloan, or else..." Ellie said, her best imitation of a television detective only a little bit shaky.

"Or else what?"

"Or else I'll find a way to make you spill your guts."

"Mmm, I'm sure we can arrange a deal." He pushed the chair back on its rollers, his arms flashing out to encircle her hips, pulling her into the crook between his thighs. She could feel the yielding softness of his maleness against her skin, could feel it tightening against her.

Ellie's heart leapt, her eyes flicking down to his lap as she remembered her earlier suspicion. But it seemed that sometime between leaving his shower and coming into the office, Ryder had deigned to drag on a pair of shorts. Ellie glanced down at the familiar logo of the Special Olympics embossed in red against the soft black fabric, just before Ryder buried his face against her breasts.

His hair made a damp patch on the cloth, and Ellie shivered as Ryder drew in a deep breath, nuzzling against her.

"You smell so damn good, Ellie. Taste so good. A man could get addicted." He tugged on her, urging her down onto his lap. She resisted for a moment, then let herself slide in against him. The shirt slipped up, her bare bottom pillowed on a hard, hair-roughened thigh.

She tried to squirm away, but Ryder's arms tightened around her, and a low groan rumbled in his chest.

"Don't do that, lady, unless you want to face the consequences."

Ellie tried to steel herself against the honeyed warmth of his voice, and the rising tide of her own need. "Rye,

I don't—don't have time for any consequences. I have to find my clothes, go get Zak—''

"Impossible."

"To find my clothes? What did you do, drop them off the balcony?"

"No. I sent 'em down to be cleaned. When I got up I noticed they were real crumpled. I think I was lying on them at some point."

"Terrific. When will they be back?"

"An hour or so. I bribed the cleaners to do it extra slow. What can I say? I love to see you naked."

Ellie knew she was a hundred shades of red. "Ryder, I have to pick up Zak from the Craigs. I don't want to impose any—"

"That's what I said was impossible. Mia has this thing for the zoo. She likes to throw grapes at the monkeys. Alex decided to take the kids over there for the afternoon."

"Afternoon?" Ellie glanced at the clock, stunned to see the hands pointing to eleven. "But Zak's medicine, and—"

"Relax, Mom. He's going to be fine. Gina was a nurse before she married Alex. Patched his finger up when some guy stepped on it trying to steal home. Alex got the out, though."

"I'm sure you were all very relieved. But that doesn't change the fact that someone should have checked with me before they took Zakary off—"

Ryder's features stilled, his eyes meeting hers levelly. "I told them it was okay. He was having a great time. They have his medicine. They know our number. If anything goes wrong—which it won't—they can call us in three minutes."

Ellie stiffened. "Ryder, that may be true, but I'm his mother. I'm responsible—"

"I want to be his father." His arms loosened, but Ellie found she hadn't the strength to pull away. If she even attempted to stand, she suspected she'd tumble into a heap on the floor.

"Wh-what did you say...?"

"I said I want to be Zak's father."

Ellie stared into the face that had been emblazoned on every sports page across America, that had flashed that bone-melting grin in sports car advertisements. It wasn't half so dangerous as the solemn glow in his eyes.

He was serious. Dead serious. Suddenly galvanized into action, she rose to her feet. Even falling into an ig-nominious heap would be preferable to sitting there, in his arms, daring to hope...

"Ryder, are you crazy? You couldn't...wouldn't..."

"Wouldn't what? Make a good father?" The eyes beneath his spiky lashes darkened. She'd hurt him. The knowledge twisted inside her.

"You'd—you'd probably make someone a terrific father. Someday. When—well, when you're ready to settle down, and—"

"That's what I'm trying to tell you, Ellie." He gri-maced. "And I'm doing a damn poor job of it. I am ready. To make a life. For you. For Zak."

Ellie dragged a hand weakly through her hair. "You can't be serious."

"Why can't I?"

"Because...well, because...*look* at you! Look at me!" She gestured ineffectually. "You can't possi-bly...Ryder, you could have any woman you wanted."

"I want you." His gaze was so steady. That mouth that should always be smiling was solemn. Sweet. "El-lie, is that so astonishing?"

"Yes. Yes, it is, I..." Ellie walked to the far wall, and braced herself against a bookcase. "Ryder, this is hap-pening so fast. I can't keep up with you."

The corner of his lips tipped up, and Ellie died a little inside.

"I think I fell in love with you the first time I saw you, storming down those stairs ready to scratch my eyes out. You were such a little thing, but I've seen less threatening eyes in players that have been robbed of grand-slam homers."

"Just because I got mad at you doesn't mean you..."

"I didn't know I loved you until later. Until I saw the way you were with Zakary. How much you loved him. And how much he loved you. I wanted to bury myself in your apartment, in your bed. I wanted you to come to my defense the way you did Zak's—all fire and fierce, fierce love." Ryder rose and paced near her. He stopped bare inches away.

"Ryder, you could find that with any woman. A woman who would give you your own son. A woman who would... well, would understand the life you lead. Who would fit in at glitzy parties, and at the ballpark. Who wouldn't mind your being away six months out of the year."

"It would be difficult, I know. But dammit, Ellie, I love you so much I'll take whatever time I can get with you. We can work it out. Gina and Alex have. They're the only thing that kept me believing in marriage and love and loyalty at all after my wife left me."

"Your wife?" Ellie urged gently.

"It was during my rookie year. She was a model—had been doing the beauty pageant circuit since she was fifteen. Everything was fine until I got an offer from a team in California. When I refused... well, let's say she stayed just long enough to hook up with the producer of one of those teen slasher movies. But it was just as well. She didn't have any desire to try what she called the All American life—kids, tree houses, dogs. She didn't have any time for my baseball, for me, or for having the baby I wanted so badly." The hurt was still there in his voice, and suddenly Ellie knew it had always lurked beneath his cocky smile.

"You wanted children?"

His laugh was just a little bitter. "We'd agreed to start a family once we were married, but when the time came, she made it quite clear that carrying my child would prove most inconvenient to her career. She convinced me to wait a little while, till things were settled. And I acquiesced. After all, I wouldn't be around to raise the baby, anyway, once baseball season started." His inflection told Ellie those had been his ex-wife's words, words with an edge of cruelty that had cut him so deeply he still carried the scar.

"I'm sorry."

"Don't be. Best possible thing that could have happened to us. We were a pair of narcissistic kids, always staring in the mirror. We had no conception what real love was. What commitment was. When we split up... well, I think we were both a little relieved. Afterward, I was glad there wasn't a child involved in the mess the two of us had created."

"What did you do? After the divorce?"

"Played ball." Ryder reached up to run his fingers over the gold baseball glove given in honor of some achievement. "Threw myself into it like a madman. Ended up Rookie of the Year—probably because I was trying so damn hard to prove something. To Marla. And to my parents. Trying to prove to them that what I was, who I was, was worthwhile. That I mattered. The only thing I had to prove it with was the way I could swing a bat."

"Your parents must have been wonderful. I mean, you're so good with Zak...." Ellie reminded him.

"Wonderful? Andrea and Arthur?" The bitterness was hard in his voice, and she ached with it. "The only thing they were ever wonderful at was planning country club luncheons and cruises to the Caribbean, *sans* child, of course. They are very nice people—polished, elegant. Never raise their voices. Sometimes I think I would have been happier if they had. At least I would have known that they were aware I was alive."

"They ignored you?"

"They paid more attention to the dust on their Dresden figurines than they did to their son. Hell, we never went on a picnic, never went to the zoo. I never even knew peanut butter sandwiches existed until I was in school. And as for my ball games, they never went to a single one when I was a kid. I had to get my attention from the other parents who had come—I learned early how to play the crowd, Ellie. I had to. I didn't have a mom who spent every summer broiling in the blazing sun, cheering for kids who couldn't get a base hit if it whacked them in the face."

Ellie stared at him, but all she could see was a little boy with dark hair and blue eyes, standing alone on a baseball field, watching other kids get showered with hugs and home-baked cookies, lemonade and encouragement. Her heart broke a little.

"But surely when you went into the minor leagues...when you were called up to the majors, your parents must have..."

"They were the guests of a guy who owned a sky box in Angels Stadium once."

"A sky box?"

"Yeah. They're like minipenthouses, with carpet and television, air-conditioning and a wet bar. It seemed that a business colleague of Arthur's thought he might like to see his son play ball. After the game, I came up, excited as hell. I'd homered twice, hit four out of five. I'd wanted to make them proud of me. Just once. Just one damn time."

He turned his back to her, and Ellie knew he was trying to hide a pain that was still far too fresh. "They hadn't even seen me hit. Didn't even know. They'd spent the whole evening in there watching a golf tournament on TV."

Ellie couldn't help herself. She went to him and laid her hands on those broad shoulders. She pressed her face against his back. A tremor went through him.

"Ellie, everything I know about dealing with kids Gina and Alex taught me. They were the ones who showed me what a real family was, how strong it could be, how warm and wonderful. I never had that when I was a kid, Ellie. Never had that security. Is it so surprising that I want to build it now? When I met you, it was like a miracle. Like I'd been waiting forever for that moment."

"Waiting to find a widow with a child? A ready-made family?" She said the words softly, not wanting to hurt him further. Only wanting to make certain that he had truly examined his motive in seeking her out.

He winced as if she had struck him, and in a way, she knew she had. "I fell in love with you, Ellie, and suddenly everything seemed possible. It was that simple."

"None of this is simple, Ryder," she protested. Her hands fell away from him. "Don't you see, I've been handling everything alone for so long. Doing everything for Zak, and for me. I've been in control...in control of our lives. And after the years I spent with Daniel, that was the most incredible feeling."

"More incredible than the way you felt when I was deep inside you?" Ryder's voice sent shivers of remembrance down Ellie's spine.

"No. I mean, yes. I..." she paused, flustered. "Being with you was beyond description. I've never felt anything like that before. Never experienced..."

"Neither have I." He was looking at her with a mingling of belligerence, and a haunting, a hurting.

She started to turn away, confusion, disbelief and raw terror roiling inside her. But at that moment the shrill ring of the telephone made her jump.

Ryder swore. Stalking to the desk, he grabbed the receiver. "Sloan here. What the hell is it?"

Ellie could hear the faint murmuring of the other voice on the end of the line. She saw Ryder's features go still. He sank down into the leather chair, burying his face against his hand. "When?" he demanded. "Did you tell them what hospital?"

Dread rushed through Ellie. "Ryder—is it Zak? Is he—"

Ryder reached out, clutching her hand so tight it hurt. "Don't worry," he said into the receiver. "We'll meet you there."

He hung up the phone and raised his face to hers. There were tears clinging to his spiky lashes.

"Ryder, what in God's name..."

"We've found him, Ellie." Ryder's voice broke. "Ellie, we've found Daniel MacCrea."

Chapter Twelve

Coils of tension seemed to wrap around Atlanta General, squeezing the air out of the tiny waiting room until Ellie couldn't breathe. She paced the white linoleum, the bright painted figures on the walls in the hallway blurring before her eyes into smears of wild, desperate hope, swirling dread, mind-numbing fear.

Sweet God, let Daniel arrive. The words rolled, a constant plea in her head. *Please, please, let him be able to help my little boy.*

And what if he can't? What if he won't? Her own terror hissed inside her.

Then your last chance will be lost....

"Ellie?"

She shook herself inwardly, trying to stem her rising panic.

Ryder's voice.

How many times in the excruciating hours since they had received the news about Daniel had it dragged her back from her own private hell?

The blue eyes that had been damp with tears in his penthouse were rimmed now with exhaustion. His face reflected her own churning emotions.

"You need to eat a little. Maybe take a drink. You won't do Zak any good if you get sick yourself."

He pushed a plate toward her. In its center was one of the donuts kept constantly in the parent's waiting room. A cup of coffee steamed in his other hand.

Ellie's stomach lurched, her throat squeezed shut. "I can't. I just . . . can't."

He put the food down and crossed to where she stood, enfolding her in his strong arms, pulling her tight against the hard wall of his chest. She felt his warmth seep through her, the steady thrum of his heartbeat calming her as he stroked her hair.

"I'm so scared, Ryder. More scared than I've ever been in my life. What if . . ."

"It's going to be all right, Ellie," he murmured, holding her closer. "I'm going to *make* it be all right."

There was such determination in his tone, such confidence, the assurance of a man who had never known defeat, who had never hurled all he was against the odds and lost.

What would it do to him if he failed? If he lost this most precious gamble?

As if he sensed her thoughts, Ryder pressed a kiss to her temple. "Zakary is going to be fine. MacCrea should be flying in any minute, if he hasn't already. His tissue type is going to match. Gina and Alex will have Zakary back to the hospital in a matter of minutes. And before we know it, the kid's going to be striking terror in the heart of Little League batters all across the city."

"If . . . if only I could believe . . ."

"Believe it. He's my kid, too, you know. Here. Where it counts." Ryder took her hand and pressed it against his heart. "We're going to be a family, Ellie. I swear."

"Ellie?" The sound of a voice from the doorway made Ellie spring away from Ryder, as guiltily as if she'd just been caught in an adulterous embrace. They both wheeled, staring into the face of the man framed by the doorjamb.

Daniel.

Time seemed to freeze as she stood there, her eyes fixed on the man who had fathered her child.

It had been two years since Ellie had seen him. Two years of hell, that had aged her until she had felt like she'd lived for two hundred. Endless days of battling Zak's disease and her own gnawing fear, of struggling desperately to keep a roof over their heads, and some semblance of normalcy in her sick child's life.

She knew that those years had changed her forever, inside and out.

Daniel had changed as well. His sunstreaked blond hair still fell boyishly about a darkly tanned face that made one think of a California surfer, a kind of agelessness clinging to his features that would always make him appear young. But for once his lips were not curved in that engaging little-boy grin that had had the power to melt her heart. The hazel eyes that had always been sparkling with eagerness for some new adventure were bloodshot, so frightened they reminded her of Zakary's when he'd just awakened from a nightmare.

She had loathed, despised and cursed this man for two years, but there was still a tie she couldn't sever, a tugging at her heart she wondered if she'd ever be free of.

"Daniel." The instant she said his name, he closed the space between them, scooping her up in a tremulous hug.

"Thank God. Thank God you found me." Daniel's voice shook. "Where's Zak? How—how is he?"

"Friends are watching him until we have some news. I didn't want to build up his hopes in case things didn't work out."

"Didn't work out? You mean, in case I didn't come? In case I didn't give him my kidney?" There was a touch of hysteria in Daniel's voice. "For God's sake, Ellie, how could you even think—"

"No, no. It was nothing like that," Ellie felt herself already slipping into the role of smoothing things over. "With a transplant there are so many variables, the doctors can never be certain until they run a full battery of tests."

"What do you mean they can't be sure? They're doctors, aren't they? It's their job to be sure. He'll be fine. Ellie, tell me he'll be fine."

"I wish I could." She swallowed hard, resentment welling up inside her. In some stomach-twisting way, it was like having to confront Zak's illness herself, all over again. "The truth is that he's sick, weak. The doctor says he's approaching a crisis."

"A crisis? You mean he might . . . might . . ."

"Die? It was a possibility. Maybe still is one, unless your tissue type matches his."

"He's my son. My flesh and blood. I'll match him, dammit." Daniel's eyes were filled with subtle accusation. "Why didn't you contact me the minute he got sick? If I'd known, I would have come right away."

"She tried to find you for two years." Ellie started at the sound of Ryder's voice, stunned to realize that she'd forgotten he was there. "But it was a little tough to reach you, MacCrea, since you didn't bother to leave a forwarding address."

Daniel stilled, his arms still around her. "Who the hell are you?"

"I'm the one who tracked you three times around the world to get you here in time to help Zak."

Disentangling herself from Daniel's grasp, Ellie stepped between the two men.

"Daniel, this is Ryder Sloan. He's been wonderful to Zakary, and—"

"So you're the man who brought me home to save my little boy's life." MacCrea's sudden obsequiousness made Ryder's skin crawl. "It was lucky a guy who worked on the offshore oil rigger I was on was a fan of yours, Mr. Sloan. He had his sister send him the clippings from Angels games in the mail. She sent all your publicity about Zak needing to find me. I can't tell you how much I appreciate all your work on my behalf."

"Whatever I did was for Zak and Ellie."

Daniel looked taken aback. His eyes flashed from Ryder to Ellie and back again. "Of—of course," Daniel said, brow puckering. "And it was real charitable of you to help them out. But now that you've found me, I wouldn't dream of detaining you any longer. My wife and I have some things to discuss."

"*Ex*-wife."

Ellie felt Ryder's arm go taut against her back, could almost hear the grinding effort it was taking him to stay in control of his temper.

Daniel stared at Ryder. Their eyes locked.

"Like I said, my wife and I have family matters to discuss."

Ellie looked from one man to the other, and wanted to crack their skulls together. They might as well have been two water buffalo with their horns locked over some poor female. There was possessiveness in blue eyes and hazel, a hard set to both mouths that made her clench her fists.

"Stop it, both of you. Zak doesn't have time for any of this idiotic male garbage, and I don't have any patience for it. He's the one who's sick, and scared."

Ryder swore softly, racing his fingers through his hair. "I guess Zak's not the only one who's scared. We're all tired, and nervous, and—hell. Nothing matters a damn except that little guy getting well. Ellie, go ahead and take Daniel down to Dr. Tyler's office and get him set for testing. I'll call Gina. Have Zak here in nothing flat.''

Calming, bracing, Ryder's voice steadied her, but there was a lurking of something in his face, a dart of something akin to uncertainty. As if he were measuring himself against Daniel, and fearing she might find him lacking.

The perception stunned her. But she had no time to deal with dueling male egos now. The only thing that mattered was Zak. Getting him well, as quickly as possible.

Her jaw clenching against the hurt in Ryder's eyes, she took Daniel's arm and led him down the hallway to where the doctor was waiting.

Ryder rubbed his fingertips against gritty eyes, then flicked his gaze yet again to the wall clock that brightened a corner of the hospital lobby. How long had it been since Ellie had vanished, her rose-colored skirt swirling about her slender calves, her hair a tousled mass of red down the back of her blouse?

While that hand... that hand that had driven him crazy the night before, was linked in the arm of the bastard who had abandoned her and Zak. The bastard who had put the pain and the distrust in those incredible gray eyes. The bastard who, even now, was leaning so hard on her waning strength, it was as if Ryder could see it draining away, leaving her nerves more taut, her fears more raw, than they had been before.

It wasn't fair, dammit, that a selfish pig like Mac-Crea should be the only one able to help the child Ryder had come to love as his own. MacCrea didn't deserve a son like Zak, didn't deserve a woman as special as Ellie.

He'd thrown them away, with no more thought than he'd give an old pair of running shoes, and now, here he was, butting back into their lives with that blasted, hangdog, guileless look that Ryder could see was already eating away at Ellie's reserves.

And, God knew, the woman had been running on empty for far too long now.

"Stop it, Sloan. Ellie's right. There's no time for this now. If you still feel the need, there'll be plenty of time to deck the jerk later."

"Whoever this jerk is, don't hit him with your throwing hand." He turned at the familiar sound of Gina Craig's voice. She stood just inside the sliding glass doorway, looking like an adorable pumpkin in her orange maternity top and fitted green leggings. One of her brood had pressed a clown sticker onto her shoulder sometime earlier in the day, and there was a crumpled spot on her left side, where Mia liked to bury her face when tired or teased beyond endurance.

For an instant Ryder wished he could do the same, pour out to his friend the conflict raging inside him. As if she'd read his mind, Gina crossed to where he stood and gave him a quick hug.

"Zak'll be in in a minute. He's helping Alex park the car—the kid can shift a stick like a pro." She drew away from Ryder, her penetrating brown eyes probing deep. "You look like hell, Sloan. Rough night?"

"The night was wonderful. More wonderful than anything I've ever..." Ryder's throat tightened at the memory of Ellie in his arms. But the pain and pleasure of what they had shared was too fierce, too fresh, to put into words. He let the sentence trail off, knowing that his silence would tell Gina all she needed to know.

Her eyes shone. She ruffled his hair as if he were one of her small sons. "You deserve 'wonderful' after all this time," she said. "But it's a long way from wonderful to looking like your batting average has plunged below Alex's."

Ryder grimaced. "Let's just say the night from heaven turned into the morning from hell."

"Nothing went wrong? I mean, Zak's father *is* coming?" The expression on Gina's face warned that if Daniel MacCrea didn't get his buns to Atlanta General, he'd most likely be dragged there by the scruff of the neck by one very pregnant, very indignant, lady.

"MacCrea is already here." Ryder tried to infuse a dismissiveness he didn't feel into his voice. "He's upstairs with Ellie and the doctors."

"Oh." There was a world of understanding in that single word. Gina squeezed his arm. "Wishing they were going to carve you up instead of MacCrea, huh?"

Ryder started to deny it, then couldn't suppress an uneasy laugh. "Something like that. I'd give my right arm for that little boy, Gina."

"Don't let the companies that use you for endorsements hear you say that."

"Dammit, I would—"

"I know, I know." She slipped her hand into his. "But in this case, your right arm won't do Zakary any good unless it's still attached. This MacCrea guy is Zak's father, whether you like it or not. He's Zakary's best chance at life. But you're that little boy's best chance at stability. Security. I mean, the kid's father has already walked out on him once without so much as a goodbye. And when this transplant stuff is all over, MacCrea will walk out again. You won't."

"Ellie and Zak are everything I've ever wanted, Gina. Sometimes, watching you and Alex and the kids, I'd get so damn jealous. I wanted that for myself, but I could never seem to find it."

"Blinded by the bimbettes," Gina commiserated. "Got to admit, it was tough to see clearly through all that lacy underwear women sent you in the mail. But you can't lay all the blame on them, sweetie. I mean, you look like a champagne-and-caviar-all-night-in-bed kind of guy. Every woman's fantasy man. Who would'a thought your own fantasies would lean more toward patchwork quilts and changing diapers when you have a face and a body that could stop a centerfold dead in her staples.''

"Gina, it's not funny. I love Ellie, and that jerk is upstairs with her, while I'm stuck down here. I feel so useless. There's nothing I can do.''

"I wouldn't say that. Here comes something that can keep you real busy—for about the next fifteen years.'' Gina gestured toward the glass doors.

Alex was striding toward them, a somewhat sub-dued, wary Zakary in tow. The boy was still dressed in the Angels uniform that had been Ryder's gift to him. His little fingers were clenched tight around one of his batting gloves.

He was scared. Damn scared. Trying hard to be brave.

Ryder's heart swelled with love, so much love that all his anger, resentment and hurt were squeezed away, leaving only the desperate hope that the arrogant jerk being tested two floors above them would at least be able to give his son something of value.

With long strides, Ryder crossed to Zakary and scooped the little boy up into his arms. Zak's thin arms twined around Ryder's neck, his hands clinging. Ryder buried his face in the curve of Zak's neck, breathing in that fresh, innocent little-boy smell, feeling the warmth in Zak, the life.

"Hey, slugger,'' Ryder said, instinctively rocking the trembling little boy. "Looks like it's going to be a big day at the ballpark.''

Zak lifted his face from Ryder's shoulder long enough to cast a dubious glance at the bank of elevators that would take them up to the urological center. "How come I had to come here? Alex was gonna take me for a ride on his three-wheeler. And it's not my day for dialysis or anything. Is—is somethin' wrong, Rye?''

Ryder ruffled Zak's curls with one large hand. "You mean besides the fact that you kept Alex and Gina up all night with your snoring?"

"No, really, truly, Rye. Where—where's Mom, and why'd she make me come here?"

Ryder carried the child over to one of the chrome-and-vinyl chairs and sat down, perching Zak on his lap. "Your Mom is upstairs with the doctors right now, talking with your father."

"Daddy? My daddy's here?" Zak's frown deepened, the uncertainty in the child's face tearing at Ryder.

"He's come to see if he can help you get well, Zak."

"*You* been helpin' me get well. You been goin' to dialysis with me, and talkin' to the doctors, and . . . and I want you to be the one that stays with me. I'll be real good, Rye. Take all my medicine and not even cry when they poke me with needles. Just don't go away."

"Easy now, easy. I'm not going anywhere." Ryder rocked the boy, pressing him gently against his shoulder. "You've been a terrific patient, Zak. You've done everything the doctors asked you to. You've been so brave. I'm real—real proud of you, slugger."

"But if I get better, you'll go away. I don't want a new kidney. Don't want you to leave."

Zak's whole body was shaking. Tears trembled on the child's lashes. Ryder closed his eyes, remembering how small and helpless Zak had looked attached to the dialysis machine, how pasty white and thin he appeared now, in comparison to the pictures of the rambunctious, healthy boy who had been in the album Zak had shown him the first night in Ellie's apartment.

The knowledge that Zak feared abandonment more than his disease was sobering, heart-wrenching.

Ryder framed the child's face between his hands and looked straight into wide, frightened eyes. "Zakary, I love you. You aren't getting rid of me, kid. That much I promise you."

Ryder felt Zak's arms tighten around him, and a heavy ache settled in the pit of his stomach. After a moment, Zak pulled away, confronting Ryder again.

Grey eyes, mirrors of Ellie's own, seemed to look straight through to Ryder's soul. "Do you love my Mom, too?"

"Yeah, slugger. I love your Mom, too." Ryder brushed a wisp of red curl away from Zak's forehead.

"I'm glad. Before you came, it was hard to make her smile. She used to cry sometimes when she thought I was asleep. It made me sad."

"I'll do everything I can to make your Mom happy, Zak. We both will, as soon as you get well."

"Then I guess I better get well as soon as possible, huh?"

Alex's laugh rumbled as he came to kneel down beside the small boy. "You'd better get well right away. Tony and Will have already been asking when you can stay over again. And pretty soon there'll be a new baby you can play with." Alex's hand reached out to smooth over Gina's distended abdomen.

"I don't know much 'bout babies an' stuff. I asked for a brother for Christmas once, right after my Dad left. I thought a baby'd help keep Mom company while I was at school. Mom said Santa doesn't bring babies. Love does. Maybe if you love Mom enough, Rye, you could give her a baby."

The child's innocent words made Ryder's loins clench, his arms ache with the need to give Ellie that precious gift.

He cleared his throat. "We'll have to see about that, sport. Talk to your Mom about it later. After—"

"I know, I know. After I get well. Well, I guess we better go talk to Dr. Jim, then, huh?" Zak climbed down from Ryder's lap, his stance, one foot slightly forward, weight on one hip, an adorable mime of

Ryder's favorite position. But even that cocky aura couldn't fully bury the dread in the little boy's face.

Gina went to him and dropped a kiss on the top of his head. "Good luck, Zak. I'll let you squeeze noodles out of the spaghetti-maker when you get out of the hospital."

"And will you make me those cookies? The ones with jelly in 'em?"

"You betcha."

Ryder saw Gina's eyes go misty. She reached for her husband's hand. And Ryder knew she was thinking of her own three healthy kids, tucked safely away at their grandma's.

"Ryder's gonna stay with me. Aren't you, Rye?"

"You bet, slugger."

"Take care of him, Ryder," Gina said, giving them each a quick hug. "And let us know if anything…" Gina hesitated, then forced a smile. "Call us, day or night, if you or Ellie need anything. I mean it, now."

"I know you do."

"Tell Ellie…" Gina cradled her unborn child with one hand, the instinctive, protective impulse wrenching Ryder inside. "Tell her I'm thinking about her. I just know everything will turn out fine. It has to."

Ryder nodded. Taking Zakary's hand, he led him to the elevators.

And to what might be the child's last chance.

Chapter Thirteen

Ryder's fingers tightened around Zak's small ones as the elevator door slid open, revealing the urological ward beyond. A laughing nurse propelled a patient of about six along the corridor at a clip that would have done a Nascar driver proud. Squeals of delight rippled from the child as the nurse popped the front of the chair up in a wheelie just inches from where a preoccupied-looking Dr. Tyler stood.

The physician glanced up with a vague smile, but there was something about his face that made Ryder's gut tangle into knots.

Easy, Sloan, easy, Ryder tried to calm the sense of foreboding pumping through him. *You're just edgy, man.*

But he couldn't stop himself from lifting Zakary into his arms.

Not certain where to find Ellie, he approached the clipboard-wielding man.

"Dr. Tyler?"

"Yes?" The physician's eyes met Ryder's over the rims of clear glasses. A line of puzzlement was carved between sandy brows. "Can I help you...oh, Zak." Recognition dawned on Tyler's face as he saw the little boy.

"Hi, Dr. T." A sliver of nervousness slipped through Zakary's voice.

"I've been in talking to your father and mother for the past few hours, doing some tests."

"I know. On my dad. To see if his kidney'll work on me. Did you have to stick him with needles and stuff?"

"Some. But not half as many as we've had to use on you."

Ryder caught the slightest hint of a grimace around the corners of Tyler's mouth. Despite the sting of jealousy Ryder had felt when Zak had betrayed the physician's interest in Ellie, Ryder couldn't help but like the man. It was evident that this doctor who had been Ellie's mainstay for the past two years had already formed the same opinion of Daniel MacCrea as Ryder had.

And it wasn't a pretty one.

As if suddenly aware his face might be revealing too much, Tyler cleared his throat. "So, Zak, maybe you'd care to introduce me to your friend here."

"Name's Ryder Sloan." Ryder extended a hand. The doctor took it with a firm, cool grasp.

"Sloan. Ah, yes, the gentleman who threw the whole pediatric ward into chaos a few weeks back. The nurses are still talking about it."

Ryder's cheeks burned. "If I upset things for them, I'm sorry. I—"

"Are you joking?" Tyler shoved his glasses up the bridge of his nose. "We only wish we could bottle you and serve a dose to the kids with their prednizone every morning. I can't begin to tell you how much they enjoyed your visit." Tyler's mouth softened into a kind of melancholy. "And heaven knows, these kids have little enough fun when they're here."

Tyler seemed to shake himself inwardly. "So, I assume you two are looking for Zak's Mom, eh?"

"Yeah. We weren't sure where to look."

"Mr. MacCrea's hospital room. Number 241. I was just on my way to see if there is any news yet from the lab."

"Thanks," Ryder said.

"No problem." The doctor started to walk away, but Ryder reached out to stop him. "Dr. Tyler, about the visit I made to the floor a while back. I was thinking, next time the Angels have a home stand I could round up some of the other guys on the team. Come in and talk to the kids."

Tyler's smile warmed, his eyes flicking to Zak. "They'd like that. They'd like that very much. Zak, you take Mr. Sloan on down to 241 for me, will you? Hopefully if everything goes well, we can have you checked in across the hall from your dad before you know it."

Ryder felt a tremor go through the little boy and was uncertain whether it was hope or fear.

Zak wriggled to get down, and Ryder gently lowered the child to his feet. Zak linked his fingers with Ryder's and started down the hall.

As they neared the room, Zak's steps slowed. The boy hung back, eyeing the number above the door warily.

"Rye, does it hurt to take a kidney out of somebody? I mean . . . I don't want to—to hurt my dad."

Ryder struggled to find the right words—needed to find them for Zak. For just an instant, he thought about glossing over things, but felt that the kid deserved honesty.

"I don't know. I imagine it will hurt some. All I can tell you is that if Dr. Tyler were operating on me, I wouldn't even feel the hurting, wouldn't care about it at all. I'd be too busy being glad that you were going to get well. I'd be thinking of all the places I'd want to take you to after you got out of the hospital. All the things we could do." Ryder's voice cracked on the last.

Zak's eyes met his, the boy achingly solemn. "My dad is lots different from you. He always wants to run around doing stuff where you can't take a kid. Rye?" Zak hesitated for a moment. "Do you think he minds? Having to come back, I mean?"

"I don't know your dad very well, Zak, but I do know this—the minute he found out you needed a kidney, he came back to help you."

Ryder didn't add that if MacCrea hadn't, he would have personally strung the man from the top of the oil rig.

Zak stood, quiet for a moment, as if trying to dissect Ryder's words and his own mixed feelings.

"Rye, is it okay to love another guy more than you love your real dad? I mean, not that you wouldn't love your own dad at all...just, is it okay to love someone else better?"

Ryder hugged the boy against him, burying his face in the tousled mass of Zak's hair. "You're going to know lots of kinds of love in your life, Zak. Have lots of people love you, while you love them back. I think you've got enough room in your heart for them all."

"I love you, Ryder." Zak's eyes brimmed with a trust that humbled Ryder. Then the boy tugged on his hand, leading him to the half-closed door to Daniel Mac-Crea's room.

Stopping outside, Zak rapped shyly on the panel.

In the slice of room revealed by the door, Ryder could see Ellie start up from her chair, her face pale, taut.

Ryder could feel the tension in her, twisting tighter, tighter, until she seemed ready to snap.

"Rye? Is that you?" Her voice was unsteady. "Is Zak here?"

"No. I just dragged in some stray kid I found wandering around by the gift shop," Ryder said, pushing the door open.

The moment Ellie's eyes alighted on her son's face, the gray depths swam with tears.

"Hey, munchkin," she managed to squeeze out, sweeping over to catch the child in a fierce hug.

"Mom, you're—you're gettin' me all wet." Zak squirmed out of her arms. Ryder felt a pang of sympathy for Ellie as her face fell. But it seemed as if the child was intent on dealing with the man who had disappeared from his life so long ago. Stiffening his spine, Zak turned to face the bed where Daniel MacCrea already lay, the man's face ashen under his tan.

"Zakary?" To give credit where credit was due, MacCrea's voice was shaky. "Zak, it's me. Daddy."

"Yeah. Hi. Nice to—to meet...I mean, see you again." Zak's gaze flicked to Ryder, as if seeking guidance. The child edged closer to jeans-clad legs. "Did you have a—a nice trip?"

Daniel's face puckered. Surprise and hurt flashed across his face.

Hell, Ryder thought grimly, *what did the guy expect from the kid? That Zak should kiss his damn feet for deigning to put in an appearance after two whole years?*

"Don't you have a hug for your old man, Zakary?"

Ryder tried not to gag.

Zak regarded his father quietly. "I'm too big to be hugging anymore."

"That's ridiculous. I'm your Daddy for God's sake—"

Obviously sensing trouble, Ellie crossed to Zak's side. "Daniel," she warned gently. "It's been a long time."

MacCrea glowered at her, a sulkiness clinging to his mouth. "It's only been...well, it couldn't have been more than..." he said, faltering and eyeing his son—a son who, despite his ill-health, had obviously grown considerably since they'd last met.

Ryder could almost see the slimy bastard mentally shift gears. MacCrea turned pleading. "Zak, you have to know that I missed you. I wanted to come to see you, but things came up. Important things."

More important than me, Ryder could almost hear Zakary cry inside.

"That's okay," the child said in a tone that left no doubt that it was not.

Zak edged over until he was pressed up against Ryder's leg. Ryder lay one hand protectively on the boy's tense shoulder.

MacCrea's eyes clouded, belligerent.

"Come on, now, MacCrea," Ryder said, trying to keep his voice calm. "It's only natural that you should both feel a little awkward after all this time."

Daniel pushed himself up off the pillows. A miraculous recovery, so swift it should have made medical history, Ryder thought cynically.

"The only reason either of us feels awkward is because there's a stranger in the room," Daniel enunciated with the burningly clear voice one would use in talking to a very dull child. "If you'd quit intruding where you don't belong, Sloan—"

Zak's hand grasped Ryder's so hard the boy's knuckles went white. "I—I'm sorry, D-Daddy. I'll give you a hug if you'll let Ryder stay—"

"Whoa, slugger. It's okay." Ryder's blood was boiling on Zakary's behalf, but though he wanted to stuff the nearest bed-pan in MacCrea's mouth, he crushed his own temper, wanting only to spare Zak and Ellie as much emotional trauma as possible. And the best way to do that, grating as it was, might well be to make the quick exit Daniel MacCrea so desired.

"Listen," Ryder said gently to the little boy. "Maybe I should be heading out. Give you guys some time to get settled."

MacCrea gave a derisive snort, and Ryder's control slipped a notch. But before he could say anything, Ellie was there, her gray eyes lit with fire, her arm curved around Ryder's back.

"No."

"No?" Daniel stared as if she'd lapsed into a foreign language. "What do you mean, no?"

"Ryder belongs here." The steel was back in Ellie's voice, the same tempered strength that had stung Ryder when she had lashed out at him the first day he'd met her.

The iron band of tension in his chest snapped, releasing a joy so fierce his eyes burned with it. He linked his hand with Ellie's, his throat tight as he thought of how much standing up to her ex-husband must have cost her.

But even though Ryder wanted to stay with her, with Zak, forever, the emotional balance in the hospital room was too fragile—Zakary's life depended on the unpredictable MacCrea's willingness to go under the knife.

Cupping one palm against Ellie's satin-soft cheek, Ryder drowned in gray eyes. "Really, Ellie, it's all right. I should probably head out."

"No!" Zak shouted, all but scaling him like a tree. "You promised you wouldn't leave me!"

Ryder hugged the boy close, feeling the trembling in him, the terror. Ryder stole a glance at Daniel, felt the hardening resolve in the other man. If the stakes hadn't been so high, Ryder would have told the bastard to go to hell. A whole damned army couldn't have blasted him away from the boy in his arms.

With more self-control than Ryder had known he possessed, he turned back to the little boy, searching for some way to make the inevitable as painless as possible.

"I won't be away for very long," Ryder explained, stroking the boy's silky curls. "Just enough time for me to hit a few over the fence at batting practice. Get ready to belt 'em out onto Wakefield Avenue when the Cardinals come to town."

"L-let someone else hit 'em over the fence for a change." Zak snuffled into Ryder's shirtfront. He could feel hot tears seeping through the fabric.

Ryder forced a wobbly laugh. "Who? Alex? Mitchell?"

"C-couldn't hit a beach ball with a whole store full of bats," Zak admitted, still, his fingers tightened on Ryder's shoulders. "But I like 'em, anyway."

"They'll be glad to hear it," Ryder said, burying his face in the warm crook of the little boy's neck. The fear tore deep in Ryder again, the feel of Zak's heartbeat against Rye's own chest seeming suddenly, terribly fragile.

"Rye." Ellie's voice. Gentle. Warm. "You don't have to go."

Ryder formed his lips into a ghost of a smile. "I'm afraid I do." He set Zak down and dragged his fingers distractedly through his hair. "There are games the rest of the week, and I'm going to have to be there."

It had started out as an excuse to save Zak and Ellie from being torn between him and Daniel MacCrea, but as Ryder watched the change come over Ellie's face—the hurt, the betrayal, stirring deep in her eyes—he realized with sudden, sickening clarity that there was nothing contrived about the conflict raging in her eyes, the stunned hurt that seemed to sting the lips that had defended him so resolutely moments before.

"You mean, if—*when* Zak has the transplant, you're going to—to be..."

Spending the next two weeks jetting between San Francisco, San Diego and Los Angeles? a voice jeered in

Ryder's head. He wanted to grab Ellie, drag her into his arms.

Explain.

Explain that baseball was his job—that it was only because of that job and the high visibility and generous remuneration he received for it, that he had been able to help Zakary at all.

He reached out to touch her, but she shrank away from him, her eyes wide, wounded. "Ellie, of course I'll be here when Zak's in surgery. But afterward, I'll have to...to..."

He faltered, searching futilely for a way to make her understand.

But before he could say anything more, there was a rap at the door. All eyes flashed toward where Dr. Tyler now stood, yet it was as if even the medical man's smile hadn't the power to penetrate the hurt flowing thick in the room.

Ryder stared numbly as the doctor strode in and swept Zakary up into his arms.

"Dr. Tyler." Ellie's voice trembled. "Do you have any news?"

"News? Yes, I have news." The physician beamed, his eyes fixed on his small patient. "So, Zak-a-roo, how do you feel about winning the lottery?"

Ellie gripped the rail of the hospital bed, as if to keep from falling. "You mean...Zak...he..."

Tyler's gaze locked with hers. "A perfect match. I'm scheduling the surgery for the day after tomorrow."

Stark, blinding relief streaked through Ryder as Ellie flung herself at her son, all but crushing him in an embrace that excluded everyone else in the room.

A magic circle of mother, child and sweet, sweet hope.

Ryder's fists clenched with the knowledge that moments ago he would have been welcomed inside it.

Instead, he stood alone, so cold, watching as Ellie rocked Zak back and forth, tears of gratitude streaming down her cheeks.

"Did you hear, Zak?" she sobbed over and over again. "It's going to be all right."

But as Ryder glanced from her face to Daniel Mac-Crea's subtly triumphant one, he wondered if things would ever be right again.

Chapter Fourteen

Exhaustion burned at the back of Ryder's eyes, blurring the infield into smears of green and brown. He stepped out of the batter's box, almost hearing the collective sighs of the batting coach and relief pitcher he'd bribed into coming in early to help him practice.

Only Alex was silent, his features obscured by the mask drawn across his face, tension emanating from the catcher's compact body as the clock ticked closer and closer to the time when Zak and Daniel MacCrea would be wheeled into surgery.

Ace reliever, Ben Mitchell, rolled the ball in his hand, forcing a tired smile. "Lookin' good, Rye. Lookin' good."

But Ryder knew his swing had looked like garbage.

He stifled an oath, knowing that none of the three men who had come out to help him practice deserved a display of "superstar temper."

God knew, Mitchell had been willing to do whatever he could for Ryder and for Zak. The sick kid had totally won over the off-kilter southpaw when Zak had confided his dreams of pitching weeks before.

It had been no small sacrifice for the notoriously late-rising pitcher to drag himself out of bed at this ungodly hour to pitch a few to Ryder so early that they had had to turn on the stadium's blazing lights. Mitchell and Alex had been doing their best to keep some semblance of normalcy in the practice routine, but the familiar exchange of banter between them was conspicuously absent, any attempt at humor falling dismally flat.

Propping the bat's pine-tarred handle against one leg, Ryder rubbed the knuckle of his worn leather batting glove against his eyelids in an effort to clear his vision.

"Relax. Don't press," the batting coach called. "You'll nail it next time."

Nail it? Hell, he hadn't even *seen* that last fastball—a gift served up belt-high by Mitchell in an effort to find Ryder's bat.

Ryder picked up the bat, shifting it in an effort to get it to settle into the curve of his palms. From the time he'd been a kid, he'd been able to make the smooth wood almost a part of him, had been able to make it meld with his hands until it felt right. So right.

But today, it was as if he'd never held a bat before. As if the Louisville Slugger had shrunk to the size of a straw, the ball seeming to dart about like some kind of crazed firefly, defying him to hit it.

"Concentrate," Alex said quietly from behind him. "Just concentrate on seeing the ball."

It was in that instant Ryder's temper snapped, spilling out all the anger, all the hurt, he'd felt in the aftermath of Ellie's rejection. A rejection that had only grown more chill, more hardened, with each visit he'd paid to Zak's hospital room.

"How the hell am I supposed to see the ball, when all I can think about is Ellie . . . Zak. . . ."

"I know how you feel, Rye."

"What do you know about how I feel?" Ryder swore, flinging the bat to the ground. "I'm about to lose the best thing that ever happened to me, and my damned batting average the past two games is almost as bad as yours."

"Whoa, Rye, easy," Mitchell said as he came off the mound. "You're acting like a jerk, bud."

"No, it's okay," Alex said, holding up one hand to ward the pitcher off. "He just needs some time to cool off." But in spite of Craig's words, Ryder could hear the hurt in his friend's voice.

He was being a bastard, and he knew it. But he couldn't seem to stop.

"Listen, Rye," Alex continued, "maybe you should just lay off for a little while, run up to the hospital and see what's happening. Didn't you tell Ellie you'd be there a couple of hours before—"

"I told Zak I'd be there when he wakes up this morning. Talk to him before he goes into surgery. I've got forty-five minutes before I have to leave. And I'm damn well going to spend them getting my swing under control."

Cliff Tarkington, the aging batting coach affectionately nicknamed Pops, paced forward, rubbing his hand against a balding pate. "Listen, Sloan, the way I see it, you're not doing anybody—including yourself—any favors trying to club the ball out here this morning. If anything, it's hurting your confidence instead of helping it. Just do what Craig, here, says, and go hold your lady's hand. Bet she could use somebody to hang on to about now."

"You got that wrong, Pops." Ryder gave a bitter laugh. "She's made it crystal clear the past two days to both me and her ex-husband that she doesn't need anybody." His voice dropped, his hands fisting. "Except maybe that kid of hers."

"What do you expect?" Alex's voice held a tinge of impatience. "She's got a child who's sick and two grown men acting like . . ." Alex cursed under his breath. "Forget it, man," he muttered, yanking off his mask and heading for the dugout. "Just forget it."

Ryder knew he should let Craig go, give them both time to cool off. But the anger surging through him was better than the emptiness, better than the fear that had gripped him since the day he'd watched Ellie start slipping away.

"Come on, Alex," he baited Craig, stalking after the catcher. "You obviously have some kind of opinion." Ryder took the steps down into the dugout two at a time. "What am I acting like? An arrogant jerk? A stupid jock? Just how am I acting?"

"Like you're hurting, man. Hurting." Alex spun on him. "Only you keep forgetting that anybody else might be hurting, too."

"Who? You tell me just who is hurting besides me, *friend.*"

"Ellie, to start with."

"Ellie? She has everything she wants. Zak and MacCrea are a perfect match. Tyler's one of the best doctors in the business. He's as sure as humanly possible that Zak's going to be tearing up the school playground before Halloween. Everything's just perfect. Except that Ellie sure as hell doesn't need me anymore."

"Maybe you're right." Alex's eyes met his with a disgust that ate at Ryder. "Ellie doesn't need you. Doesn't need anyone. That must be why Gina found her in that little garden place at the hospital, crying her eyes out last night."

Ryder felt like he'd been slugged square in the chest. His hand knotted into a fist, and he wanted to slam it

into the protective gear covering Craig's broad chest—
wanted to break windows, kick walls.

"Rye, I love you like a brother, man. Gina does, too.
But you're acting like the spoiled kid those tabloid things
label you. You can't always expect to be number one in
a relationship. Sometimes you take, but more times, you
have to give."

"Don't you think I know that? I've been giving,
dammit, until there's nothing left. All I want is some
little sign that she loves me half as much as I love her.
That she needs me. That she understands. I thought we'd
made progress the night Zak stayed at your house. I
could feel her opening up to me, opening herself to the
idea of loving me. Letting me inside all those walls she'd
built since Daniel MacCrea abandoned her."

Ryder raked his fingers through his tousled hair, and
stared, unseeing, across the field where he'd spent so
many golden, glorious hours.

His voice was hushed, hurting. "It was so incredible,
Alex, watching Ellie that night, seeing her laugh, feeling her touch me in ways that had nothing to do with
sex. Ways that were so deep, no one's ever touched me
there before. I never knew it could be like that. Never
knew I could get high from seeing her tiniest smile, from
watching the sun on her hair."

Ryder's voice trailed off, and he felt his cheeks burn.
He'd revealed too much for comfort—even to his best
friend.

He heard the sound of Alex laying his mask on the
bench, heard the soft crunch of his spikes as he took a
step nearer. "It's scary, Rye. I know. Gina and I were
seventeen and naive as heck when we fell in love, but I
can still remember how terrified I was. With everything
you and Ellie have already gone through, it must be pure
holy hell."

"I'm going to lose her, Alex," Ryder whispered. "I
can feel it."

"You can't know that. Not yet. You have to give her time."

"I have been giving her time ever since I met her. Giving her space to heal. But every time I start to believe things might work out, something happens. She shuts me out."

"Rye, I haven't known Ellie very long, but even I can tell the lady adores you. Needs you."

"Well, I need her, too, dammit." The words were wrenched painfully from deep inside him. "But she won't let me in. And, Alex, I'm not sure how much longer I can take watching her, waiting for something I may never have. It hurts too much."

Ryder started as he felt Craig's hand close over his shoulder, giving him a bracing squeeze.

"Whatever happens, Rye, know that Gina and I..." Alex's voice caught.

Ryder sucked in a steadying breath. "Yeah, I know. I'm counting on it." After a moment he stripped off his batting gloves and tossed them onto his shelf space above the bench. "I think I'd better hit the showers and head up to the hospital now. I promised Zak...."

Ryder closed his eyes, suddenly struck with the memory of his conversation with the little boy the day Gina and Alex had brought him to the hospital—a conversation filled with hope and love, and dreams of a houseful of red-haired brothers and sisters. Dreams of a family both Ryder and the gray-eyed little boy had shared.

Swallowing hard, Ryder spoke. "Tell Pops and Mitchell I'm sorry for acting like—"

"A three-toed sloth? I will. Oh, and Rye..." Alex turned to the bag of equipment he'd left on the bench earlier that morning. "Tony... he sent something along for you to give to Zak."

Alex dug something out of one of his bag's zippered pouches. Ryder saw the rising sun's rays hit a polished chunk of rose quartz that he and Tony had found on a trek through the mountains two years ago. It was the little boy's good-luck charm. Magic beyond compare.

Ryder's throat swelled shut.

"Thanks," he managed to squeeze out. "Zak and I . . . we'll both need all the luck we can get."

Ryder's eyes burned as he walked down the stairs into the locker room, the ridges of the stone digging into his clenched fingers.

Ellie stared at the blade of sunlight slashing through the crack in the curtains, her whole body aching with tension as she shifted slightly in the lumpy hospital chair that had been her bed the past two nights.

Sleepless nights, an eternity away from the magical one she had spent in Ryder Sloan's penthouse three days before. That night that had been so wonderful now seemed no more real to her than the love scenes in the movies she had adored when she'd been young and still gullible enough to believe in happily ever afters. When she'd still believed that if you loved someone enough you could conquer any differences that might lie between you.

Before Daniel had shattered her.

Before Zak had gotten sick.

Before she'd discovered that the only person it was safe to depend on was herself.

She lifted one hand wearily to knead the wire-taut muscles at the back of her neck. It had all been so clear to her before Ryder Sloan had burst into her life. All laughter. All light. Making her dream just a little. About forevers. Families.

About waking up in bed with the same infuriating, wonderful man every morning until she was eighty.

Simple dreams.

But it had been so long since she'd had any at all, that even those dreams had seemed as unattainable as Cinderella's fairy-tale coach spun out of moon dust.

Now she hated Ryder. Wanted to. For making her feel again when it had been so much less painful to be numb—wrapped up in her tutoring, her son, in milk and in monster movies and trips to the zoo. Channeling all of her energies into fighting the disease that threatened her child.

Blinking back tears, she turned to look at her son, still asleep behind the hospital bed's gleaming steel rails. He seemed smaller, somehow, more fragile, as if the institution-green walls of the surgical floor had drained his skin of all color.

She'd seen him sick so often over the past two years, had spent so many hours inside the hospital's walls. But this time was different. The room seemed even colder, as if chilled by the steel instruments awaiting Zak in the operating room a corridor away. It was as if she could feel their bite, taste the almost necessary indifference of medical staffs that saw thousands of patients each year. Zakary would be just one more chart to them, filled with prescriptions and dialysis logs and medical data to be pored over by eager interns in years ahead.

Ellie's chest ached, and she wanted to reach out, take Zak into her arms, protect him, somehow. No. She'd only wake him up, give him more time to worry, to try to be brave. She dug her fingers into the arms of her chair, her eyes tracing over her little boy.

Bright frogs frolicked across the blue of his hospital gown, his hair a tumbled mass over pinched, pale features. Fluffles, the stuffed dog that had accompanied Zak on countless other forays into the hospital, lay abandoned at the end of the bed.

But the thing that made Ellie's heart wrench most painfully of all was the baseball jersey the child clutched in the ragged dog's accustomed place. The wad of blue-and-white-striped fabric was tucked tight under Zak's chin, the child clinging to the jersey even in sleep, as if it were a tangible piece of Ryder Sloan.

Ellie buried her face in one trembling palm, remembering how much it hurt to watch Zak in the weeks after Daniel had left. The stuffed dog, his last gift, had never left the child's arms, and every time Ellie had seen it, fresh, sharp pain had driven inside her.

Would Zak drag around this reminder of Ryder the same way? A silent reproach to the mother who had failed to hang on to yet another man Zakary had dared to love?

This time, Ellie knew, the pain would be even more relentless for both her and for Zak. Even as a toddler Zak had learned not to depend upon his father, but in the past few weeks, the child had come to trust Ryder more than anyone, save Ellie.

And as for herself, Ellie thought with a sick grimness, this time she wouldn't have the emotional armor of the bracing anger and resentment Daniel's countless transgressions had built up inside her. This time, the only thing she would hold in her hand would be fragile, broken dreams.

No, she berated herself inwardly, she'd have her child's life. All she'd ever wanted. Maybe more than she'd dared hope for.

She stilled, suddenly aware of the sound of someone approaching down the hall that had been hushed with an early-morning quiet. Panic knotted in her chest, and she glanced at her watch. The gurney to take Zak to surgery? No, not yet. It was too early, wasn't it?

But the footsteps stopped outside Zak's door, hesitating there, as if checking one of the infernal charts that seemed forever in the medical staff's hands.

Ellie forced herself onto wobbly legs and brushed her tangled hair from her eyes just as the door was slowly opened.

She grasped the back of her chair to steady herself as her eyes met Ryder's blue ones.

He looked like heaven—worried, tense, yet strong enough to lean on if only she had the courage to do so. Charcoal-gray dress pants clung to the long-muscled contours of his thighs, while a short-sleeved polo shirt the exact shade of his eyes molded over his shoulders. His hair was still damp from his shower, tendrils curled around his tanned face. A face filled with pain, and tenderness, and terror. Hurt, and wariness . . . and love.

So many emotions, so much pain. Ellie winced inwardly, knowing she had put them there, yet knowing she'd had no other choice.

"You're here," she said, knowing she sounded ridiculous.

"I said that I would be." He seemed so quiet, so subdued. He walked over to the side of the bed and looked down into Zakary's face.

When Daniel had looked at Zakary, there had always been a carelessness about him, as if he were glancing at a grubby little boy, instead of at a miracle.

But Ryder . . . Ellie's throat swelled, aching. When Ryder peered down at the sleeping child, she knew he saw the same beauty she did, the same inexpressible perfection.

It was in every line of Ryder's face, in the soft curve to the mouth that could be so sexy, so masculine. It was in the way his fingers reached out toward the little boy's cheek, then drew away, as her own had countless times the night before.

"Guess I'd better let him sleep as long as he can, poor little guy."

"He'll be thrilled to see you. It's all he could talk about last night . . . your coming here this morning."

Ryder glanced back at her, the softness around his mouth shifting into the barest hint of bitterness. "And I just bet you spent most of the night explaining to him that sometimes grownups make promises they can't keep. Sometimes things come up—"

Ellie's cheeks flamed as Ryder hit uncomfortably close to the mark. She didn't say anything. She didn't have to.

She swallowed hard. "Ryder," she managed at last, "I don't want to argue."

"Neither do I. All I want to know is what Zak said, when you told him I probably wasn't going to bother showing up."

Ellie felt like he'd hit her. Maybe she deserved it. "Zak told me not to worry." Her eyes stung with the memory of the child's exact words. "He said you'd come, even if the creature from the Black Lagoon was in your way."

Ryder's shoulders slumped, and he rubbed one hand wearily across his freshly shaven face. "Hell, I'd welcome a monster to fight off, anything except these damned ghosts you won't let go, Ellie. I love you. I'm not going to let you down."

There was so much vulnerability in his face, she couldn't bear to see it. She turned and walked to the window. She leaned her cheek against the smooth, cool wall, and watched the rest of Atlanta scurrying off to jobs and babysitters and breakfasts with friends, oblivious to the fact that her life was crumbling around her.

"Ryder, you can't help but let me down. Baseball is your life—"

"Baseball is my *job*. Dammit, Ellie—"

"R-Rye?" The sleepy voice of Zakary made them both turn to face the hospital bed. The child glanced from one to the other, confusion rimming his eyes. He rubbed at them with one fist, then blinked, a slow smile creasing pale lips. "See, Mom. Tol' ya so."

Ryder smiled, the first genuine smile she'd seen since Daniel had come. "Hey, slugger, you'd better get well, and quick. I need you to give me some pointers on my swing."

Zak yawned, battling valiantly to stay awake, but his eyelashes drooped shut.

"Why don't you . . . just . . . hit the ball," he mumbled, as if it were some vast revelation. Then, snuggling the jersey under his chin, he drifted back to sleep.

It was ten minutes later that the nurses came, their hair caught up in green paper caps, their eyes gratingly reassuring.

They smiled and chatted brightly as they eased Zak onto the gurney, but all their banter couldn't hide the thick pall of fear that seemed to shroud the small room. They pulled up the side rail of the cart, the metallic click seeming suddenly, terrifyingly final.

"Mommy?" Zak's uncertain voice made Ellie want to scream, cry. Instead, she smoothed back his hair and tried to smile. "Can I have ice cream when I get back? I mean, if everything's working and stuff?"

"We'll have to wait and see what the doctor says."

The nurse started to push the car, but Zak cried out, "No, no wait."

The nurse laughed, gently, firmly, and continued to wheel the cart. "Honey, we have to go."

The gurney lurched to a stop, stilled by Ryder's strong, tanned hand. "Zakary asked you to wait."

"Mr. MacCrea . . ." the nurse began, obviously confusing him for Zak's father.

"The name is Sloan, and it'll just take a minute," Ryder said, a steely edge to his voice. He took his hand from the rail and skimmed his knuckles over Zak's cheek. "What is it, slugger?"

"Are you gonna be here when I wake up?"

"Yeah. The creature from the Black Lagoon couldn't keep me away."

Ellie watched her son smile up into Ryder's face, so trusting, so certain. Then the nurse wheeled the cart away.

For a long time the two of them stood in the hall, staring at the double doors as they swung closed behind

Chapter Fifteen

No windows were cut into the walls of the surgical waiting room. No rising sun or moon sent shifting patterns across carpeted floors that had seen the restless pacings of families and friends of patients who had come before. The room was pristine, except for the dark stains near the coffee machine. The pot was kept brimful by hospital volunteers who slipped in and out, on their way back to lives where taking out the garbage and frying hamburgers for dinner were still the highest priorities of the day.

They laughed together in the hall, bantering with the busy nurses about dates and fights with their husbands, and the idiosyncrasies of the doctors they worked with on the floor. But did they know about the little boy in the cold, sterile room nearby, battling for his life? Did they care?

Stop it, Sloan, Rye grated inwardly. You're being a jerk. Hell, yes, they cared. The nurses had cared enough to fight their way through school, to work in a job where the demands were relentless and the pay inadequate at best. And the volunteers weren't getting paid at all. If they involved themselves gut-deep in every case they were assigned to, they'd be burned out inside of a year, basket cases, strung out as tightly as he was now.

He could only hope that, despite that necessary detachment, the medical expertise housed in Atlanta General would be enough to pull Zakary through this nightmare of scalpels and retractors, sutures and anesthesia.

Ryder tried to suck in a deep, steadying breath, the mere thought of what the child was undergoing making him feel woozy. But instead of easing the tightness in his chest, the waiting room's walls seemed to squeeze him even tighter, pressing the air from his lungs.

And in that moment he would have traded three summers of his baseball career for just five minutes in the middle of Angels field. Just long enough to drink in the wide-open sweep of green, smell the fresh-mown grass, the damp tang of the dew clinging in the air.

He would have traded anything for it, except those precious scraps of time in the past hours when Ellie had betrayed that she needed him a little.

A sigh shuddered through him, and he arched his head back to ease a kink in his neck. He'd wanted so much for her to need him. God knew, he needed her more badly now than he'd ever needed anyone in his life. He needed to face this agonizing wait with her, clinging to her hand, and to the most fragile of hopes. But it was as if Ellie had enclosed herself in some brittle, bitter shell no one could breach, her stoic expression making resentment churn deep inside him.

He glanced over to where she sat, her face so pale set against Gina Craig's rosy one. Gina had arrived an hour after they'd wheeled Zak into surgery, and in spite of Ellie and Ryder's combined pleadings that she go home and rest, the pregnant woman had lodged herself on the hospital chair, as immovable as the pictures bolted to the walls.

By the time Alex had arrived at the conclusion of that afternoon's game, Ryder had long since given up trying to talk Gina into leaving. Because, selfish though he might be, he found something comforting in her presence, something soothing in seeing the new life growing inside her. As if it were some sort of talisman to preserve the life that lay in the balance a corridor beyond.

Yet even with the Craigs' emotional support, Ryder couldn't escape the fear that darkened with every sweep of the clock's hands. Time crawled past, the hours bleeding together into what seemed an eternity. He knew he should be relieved, glad that the agonizing wait would soon end. But instead of comforting him, the knowledge that the surgery would soon be over was proving to be the most horrible torture he'd ever known.

Because he was helpless—helpless to change the outcome for Zak, if things should go awry. Helpless also, to mend the rift that seemed to yawn wider and wider between Ryder and the woman he loved. The woman who sat in the harsh glow of fluorescent lamps, a resigned, hollow expression in her mist-gray eyes.

Ryder's fingers tightened on the disposable cup, half filled with tepid, murky liquid. There was so much emptiness inside Ellie now. He could feel it, growing as certainly as the child that kicked in Gina's womb. He wanted to smooth the tumbled sunset curls away from Ellie's forehead, kiss her, love her, fill her with all that he was. But he couldn't fill her if he couldn't reach her. Couldn't touch her when she'd drawn her solitariness so tightly around her he couldn't break through.

This was her pain. Her private hell, and odd as it was, he sensed she resented sharing it, even with him.

Ryder closed his eyes.

No. She didn't want to share anything with him. Was afraid to want him at all. It was clear that the pain of losing the love they shared was less frightening to her than the prospect of a lifetime of waiting for him to walk out the door.

And if Ellie MacCrea was looking for an excuse to shut him out of her life, she couldn't have fabricated a better one than the excuse Ryder himself couldn't help serving her on a blasted silver platter.

Baseball.

His job—though God knew, Ellie would never see it as anything but a bunch of Peter Pan boys, getting paid obscene amounts of money for doing something she saw as totally worthless.

Pain stabbed deep, and Ryder closed his eyes. But the image of Andrea and Arthur Sloan rose up in Ellie's place—that nightmare of an evening when he told them he was going to refuse a full-ride scholastic scholarship to Stanford in order to enter the minor leagues straight out of high school.

The agent who had sought him out had been working out the details—details so lucrative Ryder had dared hope even Arthur would be pleased for him. Arthur Sloan might not understand a childhood dream come true, he might not understand the near-reverence with which Ryder viewed the game and its rich history—a history of which he wanted to become a part—but if there was one thing Ryder's father did understand, it was money.

Yet in the end, even that hadn't mattered. It was baseball money. Tainted, somehow, by the sweat and the dirt and the vulgar publicity— Ryder could read the contemptuous disbelief in Arthur's face.

Ryder had feared the man was going to have a coronary on the spot as he paced the walnut-paneled study, while Andrea had wrung her white, perfectly manicured hands until Ryder worried she'd shred them on the two-carat cocktail ring weighting her finger.

"Enough of this foolishness," Arthur had boomed in the voice that struck terror in executive boardrooms across the country. "I forbid you to throw your life away. You're a Sloan, heir to Sloan Enterprises. You'll go to Stanford and then take your place in the company as expected."

Ryder winced, surprised at the depth of hurt the memory could still cause him. Never once had Arthur said, *You're my son, I love you. A baseball career is so uncertain. I don't want you hurt, disappointed, disillusioned.* Never once had Arthur confided to Ryder that he'd had his own dreams, of a son working beside him, of building some kind of Sloan dynasty, to look back on with pride.

No, Arthur had only told Ryder what was *expected* of a Sloan. And when Ryder had refused to fit himself into Arthur's mold, his father's eyes had chilled, his mouth pinched in a sneer that had never again left his lips whenever he looked at his son.

"It is evident your mother and I have been too indulgent with you in the past."

Ryder's fingers had clenched the Spanish leather of the armchair, and he had thought of the one summer he'd known what love was, what indulgence was— Cammy Rath, shaking her head and laughing when Ryder and her brother had made a gelatin slide on the kitchen floor.

"Let me make this perfectly clear," Arthur had bellowed. "If you persist in this absurd notion of *playing baseball* for a living, you may expect no more financial aid from us. No Mercedes. No unlimited credit lines."

"Didn't you hear anything I said?" Ryder had burst out. "I'll be able to support myself with the money I make signing. In time, there'll be even more. I'll work hard, Dad. Real hard. The scout said I could hold my own with the best someday.''

''Oh, for God's sake!'' Scorn had dripped from Arthur's voice. ''For once in your life be a man, Ryder. I'll not have my son spending his life grubbing around in the dirt, making a spectacle of himself in front of—of a stadium full of bellowing construction workers and shrewish housewives.''

Andrea's voice had cut in then, quivering with emotion. ''After all we've done for you, your father and I, surely you can't mean to humiliate us by pursuing this...this ridiculous notion.''

Ryder had just turned eighteen that month, but in those few moments in Arthur Sloan's study he'd aged ten years. With deliberation, Ryder had forced himself to his feet, trying not to show the hurt in his eyes. ''I never wanted to humiliate you, Mother. I only want you to...'' *love me.* He couldn't say the words. Instead, he dug into the pocket of his jeans and took out the keys to the silver Mercedes his parents had ordered for him the day he got his driver's license.

If you think I'll have my drive littered up with some rattletrap monstrosity, you're sadly mistaken... Arthur's voice had drifted back to him.

Slowly Ryder had placed the keys on the table and walked from the room.

Before he awoke the next morning, his parents had jetted off to the Virgin Islands so that Andrea could ''compose her nerves'' and, no doubt, avoid the phone calls of her society friends when the local paper reported that Ryder had signed on with the Angels Triple-A farm team.

It had been a year before he'd seen his parents again, and by then, he'd been driving his own Porsche, but the car hadn't mattered a damn. Arthur Sloan had looked at it as if Ryder had stolen the thing, then the businessman had stalked away and barred himself in his study for the duration of Ryder's visit.

Ryder shook himself, trying to drive away the shadows in his mind, but they lingered as he poured out the last dregs of his coffee and went to pour himself some fresh. He took a swig, glad when it burned his tongue. He concentrated on the sting in an attempt to close out the pain that bit far deeper.

Ellie. He glanced to where she sat, her hands clasped, still, so still on her lap. Yes, she'd known pain, loss, betrayal, but she didn't have a corner on the market. If only she'd open her eyes enough to see it.

"Hey, Rye."

Ryder started at the sound of Alex's voice a few steps away from him.

The catcher rolled stiff shoulders. "Sure as heck is taking them long enough, isn't it?"

"It's not like installing a new muffler in a car, Alex. If you've got somewhere to go, then get the hell—aw, cripes." Ryder slammed his fist against the wall. He heard Gina gasp behind him, felt Alex jump. Only Ellie remained silent, frozen.

Ryder buried his face in one hand, his voice low, muffled. "I don't know why you put up with me, Craig. I wouldn't."

"Sure you would." Alex cuffed Ryder gently on the arm, a gesture more soothing than one of Gina's hugs. "You do it every time Gina goes into labor."

"But this is different," Ryder said, swallowing the knot of dread in his throat.

"Yeah," Alex echoed. "This is different."

What if something's gone wrong? Ryder wanted to yell. *What if the doctor is washing up even now, trying to think of a way to tell us . . .*

"Dammit," he swore, kicking a spindle-legged chair near the emergency phone.

"That's not going to make the surgery get over any faster," said Ellie, her voice lifeless. "It's not going to change whatever happens."

"Maybe not, but it sure as hell makes me feel better." Ryder knew he shouldn't be angry at the acceptance in her face, knew that it was a defense she'd had to nurture to get through the time she'd had to deal with Zakary's illness alone. But he hadn't had the time to get used to the fact that the child he loved might die. Maybe he didn't have the strength.

He glared at Ellie. "I'm going to find out what the hell is going on down there. I can't take this damned waiting."

He turned and stalked out of the waiting room. He'd expected Alex to follow him, try to calm him, but it was as if Craig had used the intuition that had served him so well behind the catcher's mask, the instinct for knowing when to charge the ball, or when to play it safe.

Nothing Alex could have said would have stopped Ryder. And if Craig had trailed after—even in the guise of offering support, it would only have fueled the emotions churning in Ryder's gut. Emotions so frightening, so powerful, it was safer to channel them into anger than to recognize them for what they really were.

At the nurse's station, a petite brunette was making notes on a chart, her brow furrowed in concentration.

"Excuse me," Ryder said, striving to keep his voice civil. "I'm Zakary MacCrea's...friend. We've been waiting since seven o'clock this morning. Would it be too much trouble to give us some idea what the devil's going on?"

The girl almost swallowed her gum. "Oh, I...Ryder Sloan, isn't it? I watch all the Angels games on TV. That last series against the Mets was—"

"To tell you the truth, I don't give a damn if the whole National League has jumped off of the Sears Tower right now. All I want to know is what's happening to my boy.''

"Um...um, of course you do. But these things take time, Mr. Sloan. I know how hard it can be, waiting.''

"Terrific. Then you know I'm not moving until I get some kind of news.''

The woman's eyes were kind, her voice just a little tart. "Would you like me to bring a chair in from the waiting room? You might be here a long time. I can hardly disturb a doctor who is in the middle of a surgery as delicate as the one Zakary is going through. And really, Mr. Sloan, you know you don't want me to.''

Ryder swore, but the woman only reached out, patting his hand.

"I know it's hard. Just keep thinking, tomorrow this will all be over.''

That's what I'm afraid of, a voice inside Ryder cried. *That it will be over—my time with Zak, my loving Ellie. I'll be alone again. Only it will be worse this time, because now I know how it feels to belong to someone, to have them belong to you.*

Defeated, Ryder turned, making his way blindly back to the waiting room. Three faces turned to him, expectantly, and Ryder's gut twisted as he saw a flicker of hope light Ellie's eyes.

He bit the inside of his lip, and shook his head, silent, before he turned away.

If there had been any emotion left in Ellie, she would have ached for him. But she was drained of hope, drained of everything, except the tiny thread of loving that bound her to Ryder. The thread that kept her hanging on even when she didn't want to.

The nurses' shift changed, the carts full of patients' suppers glided past. When it neared six, Alex insisted on taking a reluctant Gina on a foray to the hospital cafeteria. Though they offered to bring something back for Ellie, she refused. This time, Ryder made no protest.

Strangely enough, it hurt, as if he sensed the distance between them and was already struggling to separate himself.

Ellie twisted her fingers in the folds of her skirt, unable to keep from glancing surreptitiously at Ryder. For hours he'd paced the room like a panther she'd seen once when she'd taken Zak to the zoo. On similar trips, she'd always been oblivious to all but Zak's pleasure, but there had been something in the magnificent cat that had reached out to her that day, touched her when she didn't want to be touched. If was as if the panther believed if he persisted, walked far enough, long enough, he could outrun his captivity.

In the agonizing hours since they'd wheeled Zak away, Ryder had reminded her of that panther with its haunted eyes, its fierce resolve. Yet even Ryder seemed to sense the hopelessness now. He leaned against a wall, captured in a net of shadow. Silent. Alone.

Ellie dug her fingernails into her thighs to keep from going to him. No. It was better this way. To leave the resentment, the hurt simmering between them, warning them both of the danger they'd so narrowly escaped. The danger, and the joy, she thought as she reached out to the numbness that had been her defense. But it was gone, and in its place was a chill despair.

They had started at the sound of footsteps so many times, felt the thundering hope and dread turn to disappointment as whichever member of the medical staff had hurried past, that they paid no mind to yet another set of footfalls.

Not until the weary steps paused at the waiting room door.

Ellie's heart stopped. Ryder shoved himself slowly from the wall, as they both stared at Dr. Tyler, his eyes dull with exhaustion, his face sallow against his green hospital scrubs.

Ellie's fingers felt cold as stone, and as lifeless. She was unaware Ryder had crossed the room to take them in his own.

"The duty nurse said you wore a trough in the linoleum, Mr. Sloan," Dr. Tyler said, his lips pulling into a tired smile. "And Ellie—I'd wager you haven't eaten a thing all day."

"Zak...Dr. Tyler, how—how is he?" Ellie croaked out.

"Let's just put it this way. He looks a heck of a lot better than the two of you. Sometimes I think we should admit the parents instead of the kids."

"You mean, he...everything went..."

"The kidney started functioning even before we stitched Zak up. It's early yet, and a lot can still go wrong, but if I were going to make a bet on how things are going to turn out, I'd wager half my malpractice insurance that the two of you are going to have one healthy young man to keep out of trouble a few months from now."

Healthy...the word seemed to echo and reecho in Ellie's head. She sagged back against the cushions, feeling weaker, more drained, than she'd ever been in her life.

"Ellie, did you hear that?" Ryder's voice penetrated the haze of relief swirling around her. "Zak's going to be okay."

Okay—healthy, things she'd hardly dared dream of in the time since Zak had been diagnosed. They'd won, she and Zak and Ryder. They'd beat the disease, beat it.

She knew it, sensed it, as certainly as if she had read some mandate from heaven.

Then why did she feel the emptiness seeping deeper into her very bones? Why did she feel so brittle, as if a single wisp of breeze would shatter her?

She looked up into Ryder's face, wanting him to hold her, crush her to him, but he only glanced from their twined fingers into her eyes. Then slowly, painfully, he let her go.

grossed he had little time to distract Ellie with his constant chatter.

She glanced around the room that looked more like a toy store with every passing day. A giant stuffed stego-saurus took up most of one corner, and a newly fin-ished wooden model of the dinosaur was drying on the bedside table.

Art supplies, from finger paints to origami, had been the order of the day last Tuesday, and Zak's creations were already stuck up on the walls of his room and the nurses' station with tape.

On Wednesday, there had been a stamp collecting al-bum, with a whole envelope of glossy stamps to stick in place. A miniature cassette player and a case filled with tapes had come next—musical selections so different from Ellie's own, she supposed she should be grateful for the accompanying headsets.

But none of the daily gifts Ryder sent had more im-pact than the "magician" who had arrived with a bou-quet of balloons the week before. Apparently Ryder had ordered a Houdini type, mysterious with a black cape, but the agency had made a mistake and sent Mata Hari, with bells sewn at strategic points on a very flimsy cos-tume. When the woman had discovered the mistake, she'd disappeared quicker than Ellie could have said abracadabra.

Postcards from four cities were taped where Zakary could always see them, along with get-well cards from half of the Angels team. But Ellie knew that the trea-sured letters Ryder had sent were tucked beneath Zak's pillow. Each night, before he fell asleep, she saw the child slip his hand beneath the pillowcase to touch them.

It hurt. Hurt so much to watch Zak, see his face light up any time anyone mentioned Ryder's name. The packages threw the boy into ecstasies that had little to do with the presents they contained. Rather, it was the evi-dence that Ryder had not forgotten him, that Ryder was thinking of Zak, loving Zak. Tangible proof that Ryder was going to return.

And he had.

Twice he had walked through the hospital room's doors with that long-legged athlete's stride, jetting in on an off day between the series in San Diego and L.A., and then again between San Francisco and Pittsburgh. In the time between visits, there had been phone calls—so long, Ellie figured the telephone company must be shooting off skyrockets in celebration.

But in spite of Ryder's generosity, in spite of the lurking sadness in those electric blue eyes whenever he looked at her, Ellie couldn't seem to get past the coldness that had settled deep in the pit of her stomach, the strange, sick dread that crept out of the shadows every night when Zak was asleep and the hospital hallways were quiet.

There was too much time to think, then, about a hundred changes that were blitzing through her life, leaving a yawning emptiness that had once been filled with dialysis and prescriptions, diet planning and praying for a transplant that might never come.

She'd never had to look in the mirror—see, really *see,* Ellie MacCrea, and what she had become.

Consumed.

By fear, by love of her child, by anger and resentment stored up and hoarded over the years of Daniel's numerous betrayals.

There had been no dreams, no time for them; she'd buried herself so deep in responsibilities.

But everything was different now. She could see it, sense it in every careless smile of her son, in his impatience with her when she coddled him, his eagerness to go down the hall alone to the rooms of friends he'd made.

In no time at all, he'd be racing off like the other children, eager to be independent, reluctant to be the sole focus of his mother's life.

She'd wanted it that way, hadn't she? Wanted him to revel in the normal joys most eight-year-olds took for granted.

Of course she had! She loved her son. Loved him so much she would have sacrificed her own life to save his. And yet...

For all her terror, all her prayers that Zak get well, there had been a certain selfish fulfillment in having Zak need her so much. She hadn't ever had to think for herself, of herself. It had been safe, so safe. But now...now there would be time. Time to feel the pain again, to need again, to want again.

Time to feel the emptiness close in around her.

Ellie walked to the closet and straightened Zakary's clothes for the umpteenth time, though the little robe and slippers and super-hero pajamas were already arranged with a precision that would have done a four-star general proud.

She stared blankly into the dark cubicle, feeling as if she were lost in a void she alone could see.

No, a voice whispered inside her. Ryder can see it, too, feel it. It's in his eyes and in that smile that never seems to drive away their sadness. He wants to fill the spaces, for Zak, for me. But how can I let him try when even now he's gone when I need him?

Shards of loneliness spiraled through her, making her eyes sting, her chest ache. Ryder had his own life, just as Zakary soon would, a life in which there would be little room for her.

Ellie's fingers clenched the soft fabric of the robe as if to steady herself. She'd thought of herself as strong, tough, together. Had never realized how much she needed—needed someone to depend on her, to count on her, to make her feel as if she mattered.

"What in God's name do you want, Ellie?" she muttered to herself fiercely. *I want it to be a year from now. I want everything to be settled. I don't want to hurt so much, cry so much, need so much.*

I want Ryder to hold me....

"Mom?" Zak's voice brought Ellie back from the brink. "You okay?"

Ellie grimaced. At least Zak had come up for air long enough to sense her devastation. Yet, did she really want the child to know what she was thinking? Feeling?

She forced a smile to numb lips. "I'm fine. Just straightening up."

"It's already straight. You did that about fifty jillion times. An' you got fresh water, an' you lined up the junk on the sink, an' you stuck my crayons in order. You're startin' to make me crazy. When's Ryder gonna call, anyway? Is it almost time?"

"How would I know?" Ellie snapped, stunned at how badly Zak's words hurt her. "If he calls, he calls, if he doesn't—"

"Rye always calls," the child said stubbornly. "And he *never* yells at me."

"If he did, he'd have to do it long distance," Ellie said, stingingly aware of the truth to Zak's words. "Maybe if he was spending all day in this room, trying to entertain..." she pressed her fingertips to her lips, horrified at her words.

Zak's cheeks were pale, and tears glistened on his lashes. "You don't have to entertain me. Go on outside if you want to. Go home. I'm not even sick anymore. I'll just wait by myself for Rye to call."

Quickly Ellie crossed to the bed and sat down beside Zak. She reached out to take his hand, but Zak shrank away. "Sweetie, I'm sorry. You know there's nowhere else I'd rather be than here with you. It's just..."

"You miss Rye, too." Zak looked straight into her eyes, seeing far too much for an eight-year-old. "How

come you never tell him that? How come you hardly talk
to him? An' when he comes to see me, you're so crabby.
He's real tired after the plane and stuff, and you won't
even be nice to him.''

''I'm perfectly polite!''

''But you're not nice. You don't laugh and smile and
junk like you used to. It makes Rye sad. I can tell.''

Ellie steadied herself, not wanting to disappoint her
son, yet unwilling to prolong any wild dreams the child
might have about families and forevers and Ryder as his
daddy.

''Zak, sometimes relationships between grown-ups are
confusing. Sometimes grown-ups have friends that stay
around forever, and other times there are friends we only
have a little while.''

Zak's lower lip began to tremble. ''Ryder'll always be
my friend.''

Ellie swallowed hard and glanced around the room.
The stegosaurus's cheery velour grin blurred, and she
had to clear her throat before she could speak. ''Ryder
is a special man, and what the two of you share is
very... precious.''

''He shares it with you, too, even if you are mad at
him all the time. He told me so. He loves you, an' you're
going to give me a baby brother to play catch with.''

Ellie gasped, conflicting emotions roiling inside her at
Zakary's revelation. The thought of Ryder confiding in
Zak, weaving dreams for the boy, was at once bitter and
sweet. Involuntarily her hand brushed the flat plane of
her stomach as she imagined what it would be like to
carry Ryder's child. A baby whose father would adore
it, lavish it with attention...then leave for six months out
of the year, the voice of reason reasserted itself.

Her hand fell back to her side, her fingers curling into
her palm.

Zak must've noticed the stricken look on her face, because he turned sheepish. "Well, Ryder said *maybe* I could have a baby brother. If it's okay with you."

"What's this about a baby? Sloan can't buy one of those."

Ellie turned at the sound of a sullen voice from the doorway. Daniel stood there in a patient's gown, one hand braced on the doorjamb to steady himself. He might have looked pathetic, if it hadn't been for his perfectly blow-dried hair. That, and the fact that his face was all pinched up in the perpetual scowl that resulted every time he came into Zakary's room and saw the evidences of Ryder's bounty.

Regardless, Ellie felt her cheeks burn. She wiped her palms on her jeans. "Daniel, did you ever consider knocking? Zak and I were having a private conversation."

"Next time you plan on having a private conversation, you might want to shut the door," Daniel said snidely. "But seeing as you didn't bother this time, maybe you could tell me just exactly what *baby* my son is talking about."

"There is no baby. Not that it's any of your business. Zak misunderstood—"

"I did not! Ryder said—"

The name alone had the power to turn Daniel purple. "Sloan? So that's it. Now that you've taken my kidney, you don't need me for anything anymore. Sloan can move in. Take my wife, my son. What did you do, Ellie? Get yourself pregnant with that arrogant bastard's kid?"

"Daniel, stop it," Ellie said between gritted teeth. "I won't have you upsetting Zakary."

"Upsetting Zakary? What about upsetting me? Oh, yeah, that doesn't matter, does it, Ell? It never mattered. Maybe that's why I walked out on you. I just couldn't take it anymore."

"Stop it! You stop it!"

Ellie started at the sound of Zak's voice. The video game was tossed aside, as the child raked the covers off with a thin hand. Zak scrambled down from the bed, hurrying over to grab on to Ellie's hand.

"Don't you be talkin' to my Mom that way!"

"This is between your mother and me, Zak," Daniel snapped. "And I'll not tolerate your smart-mouthing me. I know it's that Sloan's influence, but I'm not about to put up with my son turning into a spoiled brat."

"Well, now." A deep, familiar voice made Ellie gape and had Daniel spinning around to see a tall, dark-haired figure squared off behind him. "If Zak were looking for an example of one of those, he wouldn't have to look any further than you, MacCrea."

"R-Ryder! Rye!" Zak's cry reverberated in the stillness of the room. The child charged past Daniel. Zak flung his arms around Ryder's long legs and buried his face in the front of Ryder's travel-rumpled shirt.

Ellie's heart twisted as Ryder's arms closed protectively around the little boy. "Hey, Zak, how's my favorite kid?"

"Terrible. Mom was all weepy an' mad, and then *he*—" Zak poked an accusatory finger at his father "—he came in an' started yellin' at her about the baby you're gonna have an'—"

"Zak, there is no baby!" Ellie raked her fingers through her hair, exasperated, embarrassed. She caught a glimpse of Ryder, saw a dart of hurt in his eyes, and regret. The corner of his mouth lifted in a wry smile.

"Remember, slugger?" Ryder said softly, as if Zak hadn't just dragged the man's secret dreams out to be stomped on. "I said *maybe* there would be a baby someday." Ryder's eyes shifted slowly from Zak's face to lock with Ellie's own gaze. "I said I wanted to have a baby with your Mom."

Ellie's heart melted, her knees weak with longing and with the pain of impossibilities.

"Just think, Ellie, you could celebrate the kid's birthday every year to the tune of paternity suits from all over the country. New York, Houston, Montreal. How many nights did you spend in those team hotel rooms alone, Sloan? According to the papers, not too damn many. And getting Ellie pregnant would hardly cramp your style."

"I want to marry her." Ryder glared at Daniel, his fists clenched. His face, shadowed with two days' worth of stubble, was lined with exhaustion and disgust, but when he turned to Ellie, it was shaded with heartbreaking sincerity. "I want to marry you."

Daniel gave an irreverent snort. "She couldn't stand it when I left the house for five minutes. Any time I wanted to take a camping trip or go rock-climbing with my friends she acted like I was Judas the Betrayer. She wouldn't last five minutes with a man who chose to spend all summer playing with the rest of the *boys.*"

"Maybe her reaction didn't have anything to do with the trips you took, MacCrea. Maybe it was the fact that you never bothered to make yourself a part of her life when you were home that was the problem."

"You don't know anything about me, Sloan, so don't pretend—"

Ryder glanced at Zak's still face. Sloan's features hardened as he grasped Daniel's arm. "This much I do know—we're going to finish the conversation on the other side of this door." With that, Ryder propelled Daniel out of the room. With a reassuring hug, Ellie released Zak and followed the two men, shutting the door behind her.

"Listen, you selfish bastard," Ryder said, his voice vibrating with anger. "I've had it with your attitude toward Zak and Ellie. You tossed away the strongest, most beautiful woman I've ever known. Not to mention your son. And now you come in here, scaring Zak, acting like—"

"I'll act any way I want to around my son. He's mine, Sloan. *Mine*. And even if you buy him every toy store in the country, you can never change that."

"No. But nothing you can ever do will make you deserve a kid like Zak. A woman like Ellie. All I want is to give them everything I can."

"Everything except time." Daniel's lip curled, ugly. "I've got your number, Sloan, even if Ellie's too gullible to see it. You try to come off as this great philanthropist. This bleeding heart do-gooder coming to the aid of a poor abandoned woman and her sick kid. Truth is, your agent set up the meeting with Zak, and you agreed to it, figuring you would milk it for all the publicity you could get."

Ellie saw Ryder flinch as if Daniel had struck him. She couldn't stand the guilt in those hooded blue eyes. "Daniel, that's enough," she said, low.

"Let Sloan deny it, if he can."

When Ryder remained silent, Daniel continued. "Then, Sloan, you took a look at Ellie's legs—what was she wearing? One of those skirts she likes so much, that are all full and swirl around her knees?"

Ellie felt humiliation suffocate her, clogging her throat.

"Anyway, I don't blame you for coming on to her. I mean, I know what those legs make a man think of. But don't get too excited. I can tell you from experience, that you'll wind up disappointed in the—*umphf!*"

Ryder's hand shot out, grasping the material at Daniel's throat, his other fist cocked back. Ellie gave a stunned cry, diving between the two men. She grabbed Ryder's arm, but she doubted her power to stop him.

"Ryder, don't! He just had surgery! And anyway, what he said . . . it doesn't . . . doesn't matter."

"Doesn't matter?" There was a fierceness in Ryder's eyes, wild, raging, that she'd never seen there before. "Well, it may not matter to you, but it sure as hell does to me. Because this bastard treated you the way he did I may never be able to have a future with you. May never be able to sleep with you at night, wake up with you in the morning. Make love...damn!"

Ryder stopped, swallowed convulsively. With a shove, he released Daniel, gaze fixed on Ellie's face. With an oath, Ryder wheeled, slamming the fist of his hand against the wall with a force that made the fixtures rattle.

There was the sound of rushing feet, and in a moment they were surrounded by a nurse and two burly orderlies.

"Something wrong here?" one asked, looking back and forth between Daniel and Ryder.

Ryder let his hand slide down to his side. He arched his head back, closing his eyes. "Yeah. Everything's wrong. And there's not a damn thing I can do to change it."

The orderly cleared his throat. "That's too bad, man. But it might be better if you'd remember you're in a hospital. We've got enough to do around here already. Don't need to give anybody stitches."

Ryder grimaced, nodding.

"Aren't you going to throw him out?" Daniel demanded. "He grabbed me by the throat—tried to strike me for no reason."

"He had plenty of reason," Ellie said softly.

The medical personnel looked at Daniel. The nurse put on her brightest smile. "Why don't I take you back to your room, Mr. MacCrea? We can put some ice on your sutures before they swell."

The taller orderly leaned close to Ryder, and Ellie heard him whisper for Ryder's ears only, "Before they swell as big as his head."

Ryder tried to smile. Ellie saw him. But she was beginning to wonder if he remembered how.

"Mrs. MacCrea, you gonna be all right, now?" the other orderly asked, regarding Ryder suspiciously.

"Yes. I'll be fine."

She and Ryder stood, silent, as the orderlies went off.

After a long minute, Ryder sighed, his voice low, controlled. "Ellie, we have to talk. I can't... can't keep on..." his voice faded, and he looked away from her.

Heart in her throat, Ellie nodded. They walked past the waiting room filled with people and made their way down the hall. By instinct, Ellie found the rose garden where Ryder had come to her the day she had found out that Zakary's condition was critical.

The roses that had been vibrant with color then were faded, wilted by a too-bright sun. Ellie stared at the drooping blossoms, her own spirits plunging.

Her knees were shaking as she sank down on the stone bench. She looked at Ryder, really looked at him, then immediately wished she hadn't. She could see every plane of Ryder's face, the sun unmercifully revealing deep-carved lines in his forehead and bracketing his lips. The eyes that had glinted with devilish charm were dull and agonizingly tired. Tired in a way jet lag and sleepless nights could never have made them.

Ellie had read about people being "soul-weary" in the vintage novels she'd enjoyed, but she'd never seen anyone who could be described that way. She'd never suspected the depth of the barrenness, the hurt.

Ryder rubbed his palm over his face and held it there for a moment.

"You wanted to talk," Ellie said, a sick sensation in the pit of her stomach.

"Yeah. I have to. I can't seem to do much else. I can't sleep, can't eat. Hell, I couldn't hit a beach ball if Ben Mitchell pitched it underhand and slow, and *that's* sure as heck never happened to me before."

"I don't know," Ellie said, wanting to take his hand, wanting to tease him. "Your swing looked like it was in great shape outside of Zak's room."

Ryder glowered. Not a hint of a smile played around his lips. "MacCrea's been asking for that for years. I wish I'd hit him the first time I met him and saved myself the frustration."

"I know Daniel can be trying at times—"

"Trying? I'm amazed the man has lived this long without someone wringing his neck."

Tenderness squeezed Ellie's heart. Ryder had the same expression as Zak when he was being stubborn—brows drawn in, daring anyone to question. She tried to speak, but she couldn't squeeze the words past the lump in her throat.

"Anyway, I don't want to talk about MacCrea," Ryder said. "Not now, not ever again. I want to talk about us, Ellie. You and me. I meant what I said up in Zak's room."

"I know." She whispered the words, reaching out to touch his hand.

"Ellie, I want a life with you. With Zak." Blue eyes were dark with need. He squeezed her hand so tight it ached, but not half as much as her heart. "My life's a mess the way things are now. Hell, my batting average stinks, and I'm so hard to live with, Alex is threatening to room with Mitchell the rest of the season. When I'm here, you all but ignore me, and when I'm on the field, all I can think about is how much I want to be with you. You hardly speak to me when I call."

"Zak's so excited, I can't get in a word edgewise," Ellie fibbed weakly. "I hate to take away his time."

Ryder bit out a crude expletive. "Ellie, I deserve better from you than lame excuses and evasions. One of the things that made me fall in love with you was your openness, your honesty. But you're not being honest with either one of us anymore."

Ellie winced, ashamed of herself, stinging under words that were painfully on target. She twined her fingers together, tight. "Maybe that's because I don't know what the truth is anymore. I don't know what's real."

"This is real," Ryder groaned, dragging her up into his arms, crushing her against him so hard she could feel his anguish. "And *this.*" His mouth swooped down, open, hungry, as if he could devour her, make her one with him forever.

Ellie gasped out a protest, her hands pressing against his chest, but he didn't seem to notice. His tongue drove into her mouth, making her so weak she feared she'd crumple at his feet if it weren't for his arms supporting her.

Fingers, callused from the bat and glove, splayed wide, delving deep into the fall of her hair. He kissed her as if he'd never kissed a woman before, kissed her as if he would never taste another.

His breath rasped, his heart thundered, those taut athlete's muscles quaking when he touched her. A tortured sound came from his throat, then suddenly, he let her go.

Instinctively Ellie grabbed the first thing she could to steady herself. The rose bush's thorns pierced her palm, but she didn't feel them. She pressed the back of her other hand to her mouth, fighting back tears.

"Ellie, for God's sake . . . I love you so much it's tearing me apart inside. Can't you see it? Can't you feel it?"

"I'm sorry," Ellie whispered, every word torture. "I don't want to hurt you. But I have to be sure . . . so sure, with Zakary. I just don't know."

"If you don't know now, how will you ever know?"

Ellie looked away. "I didn't say I would. I just know I have to . . . to . . ."

"What? Find some mystical guarantee? Some crystal ball that'll tell your future? No tragedies, no fights, no bumps on the damned road? Life's not like that. You take your chances along with everybody else.''

I've already taken my chances, she wanted to scream at him. *And every time, I've only made myself more miserable, more vulnerable. Every time I've lost myself. I can't risk that anymore. I can't...*

She closed her eyes and Zakary's face swam before her closed lids, hurt, confusion puckering his face, stealing away the sense of security that was every child's right. It was crazy, insane, she knew, but it was as if she were frightened by the gift of Zakary's health, afraid that if she dared risk too much happiness everything would be snatched away.

She steeled herself, opening her eyes to look into Ryder's face. ''You just don't understand. I need more time.''

''Time?'' Ryder barked. ''How long? A week? A month? A year?''

''I *don't know!*''

As suddenly as his storm of temper came, it vanished, leaving a quietness about his features that wrenched at Ellie's soul.

He touched her cheek, and there was pity in his eyes.

''You really don't, do you?'' he said softly. ''I feel sorry for you, Ellie. Sorry for us. But I have to find some way to put my life back together. Find some way to deal with everything. I can't do that, driving myself crazy over you, trying to second guess...''

His fingers dropped from her skin, and she felt chilled.

His voice was gentle.

''I'm afraid that time is the one thing I can't give you anymore,'' he said.

Then he turned and left her alone.

Chapter Seventeen

Late September twilight filtered through the fire escape window, painting Ellie's apartment a soft orange. It seemed like a lifetime ago that Ryder had walked out of her life and back into the spotlight of the sports world. A lifetime since she'd firmly quashed any delusions Daniel might have of a reunion and had delivered him to the airport. He was joining some scatterbrained friend who had supposedly gotten them jobs in the oil fields in the Middle East. Ellie just hoped the two of them didn't end up toppling the balance of world peace.

At the moment, she was glad the only peace she had to worry about was her own—the peace she felt when she wasn't faced with a mountain of dirty dishes to rival Kilimanjaro and the living room was at least clean enough to walk through without ending up in traction.

With a wry grimace, she swept Zak's school books together, stuffing them into his book bag in an effort to eliminate the worst of the debris cluttering the small room.

Even after three months, it still felt good to see the scattered evidence of Zak's improved health—the baseball mitt that hardly ever left his hand, the roller skates, outdoor toys that had been relegated to the back of his closet those long, weary days when he had been so ill.

Now only his basketball was off limits, the temptation of fouling each other with the force of a defensive tackle in a game with the neighborhood kids having proved too much for Zak to resist. She'd tucked his cherished basketball away again, but this time with the knowledge that by next summer, Zak would be able to play with it to his heart's content.

She straightened, worked the zipper on the book bag and stuck it by the front door, where it would be ready when Zak dashed out the next morning to catch his carpool to the nearby elementary school. An everyday thing that still gave Ellie indescribable pleasure. Normalcy. It had been the most precious of all the many gifts Ryder Sloan had given her.

Ellie paused for a moment, running her fingers over the Angels logo decorating the bright blue bag that had been Ryder's "first day of school" present to the boy. Her mouth curved into a wistful smile.

Even still, the thought of Ryder made her ache, a bittersweet ache that mingled pain at losing him forever, with gratitude that she'd been able to be a part of his life even for so short a time. The memories of him were tucked away, as cherished as those she had of nursing Zak as a baby, late at night, as precious to her as remembrances of her son's first smile, first toddling steps.

Because in a very real way Ryder had held her hand, guided her through the maze of self-doubt left in Daniel's wake. The weeks she'd spent with Ryder had made her believe in herself again, enough to make her grow. Grow strong, grow hopeful. Heal.

But too slowly to make things right between them. Too late to have the forever both she and Ryder had wanted. She'd been so afraid of making a mistake like she had with Daniel. So instead of risking being made a fool of, she had made the biggest mistake of her life.

Regret sliced through her, but she steeled herself against it. She'd told Zak time and time again that he had to face the consequences of his decisions—be they bad or good. It was a lesson she'd learned a long time ago, but the results had never been as painful as they were now.

She drew her hand away from the logo, putting to rest the niggling emptiness that never quite left her, that sensation of always waiting. Waiting for the sound of his voice on the phone, waiting for his laughter, his smile.

She'd been starving for it, so badly that two weeks ago she'd let Zak cajole her into watching the Angels game on TV in hopes of catching a glimpse of Ryder.

She'd told herself she only wanted to know he was all right, to see for herself that he'd found the peace he had sought when he walked out of the hospital garden the day he'd said goodbye.

But she'd wanted more. So much more.

It was as if she couldn't get enough information about the man or about the game he played so brilliantly. For the first time she had the emotional energy—and, agonizingly, the time—to delve into a facet of Ryder she'd dismissed, carelessly, self-righteously, as if it hadn't mattered.

She'd followed the Angels even more closely than her son did, questioning Zak about statistics, baseball lore, descriptive terms in baseball-ese that she found more confusing than the extinct languages she had tackled in college years ago.

She'd never seen the attraction in watching nine innings of play and had smiled indulgently when Zak stared, transfixed, at the set. It was only a game, after all. Had no effect on world peace or the quality of life. She'd shaken her head in exasperation when Zak stormed around the apartment as if the world were about to end after an Angels loss. She'd enjoyed his wild delight at a victory.

She had thought it was only a little-boy phase that he'd pack away with his blocks some day.

She hadn't suspected that baseball was infectious. Not until she caught the fever.

Glancing at the clock, she called Zak from his room and crossed to the set, switching on the *Pinch Hitter,* the lead-off program before that night's game. The first night she had watched, they'd interviewed Alex, teasing him about the baby girl he and Gina had had the night before. Then they'd done a program featuring the team's top three sluggers, Ryder included.

With the close-ups the cameramen had shot, he had seemed near enough to touch—a lock of unruly dark hair tumbling across his forehead, a bead of sweat from the earlier batting practice trickling in a tantalizing path down his temple.

He'd still been heart-stoppingly handsome, with his square jaw and long, sooty lashes. But there were no more deep blue sparkles of amusement in those eyes that made women drool, and that mouth manufacturers had used to tempt women into buying everything from sports cars to men's underwear no longer curved into Ryder's accustomed easy smile.

He was changed. Painfully so. And the guilt had ground into Ellie, long and deep. So much so she'd almost called him.

Almost.

But she, more than anyone, knew that sometimes things could not be mended, sometimes the words "I'm sorry" couldn't be enough.

Still, her obsession with watching him, reading about him, tracing his travels and the course of his career had grown. It was the only way she could feel close to the man she'd turned away.

Grabbing a diet soda, she went to curl up in the corner of the couch, balancing the drink on one jeans-clad knee. She barely saved the bottle from spilling when Zak dove for the seat beside her. Trumpets blared the theme song of the show, and Zak did an imitation of them that set Ellie's ears ringing.

"Today our 'pinch hitter' will be one of Atlanta's most beloved players—a man destined for Cooperstown and the Hall of Fame," the voice of the Angels' broadcaster announced. "In the years since this man has taken the field, he has given baseball a new standard of excellence...."

"Rye! It has to be Rye!" Zak screeched.

Ellie shushed him, her pulse racing. She leaned forward in anticipation as the sportscaster went on.

"Our guest on *Pinch Hitter,* Angels third baseman, Ryder Sloan."

Zak whooped as the camera zoomed in on Ryder's face, a face the camera lenses of every sports magazine across the nation loved. But as Ellie stared at Ryder's features, it was as if Zak, the living room, the whole world, had spun away.

Ryder was dressed in the home uniform, the blue Angels cap pushed back on his head, the bright hue exactly matching the color of his eyes. A heavy gold chain winked at his tanned throat, and his blue pin-striped jersey outlined the taut muscles of his torso and the powerful shoulders that held the strength to drive a ninety-mile-an-hour fastball into the stadium's parking lot.

Ellie swallowed hard, wishing she could see his hands, just long enough to remember how it felt to have them touch her.

She shook herself inwardly, listening as interviewer Bob Darnell asked Ryder questions about the coming game and the promising young pitcher the Angels manager had just called up from the minors.

Ryder smiled when he talked about the kid, and there was a softening of the pain that had shone in his eyes the week before.

It was what she had wanted to see when she'd first begun watching him on TV—she'd wanted to know that he was all right. That he would survive the loss. She'd wanted to be certain she hadn't driven the boundless enthusiasm, the strange mixture of sensuality and innocence, out of Ryder's eyes, leaving bitterness and cynicism.

She had wanted to leave him whole, in a way she knew she never would be whole again.

But now, seeing a ghost of his old animation returning to his face, seeing a hint of that bedeviling grin, made her catch her lip between her teeth and her eyelids burn with tears.

He was letting go of her, Ellie thought with a dull throb of pain. Letting go of the misery, the hurt, the emptiness.

In a while she would only be a memory that he would look back on from time to time, wondering...

She gritted her teeth, forcing herself to focus on the interview as it progressed, hoping that the sportscaster's words and the rich, welcome tones of Ryder's voice would be able to drive back the emotions warring inside her.

"Baseball is a team sport, Ryder, but we all know how much effect individual players can have on the outcome as a whole," Darnell said. "Do you think it's fair to say that the Angels would be playing for the league championship if you'd been able to shake the slump that's plagued you since mid-July?"

Ellie's stomach lurched.

Ryder's mouth compressed, and Ellie could see the self-blame shadow his eyes. How could the announcer raise Ryder's self-doubt, now, when things were beginning to improve?

Ryder put on a plastic smile. His voice was devoid of its usual warmth. "It's impossible to know what would have happened if I'd been able to pull things together earlier. There's no denying my slump cost us. But there's nothing I can do about that now. I'm just going out there every day and trying to play the game to the best of my ability."

"Well, regardless of what the middle of your season was like, no one can say your batting's suffering now. What's happened to turn things around?"

Did Ryder's shoulders slump just a little, or had Ellie imagined it?

"I've learned to be patient. That used to be hard for me. Still is. But sometimes it's the only way."

"We heard that you were experiencing some difficulties off of the field as well that might have made a difference in your swing."

"You hear a lot of things. Believe half of them."

Darnell cleared his throat. "Well, maybe there is one rumor you could clear up."

Ellie could see Ryder stiffen, was terrified for him, that the man was going to level some embarrassing personal question, pry into the broken relationship that still obviously caused Ryder hurt.

"Word around the baseball world is that you've gone to a lot of trouble in your off time to develop a network of professional athletes who are going to donate time, money and energy into building a—" Darnell checked his notes "—a bone marrow and organ bank with an organization called the Wishful Tree Foundation."

"Wishing Tree," Ryder corrected him.

"You've always been generous, but the fans might want to know what prompted you to get so involved in this sort of thing. Didn't it start in June when you befriended that little boy with kidney problems? He's recently had a transplant, we're told.''

"Yeah. Zakary MacCrea." Ryder's mouth curved into a smile, his eyes seeming to probe the camera. "Hi, slugger, if you're watching."

"Mom, did you hear that?" Zak shrilled, leaping off the couch. "He said hi to me right there on television!"

"I heard him," Ellie said, but she was still reeling from Ryder's news, still wincing at the loneliness evident in Ryder's face.

She'd been endlessly grateful to him for keeping up his relationship with the child. Though the presents had trailed off to an occasional surprise, the letters and phone calls had been a constant source of pleasure to Zak.

Ellie had known Ryder missed the little boy, seeing him, hugging him. But she hadn't known that Ryder was filling his time trying to help other kids like Zak.

"You're to be commended for all your hard work," the sportscaster was saying. "I'm sure you're a source of inspiration to the boy."

"Me? An inspiration to Zak?" Ryder gave a hollow laugh. "No, you've got that all wrong. It was Zak who was an inspiration to me. People look out on the field when we play ball, and they make us into some kind of heroes, but I never knew what courage was until I met Zak and his Mom, Ellie MacCrea." Ryder looked away from the camera, swiped at his eyes.

"Because of them," he said quietly, "I'll never look at life the same way again. I'll always be grateful for that."

Tears coursed down Ellie's cheeks, but they were tears of the most fragile of hope.

No, she told herself fiercely. It was too late. Ryder had made it plain he'd had no time to give her, that their relationship was causing him too much pain. He'd asked her to choose—between her fear of risking everything and the love he had to give.

She had hurt him in her way as deeply as Daniel had hurt her.

What would Ryder say if she turned up in his life again? If she told him . . .

Told him what?

The truth? About her feelings for him, her uncertainty over Daniel, the strange conflicting emotions she felt about Zak?

"Mom? How come you're cryin'?" Zak fixed her with a troubled gaze.

"Nothing, honey. It's nothing. What would you think if I called Gina? Asked if you could go over there for a little while."

"But I thought we were gonna watch the game."

"Maybe you could watch it with Tony and Will. See the new baby."

"It's a girl." Zak made a face. "I wanted a brother when you and Ryder . . . I mean . . . if you and Ryder had . . ." His voice trailed off, a resigned expression in his eyes. "Oh, well, I guess a girl's better than nothin'. Yeah. I'd like to go to Tony's."

Ellie dialed the phone, and her voice shook as she made the arrangements with Gina.

When she hung up, Ellie sat a long moment, her fingers digging into her thigh, her heart quaking.

One of the things that made me fall in love with you was your honesty . . . Ryder's voice echoed in her memory.

Telling Ryder the truth would be the biggest risk of all.

The question now was did she have the courage to take it!

The locker room was its usual post-game disaster—sodden towels, dirty socks and stray batting gloves littered the room. Steam clung to the mirrors from the hot showers in which the players had scrubbed off nine innings' worth of sweat, while the smell of ointment used to ease strained muscles hung in the air.

Ryder leaned his head back against the rim of the whirlpool, the jets of water streaming against his tired limbs soothing away the aches from the game.

The opposing pitcher had come in too tight on an inside curve, and Ryder had been forced to dive for the dirt to save being hit by the ball. The ball had missed him, but his cleats had stuck, and he'd aggravated an old injury to his hamstring—not enough to miss an inning, but enough that the scowling trainer had insisted on a long soaking in the steamy-hot water.

Though Ryder had always been notoriously edgy after a tough loss, needing to get out of the clubhouse to work off his frustration, tonight he'd been content to rest, think.

About things he hadn't allowed himself to dwell on in the past weeks. Things Darnell's questions had made it impossible to shut out any longer.

Ellie.

Ryder raised his arm out of the steamy water, laying it across his eyes.

Damn, why did it still hurt so much to think about her? He'd thought he would get used to being without her, that the jagged hole inside him she used to fill would heal.

The end of the baseball season was always hectic, laced with the exhaustion that was unavoidable when athletes jetted back and forth across the country to play 162 games a season. He should have been too tired to think. He should have been too exhausted to dream about her at night.

At least he'd quit waiting, hoping against hope she'd change her mind, realize that what they had together was worth any risk he could name.

He sighed, dragging his palm down across the wet plane of his chest, to where the water lapped at his stomach.

Strange, even though he'd known that she'd leave an awful void in his life, he'd never suspected how much he'd miss her, miss telling her about funny happenings on the road trips, or Mitchell's off-color jokes, or about Alex's kids' latest antics.

Little things. Things no one else would care about, except the two of them.

He'd never had that before, with anyone—his parents or the women who had flocked around him ever since he'd made varsity squad in high school. He'd never shared that kind of emotional intimacy.

It had felt right, so right, with Ellie. It made him furious to think it was gone.

"Hey, Rye." Alex's voice broke through his thoughts. "There's someone outside to see you."

"Sportswriter? Groupie?" Ryder dragged his arm away from his eyes, opening one lid to glare at his friend. "Tell 'em I drowned."

Alex's lips started to twitch into a grin, but strangely, the gregarious catcher quelled it. "I don't think this person would buy it, partner."

"Listen, Alex, my leg hurts and I'm cranky as hell. I just don't have the energy to scrawl my name on a baseball or answer questions about how it feels to be a star on a team that hasn't won a pennant since Moses was five years old."

Alex whistled. "Temper, temper, superstar. I can almost guarantee you won't mind 'scrawling your name' on *this* baseball. Says she's a die-hard baseball fan—got a kid who's an even bigger one."

"Then tell her to come back some other time, my pen's out of ink."

"Whatever you say, Rye," Alex didn't sound in the least put out, a thread of amusement lightening his voice. "The kid probably won't be *too* disappointed. I mean, he'll get over it. You're a busy man. Got more important things to—"

"Can it, Craig."

"Sure, sure. I mean, it's only an autograph, after all. 'Course, she wanted it for the kid's birthday, but life's full of disappointments. The sooner the kid learns that the better—"

"Son of a—" Ryder bit out the oath. "All right, all right, dammit! You've made your point already." He stormed out of the water with a haste that would've made the trainer bellow.

Rivulets ran down his naked body, but he didn't stop to towel them away. Ripping his jeans out of his locker, he dragged them over his wet legs, then, with a hurried tug at the zipper, strode out into the hall, his bare feet leaving damp footprints on the floor.

He shoved the door open with such force it banged into the outer wall, making the figure standing in the pool of shadow outside jump.

"Listen, lady, I've had a helluva day," he said wearily. "I struck out twice, made an error, and almost got hit with a pitch that would've left a twelve-inch hole coming out my other side. Just give me whatever it is you want me to sign so I can dive back in the . . . what the hell!"

Ryder felt dizzy as his eyes adjusted to the dimness in the corridor, his vision clearing enough to make out sunset-red hair, a delicate oval face. He stared, taking in Ellie's slender shape, all but lost in an old baseball jersey he'd given her to wear. Its hem reached well down her thighs, while much-washed denim, torn at the knees, covered the rest of her shapely legs. Her feet were clad in scuffed-up running shoes.

He'd never seen a woman look more beautiful.

Ryder swallowed hard, trying to steady himself. "Alex said there was a die-hard baseball fan out here. The triple he got in the second inning must've made him delirious."

"No more delirious than the people in the bleachers when you got that home run in the bottom of the eight. I got here just in time to see it."

"Did you?" he said tentatively, confused.

"Too bad you didn't do that in your last turn at bat against the Reds. Might've kept them from sweeping the series."

If she'd started spouting Latin he couldn't have been more stunned. "What the devil are you talking about?"

"Baseball. Your games. I've been watching them the past few weeks. I used to tell Zak it was like watching paint dry. Now..." A hint of pink darkened her cheeks.

"Now what? It's been raised to the status of taking out the garbage? Or has it graduated to the level of a root canal?"

Ellie shrugged, looking self-conscious. "Now I can't seem to miss a game."

"You? Watch a game? I don't believe it."

Ellie gave a nervous laugh. "Neither do I. If anyone had told me a year ago, worse yet, a month ago, that I'd be spending three hours a night staring at grown men trying to hit a little white ball, I'd have told them they were crazy. But..."

"But what?"

"I am watching them. Two nights ago it was Zak who had to calm *me* down when that blind moron of an umpire robbed you of that home run."

"You saw that? The game against the Cubs?"

"If that ball was foul, I'll eat my Medieval Lit text book."

Ryder gaped. Her cheeks were flushed, her eyes sparkling with disgust and indignation. He shook himself, feeling like he'd stepped out of the whirlpool into the Twilight Zone.

"Ellie, you're making me crazy. I don't understand—"

"Neither did I. I never thought I'd be able to tolerate baseball, let alone get so caught up in it. Sometimes, I even lose track of the real reason I'm watching, the real reason I started."

He stared down into those gray eyes that had been so certain when she'd told him goodbye, and saw a vulnerability there, a tinge of embarrassment mixed up with hope.

"And what was that?" he asked softly.

"It was the only time I got to watch you. Hear your voice, see the way you move. That's what made me craziest. Seeing those long legs of yours and remembering how it felt to kiss them, how they tangled up with mine in your bed the night we slept together."

Ryder felt his body harden, strain against the fly of his jeans, and his palms were sweating as if he were sixteen again. He wanted to grab her, kiss the hell out of her, push her down onto the damned concrete and drive himself into her until she couldn't breathe, couldn't speak, couldn't even think of leaving him again.

He raked his hand through his hair, desperation clotting in his chest.

Damn it, it wasn't fair, wasn't fair for her to walk back into his life when he'd just been getting it together. God, he didn't want to hurt again, the way he had when she'd rejected him before.

"We were good together." Ryder tried to force a blandness into his voice he didn't feel. "In bed."

"We were more than good."

He felt something, feather-light, touch the bare muscles of his back. Her fingers. They burned him, so deep they seemed to touch his soul.

"I miss you, Ryder."

"I miss you, too," he admitted. "But I've come down with a case of romantic scruples recently, thanks to you.

I'm afraid sleeping with the mother of a small child without a commitment is out of my league now."

"But what if there was a...a commitment? What if..."

"I don't know, Ellie. I'd need...need to know what's changed now." He pulled away from her, kicked at a popcorn box someone had dropped on the way from the game. "I didn't know loving someone could hurt so much. I'm not sure I want to...well, put myself in ...well, put myself in the position of feeling that pain again."

"But don't you see? That's why I couldn't give you what you asked of me in the garden that day. I was confused. Scared." She grimaced. "And when I wasn't busy being terrified or stubborn, I was being just plain stupid."

"I loved you. But you put me in the same class as that bastard of an ex-husband—"

"No. I never thought you were like Daniel. That's what scared me most of all." It was a hushed admission, one filled with regret. Ryder froze, his eyes searching her face.

"Don't you see, Ryder, that's why I was so afraid? When I married Daniel, we seemed so compatible, had things in common. I don't know. I was so sure it was the right thing to do. I don't think I ever even thought about loving him. I was too busy checking off complementary tastes on some little list in the back of my head. Despite all that, despite how hard I fought to control things, the marriage was a disaster."

"So I don't fit the Ellie MacCrea criterion for a perfect husband? Terrific."

"It had nothing to do with that. The problem was, I loved you too much. You were too good to me. I guess I didn't think I deserved to be treated that way."

"That's garbage. You can't be stupid enough to believe that."

"For somebody with a master's degree, I haven't exactly been displaying much intelligence lately. Wouldn't you agree?"

Ryder almost smiled, but couldn't. This was too important. Too terrifyingly final. The possibility of one last chance.

She turned and walked away from him, her finger tracing the frame of a team picture on the wall. "Ryder, the whole time we were together, I kept waiting for disaster to strike. Things were too good, too wonderful. You were like a dream, a fantasy, every wish I'd ever made."

Ryder swore, suddenly hating the looks that everyone seemed to find so stunning, hurt that even Ellie cared about something he regarded as a quirk of nature.

As if she could read his mind, Ellie turned, reached out, touching his face.

"No, it's not *this* that made you my fantasy. It was *this*." He gritted his teeth against the sweet anguish as she slid her hand down his bare chest until her soft palm rested over his heart. "It was the way you loved me, made me feel cherished, precious."

"Why?" The pain edged his voice. "Why did that drive you away?"

"Because I kept waiting for you to discover...well, whatever it was about me that drove Daniel away. I kept waiting for you to see the real me—the one who was frightened, and needing, and...and maybe a little self-righteous. I didn't dare lean on you, because I knew that someday you'd leave me. If you did, I was afraid I wouldn't survive."

"You're stronger than anyone I've ever known," Ryder choked out, curving his palm beneath her chin. "You'd be fine without me."

"Maybe. But I don't ever want to find out. I want to love you forever, Ryder Sloan, even if I am afraid. Because I'm more terrified of what my life would be like without you."

He pulled her against him, his mouth brushing hers. Her lips parted in welcome.

"I'm scared as hell, too, Ellie," he breathed against her skin. "It hurt so much . . . thinking it was over. I'm not very good at losing."

"I'm not, either. I guess I've just had more practice."

There were shadows in her eyes. He had a lifetime to drive the last of them away.

He moved his mouth against hers, the hunger building strong.

"Rye . . . Rye wait," she said, wedging her hands against his chest to put some space between them. "What you said about losing . . ."

"Mmm?" He nibbled a path down her neck, his hands finding her skin under the loose fabric of the jersey.

"I've been . . . um, thinking about that the past few days." She groaned as his thumb skimmed her nipple. Her voice was thick, but not as thick as the desire hazing his mind. "Next year, if you make a trade for a good left fielder . . . a power hitter . . . I think you could go all the way. . . ."

"The only place I'm going is to bed with you, lady." Ryder laughed, loving her. "And when we get there we're sure as hell not talking about baseball."

* * * * *

Bestselling author NORA ROBERTS captures all the
romance, adventure, passion and excitement of Silhouette in
a special miniseries.

THE CALHOUN WOMEN

Four charming, beautiful and fiercely independent
sisters set out on a search for a missing family
heirloom—an emerald necklace—and each finds
something even more precious... passionate romance.

Look for THE CALHOUN WOMEN miniseries
starting in June.

COURTING CATHERINE
in Silhouette Romance #801 (June/$2.50)

A MAN FOR AMANDA
in Silhouette Desire #649 (July/$2.75)

FOR THE LOVE OF LILAH
in Silhouette Special Edition #685 (August/$3.25)

SUZANNA'S SURRENDER
in Silhouette Intimate Moments #397 (September/$3.29)

 *Silhouette Books*®

Silhouette Special Edition

presents

SONNY'S GIRLS

by Emilie Richards, Celeste Hamilton and Erica Spindler

They had been Sonny's girls, irresistibly drawn to the charismatic high school football hero. Ten years later, none could forget the night that changed their lives forever.

In July—
ALL THOSE YEARS AGO by Emilie Richards (SSE #684)
Meredith Robbins had left town in shame. Could she ever banish the past and reach for love again?

In August—
DON'T LOOK BACK by Celeste Hamilton (SSE #690)
Cyndi Saint was Sonny's steady. Ten years later, she remembered only his hurtful parting words....

In September—
LONGER THAN... by Erica Spindler (SSE #696)
Bubbly Jennifer Joyce was everybody's friend. But nobody knew the secret longings she felt for bad boy Ryder Hayes....

SILHOUETTE·INTIMATE·MOMENTS®

IT'S TIME TO MEET
THE MARSHALLS!

In 1986, bestselling author Kristin James wrote A VERY SPECIAL FAVOR for the Silhouette Intimate Moments line. Hero Adam Marshall quickly became a reader favorite, and ever since then, readers have been asking for the stories of his two brothers, Tag and James. At last your prayers have been answered!

In August, look for THE LETTER OF THE LAW (IM #393), James Marshall's story. If you missed youngest brother Tag's story, SALT OF THE EARTH (IM #385), you can order it by following the directions below. And, as our very special favor to you, we'll be reprinting A VERY SPECIAL FAVOR this September. Look for it in special displays wherever you buy books.

 *Silhouette Books®*

FOUR UNIQUE SERIES
FOR EVERY WOMAN YOU ARE...

Silhouette Romance®

Tender, delightful, provocative—stories that capture the laughter, the tears, the *joy* of falling in love. Pure romance...straight from the heart!

SILHOUETTE *Desire*®

Go wild with Desire! Passionate, emotional, sensuous stories of fiery romance. With heroines you'll like and heroes you'll *love*, Silhouette Desire never fails to deliver.

Silhouette Special Edition®

Stories of love and life, these powerful novels are tales that you can identify with—romances with "something special" added in! Silhouette Special Edition is entertainment for the heart.

SILHOUETTE·INTIMATE·MOMENTS™

Enter a world where passions run hot and excitement is the rule. Dramatic, larger-than-life and always compelling—Silhouette Intimate Moments will never let you down.

WRITTEN IN THE STARS

Love's in Sight!
THROUGH MY EYES
by Helen R. Myers

Dr. Benedict Collier was the perfect Virgo—poised, confident, always in control . . . until an accident left him temporarily blinded. But nurse Jessica Holden wasn't about to let Ben languish in his hospital bed. This was her chance to make Ben open his eyes to the *love* he'd resisted for years!

THROUGH MY EYES
by Helen R. Myers . . . coming from Silhouette Romance this September.
It's WRITTEN IN THE STARS!

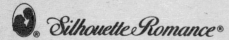

Silhouette Romance®